MY NAME IS PROMISE

The Scream Series
Book 4

Marissa Rivera

Three Dragons Publishing

This book contains violence, death, human trafficking, and closed-door romance.
Viewer Discretion advised. For viewers 15+

"The goal (of traffickers) is to strip a person of their ability to resist, so even if a person isn't physically restrained, they've been psychologically tormented to the point where they're too afraid to run."

CHAPTER 1
New World

EMBER (SCREAM)

IT'S EMPTY ON THE other side of the walls, like a dead planet. I thought the United States had millions of people inside it, so how is there so much room out here? How can there be miles and miles of emptiness?

I stare out the window, searching for life. Our bus travels a one-lane road heading for the horizon. For four months, I was trapped in a half mile of a town full of rotting buildings. Over six hundred kids from the ages of eight to eighteen were trapped with me, and though we never got along, I never felt this extreme sense of loss. I'm falling into a dark hole with no idea if there is a bottom.

If I didn't have amnesia, would I be excited about where we are headed? Because even though I've

1

destroyed the school, fought with a rebellion to escape, and stayed alive until the police came, I'm terrified. I want to run back to my little home behind the Coal building and hide underneath my mildew, ripped blanket. I want to know what to fear. Out in this brand new world, I'm more lost than before.

It's wrong, isn't it? That reaction is wrong. Because my future finally looks promising. No more Tobias, a boy who tried to control me in everything. No more Myers, a man who wanted to sell us to the highest bidder. No more school, where I was taught I was despised and unloved.

I am starting fresh. If only I knew my name, I wouldn't have to go by Scream or Ember. I could be somebody completely different, completely worthy of love and friendship.

Like Jennifer.

I sit in the front of the bus, clenching the chocolate bar in my lap, stiff and ready to spring to my feet if I have to fight. I'm in the worst possible place currently. The bus is jam packed with over forty Coal members, and these kids do not like me. They wear black and gray clothes to represent their unity.

If they didn't hate me before when they believed I was a girl called Jennifer, then they definitely hate me now. I don't know if it would mean anything if I swung around in my chair and shouted, "I am not Jennifer!" It would be full of bitterness and self-loathing, but the painful truth. I am not Jennifer, the girl that was sent to save them. I'm just me.

It's ironic that they hate Jennifer when she was a Coal Member and a Snatcher. She worked with them while working against them. She deserves all their contempt. And if she wasn't dead, I would readily point the finger in her direction, hoping they'll let go of their aggression. But it's too late. I have blown up the school and destroyed their home.

And Coal does not believe in forgiveness, only vengeance.

The cop standing next to the driver keeps looking over her shoulder, a smile wide on her lips. She sees only startled little kids, secretly excited to be finally found. Any other bus would be celebrating, but she doesn't understand that Coal members never wanted to be let out. They enjoyed the terror and enjoyed causing it.

"There it is." The police officer points.

Like a single unit, all our heads turn.

Off in the distance, two buildings stand side by side. There are equal heights, six to seven stories, with paved parking in the front and a luscious, unnatural landscape full of freshly planted trees and shrubs. It's a new building, untainted by the brutal Oklahoma heat and wind. It's beautiful, and I press my face against the window.

Do you see it, Charles?

Tears burn the back of my eyes, and I blink rapidly, trying to dissolve them. Charles would have been bouncing on the seat, laughing and pointing out everything he loves about it. The blooming flowers, the crisp black road, the beautiful big windows in every room. My heart fills with joy.

But my smile slips away.

There's a fence around the building. Our bus waits for the gate to open. It's chain-link, see-through, very different from the walls surrounding our town, but still, it's a blockade with spiral barbed wire on the top.

I look up at the officer again. She grins. "This is a new hospital. Never been used. We are borrowing it until we get you all home. And since many of you need medical attention, it was the best last-minute decision."

I nod, allowing her excitement to replace any doubt. A fence is not a wall. I can get through a fence. I push a smile and take a breath of air. I'm ready to begin. Maybe these doctors can figure out what's wrong with my head.

The bus stops, and the door opens, but no one moves. I thought I would jump up without hesitation, but what am I supposed to do? Where do I go? When can I see my friends, the family I've come to know?

Shakes, James, Mary, Brick, Vapor, and Light have become part of my life, and I'm separated from them.

The cop goes to the entrance. "Follow directions. And trust the process. We might be slow in the beginning, but I promise, you all are gonna get a new home very soon." She waves to me, and I surge to my feet, ready to find my way.

Stepping foot on the ground, all my momentary confidence dies. There are nurses dressed in green, covered from head to toe with masks on their faces and hoods over their heads. I slip to the side, pressing my back against the bus, unwilling to move closer to them. My heart pounds in chaos, and I shake my head, searching for a friend.

Coal members trickle out of the bus. And there is no sympathy.

"You're dead, bitch."

"I'm gonna slit your throat."

"We're gonna make you scream, Scream."

It becomes repetitive and boring. I have been ridiculed every day since I came to Myers' School for the Unwanted. Their threats are like bubbles. They pop without a sound.

"Boys on the left, girls on the right!" The nurses begin to chant.

The crowd of Coal just stands there, unwilling to do what they asked. It's a police officer that physically begins to move them. "Boys on the left, girls on the right!" He shoves a child, pulling hands apart. Outrage begins, but there are too many nurses and cops. "It's not forever. It's for safety purposes. You'll see each other soon."

Another bus pulls up behind us, adding more people to the confusion. The officer from my bus tries to peel me away. "It's okay, honey. They'll take care of you, trust them." I keep my back pressed against the panel, slapping at her hands.

It's not until I see Light, my maybe-kind-of boyfriend, that I take off. "Light!" I dive in between the waves of Rain, members with blue and white shirts. Light is taller than most of them. He's black, gorgeous, with brilliant blue eyes, and they pop out, pinning me where I stand. Relief pours over his face as we embrace. His strong arms hold me to him. "You okay?"

"I'm okay," I assure, but tears are coming anyway. This is overwhelming. There are so many people. Anyone of them can come up from behind and shove a blade in my back.

"Boys on the left, girls on the right!" The guard grips Light's arm, and he complies, keeping my hand in his. He's my only lifeline, and I cling to him, but as we get closer to the entrance, it's clear he and I are going to split up.

"It's alright," Light promises. But he doesn't know that. He doesn't know where we are or where we are going. He doesn't know if we'll see each other again. Behind those doors could be a gas chamber meant to put us to sleep and never wake again.

"I got her," Drop's voice interrupts, and I swing back to look at her. Drop is the leader of Rain and Light's friend. But she isn't mine. She betrayed me once; she'll do it again.

But what's my option right now?

Light smiles and releases my hand as if her word is all he needs. I shake my head, trying to reach him, but the nurses push him, and I'm shoved in another direction. Drop keeps beside me, looking back constantly to keep me close.

I go with the flow of the crowd; more cries follow behind me. They separate every couple. It's stressful listening to it, so I focus instead on my surroundings.

The first-floor entrance has a bright, luminescent lobby, a closed gift shop, a metal gate clenched tight over it, and a closed cafeteria, but it only has a sign out front and the lights off. We move through doorways and into a stairwell. I notice a hallway leading to offices. All the doors are shut.

We stay in single file, and for a moment, we stop in the middle of the stairway. Excitement echoes up the six floors, and I lean over the banister, wondering what's on the top. I don't think. I listen.

I need information and the girls will understand what's going on better than I will.

"Why do you think they split us up?" one girl asks.

"Keep us from screwing around." The girls giggle.

A whisper into Drop's ear, "What are we going to do with Coal?" Ahead of us are the female members of Coal. They keep glares on their face like they are glued on.

"We got other problems, Daisy."

"Like what?"

I lean around Drop to look at Daisy. She has white dyed hair and a yellow bandana wrapped around her neck. I've seen white dyed hair numerous times, but I don't know what it means. It's not a clan trait because Coal and Boundary both do it. Drop looks over her shoulder at me, and I shrink back. "We'll talk later."

Once we are in the hallway, boxes line up against the wall. Each one is different from the next. Shoes in various sizes. Bras and underwear from small to large. Then it went on to shorts and pants to shirts and long sleeves. An instructor called out to pick two of each.

Free clothes.

Without anyone hurting each other or pulling out a weapon, they offer us free clothes. I don't move, unsure if this is a test. If I reach for it, will she pull a ruler from her back and slap my knuckles?

The lady keeps insisting we pick our clothes and hurry up. I grab the first thing on top, barely looking at the size. But the clan girls are much pickier than I am and squish their noses up in distaste. They talk back to the nurse, asking for more suitable clothing, but she disregards their snotty attitudes and continues shouting.

I am so enthralled with my clothing collection that when I step to the front of the line, I am taken aback when the nurse stops me.

"What's your name?"

"My name?"

"Yes. Your name," she enunciates with annoyance.

"Um—" Should I give them the one Tobias gave me or the one I was given by Light? Do I tell them I can't remember my real name? Or would they prefer I pretend I'm Jennifer?

"Ember," Drop interrupts. "Right? Your name is Ember?"

I stare at her. Why does she care what they call me?

The nurse scribbles Ember on a wristband and wraps it around my hand before writing the same thing on a clipboard. "You are in room 232."

I clench my clothes tight, walking the white-tiled hall. I feel small in its extravagant light. It is so bright. So clean. I am dirtying the place just by breathing. There are too many doors. Too many rooms. So many places to hide, to lurk, to watch, to sneak out and stab you when you're not paying attention. Every door I pass, I glare at, waiting for someone to jump out. I pass the elevators and stand in front of my room.

Drop stands at the door beside mine. "I'm in here. If you need, you know, something." She dives into her room before I can give her a look of contempt. I don't need anything from her. As far as I care, she's not even here.

I enter timidly, shutting the door behind me. I stare at the knob, listening to the silence, waiting to be reprimanded. Like a slow-moving slug, I press in the lock. It's fascinating. I lock my door and no one says a thing.

The room is small, but perfect. A bed lays in the center with the headboard against the wall, floor-to-ceiling windows stretch the back, and next to the bed is a comfy, fat chair. A small flat-screen TV hangs on the opposite side of the bed. Then I notice the best thing I've ever seen to my right: A private bathroom and shower.

I go inside, flipping on the light, and simply marvel at it. It is too good to be real. Is it mine? Can I keep it?

My reflection finds me in a mirror above the sink. My brown hair is erratic around my face. Dirt had somehow gotten nearly all of me. The red of my shirt stands out. It's shocking the contrasting colors. My face is pale. I have black circles under my blue eyes.

I look traumatized.

I look broken.

I look lost.

I step in the shower, and I finally allow myself to cry.

Chapter 2
Choices

Ember

I fell asleep wrapped in a towel, tucked in the corner of the locked bathroom, my hair still partially wet where it rested against the wall. I stare out, trying to remember everything that happened. There was so much piled into my head, like an overpacked sand bucket.

I blew up the school.

Even now, I can see it. I'm standing on the roof of a bus in front of everyone in school. And I pressed that button. My heart explodes with the power of control. I made something happen. I changed the course of my life because I took possession of it. I'm addicted to that feeling. I want more of it.

Bu there are more emotions piling into me as I replay all the things that have happened. I can see bodies. I can see blood. I hold my arms around myself trying to keep the cold at bay. It's deep in my chest, freezing me from the inside.

Stop, I order myself. James' teaching coming at the right moment. I repeat this word a dozen times until the anxiety in my chest begins to fade. I don't want to wallow in sadness. I want to find my family.

I know two things: Shakes was shot and taken away in an ambulance. Mary was on a bus and should be on this floor with me. But the whereabouts of James, Brick, Vapor, and Carbon are unknown.

I dress quickly in the odd clothes I have. They are a little too small for me. The jeans fit loose, but the shirt squeezes around me. I was smart enough to grab a large bulky jacket, and I pull it over to hide my chest. Breasts are aggravating to have.

I peek my head out the front door. There are ten women congregated at the nurses' station. They wear matching blue slacks. They chit-chat, and I stand there listening. One of my strong suits, according to James, is observation. I'll need that skill here to assess my situation. They talk of random things: their home life, why they joined this nursing contract, and every single one said it was for the money. A five-thousand sign-up bonus, unheard of apparently.

No useful information, I groan.

Across from me is the elevator. The stairs are down the hall and to the right. But I couldn't get there without passing the nurses or running into potential threats from Coal.

I dart across the hall and press myself against the wall, poking the elevator button. It makes a ding when it arrives, and I cringe. There's no way they didn't hear that. I throw myself through the doors anyway and hit a random number. But nothing happens. I press different numbers, the doors adamantly disobeying, kept wide like a child's hungry mouth.

A nurse pops in the doorway. "Hi, honey. Where are you going?" She smiles tenderly, almost robotically, and I press against the wall, terrified. "It's alright, look—" Her fingers tap a panel. "It's for security; you need a card." She points to the thing around her neck. "Come on out."

She backs away, giving me space, and though hesitant, I move simply because I'm trapped otherwise. "I'm Janice. We are going to be making our rounds soon. Stay in your room until you've seen a doctor, okay?"

I notice other heads stick out of doorways. Drop meets my eyes from her room. I don't want anyone to see my fear, especially enemies, so I push off the wall and straighten my back. "I want to find my friends."

Janice glances at the other nurses, and they shake their heads, looking down at their papers. She surveys the hall, noticing other girls listening, and swallows her apprehension, plastering on her smile. "There's a gaming room down the hall we've installed for you. Maybe tomorrow there will be more information on your friends. But right now, we need everyone to stay in their rooms until we've made our rounds."

"I just want to know if they're okay. They're boys. James and Sh—" I cut myself off. I don't know if saying Shakes name is a good thing or not.

"The boys are still being divided. There were a lot more of them. We can't have anyone exploring until we get things in order."

Someone else shouts out, "When can we go home?"

Janice sighs, and a nurse mutters under her breath, "I told you not to talk to them."

"We are submitting your names, and the police will start calling your parents. That's more a cop thing than us. I don't know things like that. It will take time, and you need to be patient. We still have to perform health exams on all of you. We will explain it when we do our rounds." Her patience has run out, and she returns to the station with her back to us.

I look at the girls. I can't tell anymore who is from what clan. Without the colors, we are no longer divided. In a prosperous world, that's a great thing. We can be equal. We are girls, and we are all in this together.

But it is not reality. We are not the same.

Drop slips over to me. "What do you think?" she whispers, leaning against the wall. "Should we trust them?"

I ignore her.

Daisy comes up on the other side of me. "They trapped us. We're sitting ducks here. How long until the boys figure out we're trapped? Think they'll sit and do nothing? We need a backup plan, an out. I don't like being inside without a damn window that actually opens."

"What's the plan?"

They both stare at me like I am the one with answers. "What are you looking at me for?"

"You're in charge, aren't you?"

"Since when?"

"Since you blew up the school? Aren't you a Power?"

"What do you care about rebellion rank? You turned on us."

Drop flicks her black straight hair over her shoulder. "I couldn't support you. That doesn't mean I didn't believe in the rebellion."

I step up to her. "You tried to turn everyone against us."

"You think I had a choice? Myers threatened my clan. I did what I had to do."

"You wanted to kill me."

Drop stands firm. "You were a danger to us."

"And now you want me to help you."

"We aren't in school anymore, Scream."

I fling away and slam the door to my room.

What a stupid thing to say. Does she really believe it all goes away?

Does everything get tossed aside because we aren't in school anymore? Murderers are forgiven? Rapists forgotten? Bullies turn to sheep? Is that how it is? Is that reality? Or am I holding a grudge? Do I let it all go? Forgive unforgivable sins?

I curl up on the bed, and I watch my locked door until my eyes can't keep open any longer, and I fall asleep.

· · · · ● · ● · ● · ·

When I wake, it is to a sharp knock. It starts my heart, and I sit up, panting. I search for a weapon, and questions pop up: where am I? How do I get to safety? Where's Charles? And in that brief split second, there is a cut in my heart, and I sit, dwelling on his loss.

The knock comes again.

I grumble, asking who it is before unlocking it, and Nurse Janice enters with a pleasant smile and sets about talking. It's early morning, but somehow, she manages to have such excitable energy. She checks my wristband before she begins her instructions, asking me to change into a medical gown to remove all my clothing.

"No," is my quick reply, and I sit on the bed, stalwart.

She goes on to explain the necessary need for it to do a physical.

"I didn't ask for a physical nor do I want one."

Getting rather flustered, she moves on, and I'm victorious. That is until she rolls over a machine. She must see the look on my face because she giggles and quickly explains the device. Janice takes my blood pressure, my temperature and asks me questions like if I am on medications, when my last period was, and if I'm sexually active. I squirm, and my cheeks burn red, but she seems careless, simply reading these questions and really listening to the answers. It makes it easier. But I still have nothing to give.

I don't know any of these answers.

Before she can finish her interrogation, the doctor walks in. Whoever is in charge is smart enough to ensure the girl's unit has all female employees. I would have bolted out of the ten-inch glass behind me if a guy ever walked through my door.

"My name is Doctor Yugi. What happened? How come you haven't changed?" The nurse whispers something unintelligible. "It's alright. We'll just talk then." Doctor Yugi sits on the bed beside me. "Ember, what's your last name?"

I never thought of a last name. But I should have one, shouldn't I? "Um—" I look around the room. "Stone."

"Ember Stone, perfect. I'm a doctor here, Ember, and what I want is to take care of your physical health as well as your mental health. But right now, I want to ensure your body is healthy. So why don't you lay down? If you are uncomfortable, tell me to stop. But know you are safe. No one here is going to hurt you. Those bad people are going to be punished. Okay? Can you trust me a little bit?"

Chewing my bottom lip, I nod. Doctor Yugi pats me on the back with a bright, happy smile, and I feel like I just made her day.

I am assured with every move they make because they don't approach without describing the reason. I like them. They know how to deal with me. But it also makes me weary.

Why do they need me to trust them? What do they want from me?

The doctor continues describing the procedures and the ensuring it is all normal. They ask me to pull up my shirt, giving me control. Upon noticing the bruises, random scraps, and cuts, they bombard me with questions. I find myself opening up, telling them who did what and when, without giving away who I am or who I am helping. I show them the stab wounds in my thigh and left shoulder.

They make me feel special by saying my pain tolerance is incredible.

One thing I notice mentioning again and again is James. Tears spring unwanted, and I rub at them, embarrassed.

"Can you find him?" I beg, and they promise me they will, but it's patronizing, and I lose my faith in them.

"Ember, can you tell me what happened to your back? There's a lot of scars."

I don't want to talk anymore.

Doctor Yugi sits beside me. "Now something else we do, but I don't think right now is appropriate because you seem to still have a bit of trust issues with us, but it's a procedure that's quite common for females at your age. Have you ever heard of a Pap smear?'

I shake my head.

The doctor takes a breath. 'It's a procedure where we look at your vagina to—'

I dart off the bed and lock myself in the bathroom.

A soft knock taps on the door, and I flinch away from it, searching for a weapon. "It's okay, Ember, you are safe here. A nurse is going to bring you more information about physical exams. We're going to go, Ember. Just, are you okay?

I press my forehead against the door, humiliated. "I'm fine."

"Alright, Ember. We have a specialist that's going to come by in the morning. Is it okay if I have her come talk to you?"

My hand fists against the door. "Okay."

"Okay, Ember. Have a good night.'

I lower to the floor, with my back against the door, and hug my legs.

We're not in school anymore, Lisa claimed. But that didn't make it all better. She was wrong to talk to me like we were comrades in arms. We are not in this together. We are not equals. There's an overwhelming gap in why we will never be the same, and it has everything to do with our choices.

She chose to be a clan leader, and I decided to be clanless.

And now we have to live with those choices.

CHAPTER 3
Found

EMBER

THIS ROOM BECOMES THE first and only safe location where I have complete control over who is allowed near me. It's a place I would have given my soul for back in school. What I'm realizing though is how the quiet echoes with voices, with memories. I sit in a corner, staring at the door. It's locked and there's a chair against the knob, but it doesn't keep out the monsters in my head.

"Listen to me," Tobias whispered in my ear. *"I'll protect you. But first, I'm gonna make you scream."*

I hear Tobias the most. Over Charles' laughter, he speaks in repetition, saying the same things, over and over again. *'But first, I'm gonna make you scream.'*

I clench my hands over my ears, but it's still there, loud and clear. Tobias continues to follow me and not even death keeps me from his hold. How do I defeat against him? How do I conquer a ghost?

I stand up and though I want to stay in the room, I can't. I won't drown in his memory. I won't let him pull me into Hell with him.

I remove the chair and unlock the door. Nurses chit-chat at the station, laughing and tossing papers back to each other. Janice looks at me and waves sweetly. She points to the opposite end of the hall. "A lot of your friends are in the game room. Breakfast is ready."

"What about the boys?"

Her brows depress. "Not yet, honey, I'm sorry. We'll figure something out."

I think about returning to my room, but the word 'breakfast' stands out. I wonder what that all entails. My stomach grumbles in hopeful desire, and I move slowly against the wall, stopping before every door, making sure it's shut or no one is lurking if it has been left open.

I come into the game room. It's a massive space with multiple areas of recreation. From the right is a large flat-screen TV with a gaming system attached and a leather couch facing it. In the corner, against the windows, are bar stools and table tops. Several girls sit drinking coffee and eating their breakfast. In the center of the room is a gaming table with sticks poking out the sides and little men erected on poles. There are multiple places to sit, and tables with magazines spread on top and books underneath. On the left side is a buffet table, and it is covered in breakfast foods. Cereal containers, milk and juice boxes, large metal pans full of eggs, bacon, pancakes, fruits, and an array of muffins pack the table. And the best thing of all: it is free. I don't have to spend hours in the wastelands to come up with measly tickets to buy any of it. It is the most amazing sight I've seen.

I don't care about the dozens of girls staring at me or how they've stopped talking or eating to stare. I walk to the table, ignoring clan members with ease.

I don't know where to start or what I want first. But what I do notice is a knife. It's a butter knife, and it's just lying there like it's not dangerous or a useful weapon in this world of criminals. I slide a granola bar across the table, pick up the butter knife, and slip them into my pocket.

Drop comes up beside me. "You don't have to hoard, you know. We get as much food as we want."

I don't say anything, grabbing two juice boxes to save one for later. She's more naive than I am if she thinks food can never be taken away. Her clan-like mentality is brighter than the sunlight streaming in, and I don't have the patience for it.

Drop leans back against the table, sighing. "I think it would be a good idea if we became friends." She holds out her hand. "I'm Lisa."

I scoff, chewing on a grape, and moving down the table.

She drops her hand. "I have a lot of weight still. You want to find your friends, right?"

I reluctantly look her way. She might know something, and though I hate her, I'm not against pretending to like her to get the information I want.

"An ambulance came this morning," she reveals. "Two guys and a girl."

"How do you know that?"

"I have eyes everywhere. If something is going down, I'm going to be paying attention. And something is going to go down if we don't find a way to get to the boys. There is already talk." Lisa moves in and whispers, "I know faces of Coal members too."

I chew my food, contemplating. With all our new clothes, I wouldn't be able to pinpoint who is who. And though I consider everyone here dangerous, Coal members are particularly worse. I glance over my shoulder, searching for one.

"They aren't here," she assures. "Even Rain members don't get along with Coal. They keep to themselves and gather on the other end by the stairwell. We have the elevator, at least."

"We can't use the elevator. Not without a card the nurses have."

Her annoying stare lingers and a smile stretches. "See that? We are helping each other already."

I grumble and sit on a sofa. I feel like I got tricked somehow. I observe everyone in the room. So many people I've never taken the time to get to know. I've seen their faces randomly over the months. Most of them glared at me or cursed me at some point for something I did. I know the basketball players still have a little grudge.

Lisa leans over my chair. "Don't be so stubborn. This is a different world. Adapt. Look at everyone in this room. Remember their faces. You are among friends here. Even if you don't feel like you are. A lot of them wouldn't mind getting to know you. You freed us. You blew up the school. We just want to say thank you."

That sounds nice, but it doesn't sound realistic. Clan members aren't friendly for no reason. What can I provide for them in return is the question.

Screams echo down the hall. I slip to the floor, my food tossed, and I dig into my pocket for the knife. Lisa crawls beside me while members of her clan gather around her, around me, waiting for signals. I assume Boundary members split because they congregate around someone else. I notice one of them looks at me, looks at Lisa before she moves her clan down the hall. I wonder who she is in Boundary to have leadership over the girls. We go up the left hallway and they go up the right. The commotion is coming from the nurse's station. It's just a bunch of female screams, nothing coherent, nothing that makes sense, and it's to a point annoying. Do they understand that screaming does nothing? It doesn't ease the pain. It doesn't stop the actions of cruelty.

I crawl down the hall with my butter knife in hand. "Please don't shoot us." One of the nurses begs. I poke my head around the corner.

James stands before them. Dirt and blood cover his entire body, transforming his once porcelain white skin to nearly black. He somehow lost his shirt and his shoes. He has a gun pointing at the nurses while his other hand remains tucked into his chest, wrapped in a makeshift cast. He reads a chart on the desk, his eyes rapidly flipping along the names.

I slowly get to my feet. "James."

His head spins, and the moment he sees me, his brown eyes lighten, and stress begins to recede. James steps toward me, barely keeping to his feet. He scans me from head to toe.

I force out what he's silently asking. "I'm fine."

His brows knit, and his eyes squeeze shut for a moment in relief. The gun drops from his hand. He collapses to his knees, and I catch him before he falls over. "Help!" I call out, and the once terrified nurses now spring into action.

I hold him close, my hand going over his face, my tears slipping down his cheeks. "You're alright," I murmur. "You found me." The last thing I told him to do was find me and like I knew he would, he didn't fail. James presses a square trinket into my hands and closes it. The tension in his hold is all I need to tell me to hide it. "Rest. They'll help you." James closes his eyes and succumbs to unconsciousness.

The nurses swing a gurney over and lift him up. I follow, clinging to it as they roll to the elevator. It's here however, they push me back. "Please," I beg, but they instruct me to stay. The doors shut before I could do anything more, and he is gone.

I stare at the closed doors.

I hadn't realized how much I cared until now. I'm thankful to see his face again, knowing he is here and safe. I slap a hand over my mouth when a sudden sob escapes, and I rush to my room, shutting the door and locking it. When did I become so attached to his being? To everything that he is and everything that he does? I want to be with him, in his presence, and him in mine. Anything else is unbearable. I sit on the bed, contemplating how I am going to make it to him again. What can I do to escape this room and be by his side?

I hold the square trinket out. Whatever this is, James risked his life for it. I curl my fist and search for a hiding spot.

CHAPTER 4
What's in a Name?

EMBER

I RUB AT THE crusty tears at the corner of my eyes, shoving my crazy hair from my face. It's morning, a new day already. I've slept hours and hours, and I double-check the time in disbelief that I could sleep for so long. My body was deprived of peaceful rest for five months. Now I'm soaking it up like a plant devoid of light.

I don't move while the echoes of my nightmare flash in my mind. Ash's face comes in and out of view, transforming with every ray of light, starting off with a nasty smile and ending as I choked the life from him.

I look at my hands. I can still see the traces of scratch marks.

I almost killed him.

Then the image changes and Ash is above me and blood splashes on my face. The warmth makes me nauseous. In his face, he doesn't understand yet that he's dead already. There's fear and confusion. I can hear him struggling to breathe and the wet intake of breath as he drowns in his own blood.

There was no saving him. But I should have at least attempted.

A muffled voice sounds on the other side of the door, breaking me out of my stupor. "My name is Sarah. I'm a counselor here. May I come in and talk to you?"

I really don't want to talk to anyone. I know I'm screwed up, but pointing it out isn't going to help. I'll learn how to ignore the wrong thoughts in my head, and someday I'll stop hearing Tobias' voice in everything I do.

Someday, just not today.

I yank the door open, and she plasters on a fake smile. I already don't like her.

Sarah sits across from me, waiting patiently. She has a clipboard on her lap. Her legs crossed, and a foot dangles in white heels, jiggling lazily. She wears glasses, her blond hair up in a bun. She has dew drop earrings and a gold necklace. Her maroon pantsuit is wrinkle-free and looks good on her. Green eyes weave over me, analyzing my body language. I hope she's good enough to see I'm not going to make this easy.

"You know what a counselor is, yes?"

I roll my eyes, cross my arms, and let out a loud, annoying sigh.

"Okay." She shifts and tries a different approach. "You don't have to talk to me. But Doctor Yugi seemed very concerned about you. They want you to know you have someone to talk to."

"If I want to talk to someone, I'll talk to my friends. But you all won't let me."

Her brows knit before understanding. "I thought they allowed you to hang out in the game room?"

I sneer. "They aren't my friends."

"I take it then your friends are boys. What clan are you in?"

I can't say it. I'm naturally skeptical, something ingrained in me over the months. I don't trust easily, and I definitely don't trust teachers. If I could be logical, I could admit she doesn't look like a teacher, and we are no longer in school, but adults, in general, are scary to me.

Although she seems young enough.

"Boundary," I lie, but I made a semi-step towards trust, so I'll settle for it.

"Now Ember Stone isn't coming up in our database, but you aren't the only one. There are many kids here that don't want to be found. Is there something you're afraid of? Bad parents? Foster care?"

"No. I don't—" I pause, unsure if I should be honest. But if I want someone to help me, I need to tell them what's wrong. "I don't have a memory."

Her brows knit. "What do you mean, like amnesia?"

I nod.

"Oh, well, that puts a hold on things. Did something happen?" When I shrug, she smiles. "Probably don't remember." Sarah giggles.

"I know things."

"Like what?"

I bite the inside of my cheek. "I've never been inside a car. Or seen one for that matter. But I know there's a gas petal and a break. A steering wheel. Things like that."

Sarah taps her pen. "'*Retrograde amnesia is a loss of memory-access to events that occurred or information that was learned, before an injury or the onset of a disease. It tends to negatively affect episodical, autobiographical, and declarative memory while usually keeping procedural memory intact with no difficulty for learning new knowledge.'"* She pauses, and then flips on a personality. "From my understanding of something I read in a dictionary. It basically means all your typical functions, i.e. talking, personal hygiene, eating, you knew how to do without being taught again. While having no idea who you are."

I shrug. "Sounds right."

"How long have you been in the school?"

"Five months."

She nods and clears her throat. "The doctor mentioned you have a lot of injuries."

"They told you?"

Sarah softly smiles. "It's in the file. Everything gets written down, and we share it. It's how we keep track of everyone. But we are all doctors and it stays within our medical profession." She waits, allowing me to accept these terms. "We are searching for a boy named Shakes? I've been hearing this name a lot. But no one has told me what he looks like. Do you know? I'd like to find him. It's said he is the leader of the rebel clan Anarchy."

And it is instant, any trust developing in her falls apart and I spout out an easy lie, "He died a year ago. Someone took his name for a while, but he's dead too."

She writes this down, mulling over it for a time. "Okay. Because you seem to know a lot, does that mean you were part of the rebellion?"

I clamp my lips shut. I'm such an idiot. "I don't want to talk anymore."

Sarah rests her hands down on her lap, looking me over. "I'm here to help you, Ember."

"I'm doing just fine, thanks. If you want to help so much, find my friends."

She takes in a breath. "I'll make a deal with you. I'll find your friends, and then you tell me something about you. We build trust one step at a time."

I chew my lip. What's the downside to this? I'll have to talk about something I want to suppress, but finding my family outweighs the negative. "James. Jam-Jam. I don't know his last name." She surprises me by snapping to her feet and walking out the door. I stare after her, confused. Within minutes, she's back in the room and takes her spot.

"James, the boy that came in yesterday and scared the nurses. He's in surgery. He broke his hand after being nearly crushed by a building. But otherwise, he should be okay."

It isn't enough, but now I know her power. She can find the others. If I pull back on our agreement, she won't find anyone else for me. "What should I tell you about me?"

"Well, um, your injuries are pretty extensive. Doctor Yugi said you shut down after she asked you about the scars on your back. May I see them?"

I chew my lip. I'm obligated now, and I force myself on my feet to lift my shirt. I don't remember being whipped. I know it happened. I know who did it, but I've blocked it out. Sometimes I see it in my nightmares. Sometimes I remember the pain. If nothing else, I remember the aftermath, laying on the frozen ground, hearing Tobias talk above me like I was dead.

"Who did this to you? This isn't normal practice from what I can tell from the school."

"It was a boy named Tobias."

Her head snaps up. There's confusion on her brow, and her green eyes dance from side to side until she swallows and looks back down at her paper, writing. "And who is he?"

"He was the leader of Respect."

"Was?"

"He was killed."

Her pen doesn't move. "How?"

"Myers shot him a few days ago. I don't know how much you know of everything, but it's a long story." I slouch, picking at my nails. It's at that moment I realize they don't have dirt underneath them. They almost look like normal, healthy hands.

If not for the scratches from a kid I tried to kill.

"Did he..." She clears her throat. "From your disposition, your lack of trust, and from the doctor's notes, they assume you were raped. Was he... Were you?"

I smile, perhaps evilly. "You gotta find another friend for that answer, doc."

She narrows her green eyes but concedes and waits for a name, but Brick, Vapor, and Ink, I don't know their real names. I notice she is writing something, and I lean up, trying to see what it is. She flips her clipboard around, and in big bold letters, are the words, *'Are you Scream?'*

Panic streaks across my face. Where would she have heard that name? Why does it matter? Why is it secret?

She puts a finger to her lips and points that same finger to the TV above her head. The TV that's looking straight at me. "Any name for me to find?" She continues casually. "Or are you going to give me an answer?"

What's wrong with the TV? I stare at it. A red dot is at the bottom, but I assumed it was the power button. But what if it is a camera? The cameras at school all had red dots.

The eye of God.

When she asks again, I numbly answer, "Yes."

Yes, I am Scream.

She puts the clipboard down and writes something else while she talks casually. "Who would you like me to find?" Sarah lifts the clipboard up again. *'I'm a friend. Tell no one. They are searching for you.'*

I shake my head. I'm nobody. They had the wrong person. I am...

I am just the girl who blew up the school.

I'm somebody now.

A knock on the door interrupts. "Ember?" Janice enters. "The investigator wants to meet you. I'm gonna escort you down."

Sarah stands up. "I can do it."

"That's alright. Come on, Ember."

I glance back at Sarah, but she wears a forced smile, waving pleasantly. "I'll check back in with you later. You still owe me some answers."

How does she act so well? She's multiple people at the same time. I've never seen someone so good at pretending. I want to learn from her. I would love to know how to be someone other than myself.

I lean against the wall of the elevator.

"I figured you wanted a break." Janice smiles and tries to be friendly. "Councilors, ugh." She waits for a response, but I have none to give her. "You happy to be out of that school?" She winces, holding her head. "I'm sorry. That's stupid, of course you are. I'm sorry. I just don't know what to say to any of you. They tell us we're not supposed to talk to you, but you're just kids."

The doors open, and she takes the lead. I make a note of every turn. Every person's face and every door I pass. I ignore Janice's rambling voice. None of it is worth remembering, but it leads me to assume she is as ignorant of my situation as I am of hers.

We step into an office. The wall on the right is covered in papers, names, and pictures. The words Coal, Boundary, Rain, and Anarchy with red strings pulling to different things. There is a cluster in the corner of pictures with the word 'Specials' written in bold black font. I search for images for James.

Only four photos are under Anarchy. And Kevin is one of them.

Behind a desk sits the investigator. He is wearing a navy-blue suit and an off-white tie. He is older, perhaps thirty or more, and gets to his feet with a smile. "*Hola.*" He holds out his hand. I lean back into Janice, intimidated. He stops approaching. "Sorry, I'm too tall for my own good." He puts himself back behind the desk. "Please, sit. My name's Jose. I'm one of the detectives for the school. Are you liking everything so far?"

This is a grown man. The male teachers I've met have been nothing like him. They were short and fat, ugly, and smelt like sweat. I was starting to think all adults became obese. But Jose actually looks attractive.

That's a weird thought to have about a teacher.

Jose coughs, uneasy with my silence. "My job is to interview the students, take testimony against any teachers, and—" he hesitates to find his wording. "Against any of the students." His eyes trace over me, searching for something in my face before he continues. "Doctor Yugi sent your file down to me, so I thought perhaps you would make a good candidate for what I'm trying to do."

Jose stands up, but the moment I shift, he stops and leans against the desk. "We have to make a tough decision. We are quite aware that some of these kids are beyond rehabilitation. As sad as it is to admit it, they were in the school too long, affecting them to a point where they would not do well in modern society. And we need someone, someone that knows these kids, to help us weed out the bad seeds."

My heart is racing. Why does that sound familiar?

"Now, please, don't get us wrong. We are going to do everything we can for you kids. We have programs lined up. We will get you back to normal schooling. We will provide homeschooling if preferred. We will move some of you into witness protection. We will have financial aid for all of your medical needs for the next two years. We want to erase this horrible thing from your memory. And for the kids that need extra time, we are dedicated to that. We will give them that extra love. However, at this time, we cannot allow them to go home. Do you understand, Miss Stone?"

"You... You're bringing us home, right?"

"Yes, yes, of course." He pauses, and than changes his tone. "It's too much, let me start over."

"No." I couldn't listen to him ramble again. "You want me to tell you—" I hesitate because it sounds good, but it feels wrong. "Which ones are the bad ones?"

"Yes. Yes. Precisely."

"We're all bad."

His brows dip in sympathy. "No. No. You're not. I just need the list of people that have committed serious offenses. Like murder. Like rape."

He wants me to be a snitch.

"I can't...I can't do that."

"Okay." He tapes the table. "Let's start simple. I don't mean to be insensitive. But, I heard particulars about your case. You have stab wounds, whip marks. And um.. there's belief you were...mistreated otherwise. Do you know who hurt you?"

"Yes."

"Okay. Give me that name."

"Tobias." It's an easy name to give. Even if he were alive, I'd still throw him under the bus.

Jose quickly scribbles the name down. "Anyone else?"

"Ruler."

"Do you know his real name?"

I shake his head. And when he asks for another, I say, "Cloud. He had his friends hold me down. Does that count? I don't know their names."

At first, he doesn't know what to say. He sits back in his chair, inspecting me. I look down at my feet. He sighs and rubs his face. "I'm sorry, I'm being a *capullo*." The chair squeaks as he sits up and rests his elbow on the table. "But names are important. Do you understand why I'm doing this? What if I let these boys go, and they do the same thing to someone else? How can I live with that on my conscience? Could you?"

Isn't that why we were in the school in the first place? Because we were bad? I don't like this. Why

47

did he come to me? There has to be someone smarter who understands what's happening for him to talk to.

"They're not going to go to prison," he assures. "I can't send juveniles to prison, especially without proof or evidence. But I can send them to a rehabilitation program where they are retaught how to live in normal society. They relearn the right way to treat human beings. You all have lived in a world where normalcy was *loco*. If I could, I would send you all, but the program can't afford so many. So don't think that you're taking their freedom. Think of it as giving them another chance to be who they were supposed to be. You're doing them a kindness."

"I understand now." I face him. "You are sending them to a school."

He's disappointed of my dece. "It's not the same, Ember. I promise."

A promise...as if that holds any weight.

I shrug and take a seat. "All my attackers are dead. I don't think rehabilitation is going to work."

He cracks a smile. "You got a sense of humor. That's good."

Me? A sense of humor?

"It's a good thing to have with a situation like this. But you understand what I'm trying to do right? You think you can help me out a bit?"

If anything, he wants something from me and I want something from him. "Find my friends."

Jose chews his lip, glancing up at Janice. "She's a spitfire, isn't she?" He grabs a piece of paper, and I give him all their code names, but he sighs. "Without real names, I don't know if I'll be able to help you."

"Then maybe..." I shift in my chair. I don't know if I'm pushing too hard, but I try regardless. "Allow us to talk to the boys."

"I don't know about that, especially after learning what they can do."

"You're caging us in, and we don't like it. We haven't had normal rules and regulations and applying them all at once is not a good idea. Let us go outside. Let us have a way to communicate with the boys. You can have guards up or something. Or you won't have time to do any of this. They'll riot, and people will die."

His eyes widen. "Is it that serious?"

"There's a reason Myers allowed us our freedoms. We are fighters. All of us. There is already talk."

"Noted." He came around the desk, sitting on the edge. "There's a rumor that you might go by the nickname Scream. Is this true?"

I rapidly shake my head. "No."

He glances up at my nurse, and she agrees. Jose shrugs. "I'm just trying to find her. She probably needs some protection from Coal. We had to take Kevin, a boy from Anarchy, into protection because Coal was terrorizing him."

He took Kevin. He did something to Kevin. I try not to let the worry show.

"If you know Scream, please let her know I can help her."

Like Sarah smiled so perfectly, I force it on my lips, suppressing the panic and the fear. And with a voice so calm and sweet, I reply, "I don't know Scream. Someone should tell her that's a terrible nickname."

CHAPTER 5
Logic

EMBER

I STAND IN THE shower, afraid of my room, the people in this hospital, and everything else except for this tiny little box. The hot water sprays on me, drenching my clothes, hair, and face, but it doesn't filter. I can't get Jose out of my head. He sounded like Myers. He acted like what he was doing was for the good of humanity. Like he was doing us a favor by eliminating the 'bad ones'. But the route he was taking was so similar to Myers. Every day, we were told we were no good. Our parents brought us to Myers and asked him to take us because society could no longer handle us because we were evil.

Now, Jose wants to pick through the school to find the most corrupt. To send them away. Because society says they are evil.

But Myers was an evil man.

And Jose is a good one.

Is that the right logic? Does that make one right and the other wrong?

There is a heavy knock on my door. I get dressed before I answer it to find Lisa standing on the other side. I roll my eyes in annoyance and leave her in the doorway. I don't know why this girl suddenly thinks I want to have conversations with her.

Lisa invites herself in and makes herself at home, plopping in a chair. "Guess you figured it out. The Special came in the ambulance."

"His name is James."

I feel the weight of the TV pressing on me, like a Coal Member glaring across the desert. Every move I make, and every word I say is taken under scrutiny to be ridiculed. I blink blindly at the ground, hoping that none of my movements give way to the fact that I know.

"We're trying to find ways to get messages to the boys," she reveals. "They won't let us communicate. I don't like it. They won't let us go outside either. That's two strikes. I don't know if the guys will put up with it."

"I spoke to the detective. Maybe he'll help us."

Lisa sits up with knit brows. "The detective? What do you mean you spoke to him? What did you say?"

The accusation in her tone doesn't go unnoticed. "He's searching for Scream and Shakes. I don't know them, but maybe you can help him."

Lisa moves to the edge of her seat, understanding what I'm not saying. She taps her ear and mouths, '*Listening?*'

I flick my gaze to the TV, and she twists her head up above her. Mimicking Sarah, I keep talking, moving right on with the conversation. "This detective is pretty nice. He seems real. He's looking for bad kids. Kids that have killed or hurt others. I could only give him the names that affected me, but they are all dead, so I had nothing to offer him."

Worry creases her pretty face, her black brows squish together as she chews the side of her cheek. "Thank you." She darts out of the room.

I wonder if Lisa is genuine. I want to trust her because she is my only ally on this floor. She has connections and can keep me protected. But she turned her back on the Rebellion when we needed Rain's help. They had people, and they had weapons. The war might have gone differently if Rain had backed us up. Our people hiding could have been kept in Rain's building and never been found, nor been hostages in Myer's possession. I want to be like Shakes where I can kick people out and never trust them again, but I'm not in such a position to do that. He has an abundant of resources and people around him where he can kick out someone, and another is quick to take their place. But if I do that, I'll be alone in seconds.

Hunger makes me move to the game room, and the buffet is there with lunch food. Sandwiches, salads, and soups. I try everything simply because I can, and by the time I'm done, I've never been so full. A couple girls wave to me or greet me shyly. It confuses the hell out of me.

"Momma Mary!" Someone shouts, and the girls in the room fling out of their chairs, darting down the hall.

I hear her then, her loud booming voice, "My girls! Look at you. You are so pretty. Come here, give me a hug. Oh, Lord, we've been blessed."

I don't move. I have no desire to rush my fate. If Shakes has decided to kick me out of the family, I don't know what I'll do. If he's dead, it won't matter because I won't survive Coal's backlash without him.

The girls are spilling back into the game room, and I sit there waiting for a verdict. They pull Mary in, asking her where she's been, wanting her to do their hair, or to talk to her about a problem. She sees me, and her movements stop. I hang my head, shivering.

"In a minute," she murmurs. "Just give me a minute, girls."

I'm so happy to see her and so terrified at the same time. Mary approaches and grabs my arm. "Give me a hug, you crazy girl." I bury my face in her shoulder, squeezing with all my might.

"Is he-"

"He's fine, sweetheart. He sent me to find you."

I choke on a sob. "He doesn't hate me?"

"No, no, of course not. He cherishes you, Ember." Relief pours over me and my knees weaken. Mary pulls away to grab my face. She rubs the wetness from my cheeks. "Oh, honey. You did good. Carbon died, and it broke him. He knows that you did the right thing." We sit down, but she keeps my hands in her lap. "He's been so worried about you. You know to keep your door locked. Don't go anywhere with anyone."

I nod dumbly as she goes on with random rules, but I'm stuck back in relief. I'm still in Shakes' favor. He didn't kick me out of the family. I'm still loved. All my fears don't matter compared to that.

"Do you know about anyone else?" she asks.

"I saw James. Jam-Jam."

"So we are just missing Vapor, Brick, and Tara."

I don't know how to break bad news, but I make myself say it. "Tara didn't make it."

She throws up a hand, a sudden wave of grief. "Of course!" She blubbers and collapses against me. I pat her shoulder, loving her despite the wetness soaking my jacket. I've missed her like crazy. She wipes her face, takes a breath, and stands. "I should get back with Adam now that I found you. Don't use his nickname anymore. And don't use yours. It's safer this way. What's your room number?"

"232. Wait, where is he? Why can you be with him?"

Her face flusters. "Adam wouldn't let them take me away." She squeezes my hand. "We are in room 670. Sneak your way soon. He'll be so relieved to know you're safe." It takes her a while to leave as the girls continue moving around her, loving her like any daughter would a mother. It's so funny to watch these young women chase after Mary. Mary is the opposite of a typical clan member. She's polite and respectful, she's outgoing and sociable. She's funny and has a big, contagious laugh. Everyone wants to be her friend. They want just a little of her light to brighten up their day. It's easy to understand how Shakes fell in love with her.

When she leaves, I lean back into my seat and hold up a book on the country's best parks. It has beautiful pictures, and I go through each one, trying to put them all to memory so that one day when I get free, I can visit them. The girls slowly return to their activities, reading, writing, chatting, playing video games as I become invisible in the corner.

Jose breaks into my thoughts here. He wants a list of all the bad people, and I trace each face, trying to remember them back in our crazy world. Boundary and Rain stay separated. They have individual clusters, and they are easy to figure out from someone's tattoo. I know Boundary requires killing to join their group simply because it's a

dangerous job. If the need arises to shoot someone, they can't be afraid to do it. But they don't
just shoot randomly into a crowd. So where is the
dividing line? They kill because it's their job. It
doesn't make them evil.

Or doesn't it? A month ago, I would have called
them the devil's reincarnate. But I think differently now. And I wonder when that changed.

I bow my head, suppressing a smile. It's when
I met Shakes and his family of rebels. But most
specifically when I met James.

How can I go on to judge others? Unless I talk to
them, get to know them, figure out who they are
inside?

*That was something Charles was good at. He
wasn't afraid of strangers.*

Lisa enters the room and notices the segrega-
tion between the clans. She attempts to break this
by talking to Boundary members and then Rain
members, but they look at each other with dis-
dain before she gives up and approaches me. "Why
won't they talk to each other? It's not about clans
anymore. We are stuck here together. We have to
get out together."

I keep my book propped just right so she can't see the names I've written. For the most part, they are names that don't need the help, like her and a few of her friends. Rain was the least violent of the Clans.

I point to a girl in Boundary. "What's her name?"

She is tall and skinny, with blond hair and freckles. She is becoming the mascot for Boundary's little circle.

"That's Heather. She dates one of the leaders of Boundary. Blockade or Brick, I can never remember which."

The mention of Brick makes me shift. I still haven't heard anything about him. But I doubt the girls know any more than I do.

"She's definitely a cause for concern," Lisa agrees. "I'll talk to her when she's not around her group of hens."

"Do you know-" I roam my eyes over the pages of my book. "Has she killed anyone?"

"What Boundary member hasn't? They maintained the safety of the school. It came with the job."

I stare at her name on the good side of my list. "Have you killed anyone?"

Her eyes rest on me but I pretend that I don't notice. "What's with you? Are you helping *him* make that list?"

I slap the book closed, getting to my feet. "Don't talk to me like we're friends." I head to my room, but she aggravatingly follows me.

"We have to be on the same side."

"Why?"

"People trust you. They're scared of you, but they trust you. I need you if I'm going to keep them safe."

I swing around, walking backward. "Safe from what? This is the end, Lisa. We're going home." I shut my door, snapping the lock.

I hear her muffled voice through it, "You don't really believe that. You wouldn't have a knife in your pocket if you did."

Chapter 6

Safe

Ember

I WAKE TO A sharp knock, and I groan. Why am I so popular? Back in school, I could go a whole week without anyone talking to me, and now I can't go for a few hours. I roll off, noticing it's two in the morning. I hang my head, calling out, asking who it is.

Janice greets me with an ever-pleasant smile on her face. She had been gone all day. She must be part of the night crew. How long are their shifts? How do they leave? Where do they go?

"Sorry to bother you, can I see your nametag?"

I hold it out, and she reads my name before nodding and wrapping a green band around it. "This allows you to go between floors. Room 512." She begins to walk away, but I snag her wrist.

"What's going on?"

She looks down at her paper. "Sorry, hun, they didn't tell me."

"Janice, can I ask you a question?"

Janice glances down the hall to the nurses' station. "Yeah, sure."

"What did they say this was? Who we are?"

She sticks her hands in her pockets, leaning against the doorway. "You were kidnapped and kept in a prison. It's not a secret, honey. The police are working very hard to get you home. We are here to make sure you are healthy enough to leave. That's one of the reasons we need to do a physical. Have you read those papers I left you?"

The talk of the physical pushes me away, and I back up, dismissing her. She tells me to hurry to room 512, but I take my time, washing my face first and then brushing my teeth and hair. I stare at my reflection. There was nothing to be done about the bags under my eyes, but whoever was 'summoning' me in the middle of the night deserved my tired expression. I stand in the elevator, waving my wristband in front of the screen and the button glows. Before my finger lands on the button, I hesitate.

Could this be a trap?

I have done a dozen stupid things in the past, but I trust the nurse.

I hug my jacket around me, stepping out on the fifth floor. A pretty blond nurse notices me and waves me over.

"Are you Ember?"

"Yes?"

She pumps her fist and looks back at her friend. "I told you I could find her. Follow me. Sorry for bothering you so late, but it's been awful. He needs to rest. He's had a rough surgery. He won't eat. He keeps asking for you. So I promised if he ate something, I'd find you." She knocked gently on the door. "Please, get him to sleep."

I peek inside and follow her pointed finger toward the curtain. The room is more extensive than mine, but it fits two other boys sleeping. I pass their beds and stand on the other side of a curtain. With a deep breath, I peak inside.

James lays staring out the floor-to-ceiling windows. The moon shines on him, exposing his chiseled jawline. His bare white chest glistens and every rippled muscle makes a small shadow. He looks stunning lying there, clean and unsullied, like a Greek statue made of marble. His broken hand lays on a pillow with an ice pack on top.

I step in, and his head swings to meet me. He relaxes visibly, his head sinking into the pillow. It's silly how we simply stare at each other. I can't believe he's here, and I'm here, and we're both out of the school. It doesn't seem real. It's a dream, and yet I chose this over anything. I don't want to leave it. It doesn't have to be real. Let me stay asleep forever.

"Are you giving the nurses a hard time?" I managed to get out. My voice cracks, and a tear drips down my cheek. I rub it quickly away, smiling.

"How are you?"

My brows knit. It is such a simple question, but the way he asks, it's like my health is the most important thing to him. "I'm fine. What happened to you?"

"The computer I took from Zack. I needed that information. The building collapsed as I was leaving. Do you have it?"

I approach. "I left it in my room." His look of panic quickly makes me assure him, "It's safe. I hid it. But why did you risk your life for that?"

James stares at me distantly, like the drugs in his system aren't letting him think. "They haven't hurt you?"

"No." I smile warmly, my cheeks heating up from silly thoughts. "It's safe here."

"Safe," he murmurs, shifting his attention toward the window.

"What's going on with your hand?"

"They are naive," he responds coldly. "They want to save it."

"Well, of course, it's your hand."

"Two more surgeries, they predict. Three months to heal. Six months of physical therapy. No. Cut it off and be done with it."

I wonder if he says this because it was the same hand that Zack injured. "James."

"How can I fight like this?" He looks at me. "How can I protect?"

"You don't have to do either. We're out of school."

"If you think that school is the only horror in this world, then you are more gullible than a child."

"I think I know horrors."

There is a pause as we stare at each other. I'm seconds away from running. If he wants to fight,

I'll fight, but he will not disrespect my struggle through hell.

James relinquishes. "Yes, you do. I'm tired. I did not mean that."

I bow my head, shoving the aggression out of my chest. I look up at his face, but his eyes are closed.

"You need to sleep."

He nods in agreement.

"I'll go."

He snatches my hand, suddenly wide awake. "No. Stay."

I clench his fingers. I don't want to let go. "Okay. I'll stay. But you have to sleep."

He shifts on the bed, making room, and gently tugs.

I'm stiff, unable to do what he wants. I can't sleep next to a man. Even a man I'm not afraid of. But James ignores me, scooting over more. Nervousness festers in my gut, and I stare at his tired face. He tries to keep his eyes open, but he struggles.

I sit on the bed with a stiff back. Logically, I know he can't hurt me even if he wanted to. His arm is detained. All I'd have to do is touch it, and he'd become immobilized in pain. But this is foreign territory. The only person I've ever slept next to was Charles.

I lay down with my back toward him and use his arm as my pillow. He curls it around me, holding on to me. I'm uncomfortable and uneasy, staring out ahead of me. I'll never sleep like this, especially with his breath on the back of my head.

I sit back up, and it jolts him awake. His eyes are wide, staring at me, barely comprehending. I kick off my shoes and take off my jacket, and this time, when I lay down, I face him, laying the coat on top like a blanket. His arm once again curls around me, keeping me snug against him. My head fits perfectly in the crook of his neck. He still smells like antibacterial soap. I have my hands curled against my chest, terrified of touching while wondering what it would feel like if I did. He breathes soft and slow, already asleep.

I've always looked at boys like dangerous snakes waiting to strike. It's hard to see James like that while he sleeps so soundly. Every muscle in his face is relaxed. His lips barely open. He's harmless here, and a swirling in my stomach begins to stir. He is attractive, and no amount of fear can block that out. Attraction is new to me. It scares me more than the man himself. How do I stop it? I can't develop feelings for him. I'm supposed to be Light's girlfriend.

With shaking fingers, I reach out, watching his face, making sure he's asleep. I press it against his pectoral. His skin is soft and warm. The tattoo on his pectoral of the number '28' is invisible under my hand, and I could pretend he's a normal boy I met at school.

James has been warming his way into my thoughts more and more. It's the things he says that have no shame. He admits to things I'd be too embarrassed to say.

'I stopped following the mission the day you came. Everything I've done since that day has been because of choice. Is it that hard for you to believe I want you safe because I want it, not because of someone else?'

I wanted to kiss him then. I look at his lips, and a heat builds in my chest.

I shouldn't be here. Light considers me his girlfriend, and even though it's a terrifying term, I understand with it comes loyalty. Tobias never liked it when I spoke to another boy. But I can't find the ability to leave.

I'm not here for a malicious purpose or even a sexual one. I'm here to comfort my friend. There is nothing wrong with that. The feelings that are growing within me can be snuffed out. And for all I know, they are one-sided. James and I have a connection because of trauma. Perhaps once this is over, he and I won't matter to each other.

Or at least, I won't matter to him because I'm realizing he will always matter to me.

Chapter 7
Manners

Ember

Before the sun rises, his nurse walks on, apologizing, "Sorry, guys. I need to check his vitals. Make sure his fever is gone and blood pressure's back to normal."

"It's okay." I roll off the bed, clinging to my jacket and trying to hide my awkward embarrassment. James watches me with humor, as if he's been awake for hours and finds me slinking off to be comical. "I'll be right outside."

"Don't go far."

I step out into the hallway and to my further horror, a bunch of boys are milling about and the moment they notice me, they hurry my way. I step against the door with my hand on the doorknob, ready to bold before one of them says, "You're Scream, aren't you?"

Like they don't know who I am. The boy is a part of Rain, exposed by the 'R' tattoo on his neck. "What do you want?"

More boys step toward me. "Do you know where Lisa is? Is she okay? Have you seen her?"

I flip my eyes between them, searching for maliciousness. "She's fine."

Grins spread between them, and they nudge each other happily. One reaches into his jacket, and I prepare to stab him in the neck with my butter knife, but then he holds out a piece of paper. I stare at it, unsure what he wants. "Can you give this to her?"

Another boy reaches into his pocket. "And Daisy? Do you know Daisy?" He holds out his note.

"And Blizzard." A different boy holds out his own letter.

Chewing on the inside of my lip, I release the knife. "Do you guys know where Light is?" I take each note and put them in my pocket.

A boy runs off, yelling, "I'll get him."

"Yo, Scream."

I spin around. Blockade, the leader of Boundary, comes my way, smiling in greeting. He's a big, stubby guy with a big smile. "Can you get a message out to Heather?" Others shout out names, but I can't remember all of them.

I point to the nursing station. "Write all your messages with the name, and I'll pass them out." They bombard the station, forming a quick, unpleasant line as they shove each other.

The nurse exits James' room, and I shove in, hiding. I wasn't prepared to be the center of attention. One would think blowing up a building would be a welcoming spotlight, but any of them could be a Coal member. I have to keep my guard up.

James sits on the bed with his legs dangling over the edge. He has a black shirt on now with gray sweatpants. He's staring at his food, mindlessly tapping with his fork as if he's scared to eat it. "I gotta go downstairs. I'll be back soon."

"Where's Shakes?" James asks, disregarding what I said.

"He's on the sixth floor."

"Alive," James whispered, relieved. "And Carbon?"

"He didn't make it."

I'm not ready for the sudden flash of pain across his face. He swallows it the best he can, but I can see it. He is silent and stiff, but every muscle is tense, and his breath begins to increase.

I thought James hated Carbon. His reaction confuses me. "James—"

"I should have gone with them." He shoves the food cart, and it flings to the floor. The action scares me, and I step back. "We should not have separated."

"You can't save everyone."

"Why?"

I sputter, unprepared. "It's not realistic."

James turns away from me. "I thought you were leaving."

With a thick inhale, I turn. "I'll be back in a bit."

I don't think much about James' mood. He's rarely ever been pleasant since the moment I met him. Not that I blame him; he hasn't had the greatest life. I've only lived in the school for four months. James lived there for eight years. To expect him to be amiable and cheery is illogical. I just don't like dealing with it so I don't. I let it go and hurry back to my room.

It's unsurprising when I find Lisa and a few girls hanging around, waiting for me. They attack with questions, shouting out the names of their boyfriends. I continue down the hall to the game room and drop the batch of letters on the table. "Find your name." They dig in with vigor, smiling when they find a letter, and sit on the floor to read. "I'll take replies after I shower." I snatch food off the table, taking a soda out of the bin.

I get some satisfaction out of their happiness. If I cared, I would, anyway.

After I shower, I dress in my second pair of clothes, finding these fit better. It's a black T-shirt and light jeans. I'm comfortable enough that I leave the jacket behind. The worn clothes are tossed in a laundry bag and hung on the door for the nurse to care for. I make sure to grab the small square to bring back to James.

Lisa is standing outside with a bag full of letters. "Good job. Made a lot of people happy today."

Yeah, that's my goal in life.

· · · ● · ● · ● · ·

I have a pillowcase full of letters, and I toss it to Blockade. "My favorite person!" he claims. "Boys, love letters!" He laughs and empties them on the floor.

It's insane to me how the boys go for it with just as much eagerness as the girls. It's cute. And weird.

"Ember!"

Light greets, jogging my way with a warm smile. He wraps me up in his arms. "I came earlier but you already went downstairs."

I had forgotten Light was supposed to come. James distracted me.

Not a good thing.

Light takes my hand, leading me down the hall. "How can you come up here? I know they keep the girls' rooms locked to keep the guys out. But the boys are allowed to go to different floors. How are you? Do you like it here?"

His bombardment of questions leaves me quiet. Light pulls me into his room and shuts the door, leading to a semi-panic attack. He has the only way out, and he approaches me with a look in his eyes that screams a warning.

Light cackles. "Sorry I'm hyper. I'm happy. Why wouldn't I be? We're going home. I can't believe it. I didn't think this would happen." He hugs me, twirling me around, and I push out, stumbling back. He keeps his hands on my arms, mindless. "Three guys already were sent home. I'm totally jealous. I can't wait. What about you? Any girls out?"

I have a knife in my pocket. But this is Light. I'm not in danger. The long pause forces me to say, "No one."

"That sucks, but just wait. Have you figured out your name? I'm sure they got DNA tests or computer tests or something. You got to be on a list somewhere." He cups my cheeks in his large hands and brings my attention back to his blue eyes. "Come home with me. My parents have a huge house and are never home. All my brothers are older and gone. You can have one of their rooms and sometimes maybe—" He eases closer, his hands slipping behind my back. His lips come closer to mine. "You can join me in mine." He kisses me boldly, and all too soon, his tongue slips into my mouth.

I press my thumbs into his eye sockets, and he rips away in pain as I step back, stumbling behind the gurney, hating how now there is a bed between him and me.

"What the hell was that?" he groans, sitting on the bed.

As he holds his face, I chew my lip in regret. Probably shouldn't have chosen the eyes. "Sorry," I squeak.

Light squints at me, trying to blink through the pain. "I guess I moved too fast. Next time, just talk to me, alright? Don't go crazy on me."

Crazy? Is that what I am? It's an insult, but I don't know if he meant it that way. Guess I owe him a freebie.

"Can we, can we start over? This isn't going the way I imagined it."

Guilt flushes over me. I knew I was being stupid acting like Light would hurt me. He cares for me. He's shown it in so many ways. It's unfair to treat him like a criminal for having feelings for me. But such things are foreign to me. Tobias was my only example of what a relationship was, and it's diluted all the good stuff.

I take a seat on the other side of the bed. There's a distance, but I'm fine with it. He takes a breath, looking over his shoulder. His eyes are a little bloodshot, but he smiles nonetheless. "Hi."

I forcefully smile. "Hi."

It goes better from there. My fear fades as I watch his face. His handsome features, his dark hair, his thick jawline. His laugh sounds better without me being so stressed. I can laugh, too. And when he reaches out to hold my hand, I curl my fingers around his. His hand is bulky and thick. It is so different from James' skinny fingers. Light can crush bricks with these hands. But his personality makes him softer than a kitten's fur. My belly begins to ache with the familiar rush of yearning. And when he attempts to kiss me again, I find myself wanting it, leaning into it. His giant hand covers my cheek, his thumb brushing my skin. His lips feel good, erasing Tobias with each gentle caress.

Light rests his forehead on mine. "That's how it was supposed to go," he murmurs.

I smile, enjoying his affection. I don't deserve it and yet I want it for myself. It's terribly selfish.

"Why do you like me? We're so different." I lean back away, keeping a hold of his hand.

"Why do you like *me*?" he throws back at me.

I shrug and laugh. "Because you're not like me." He smirks but waits for more. I think about it harder, knowing it's crucial. Perhaps not to him specifically, but I need to figure it out. Because I'm starting to slip into dangerous territory as I develop feelings for James while I sit here and make out with Light. What do I want? What am I doing?

"You're funny, and I like laughing. I don't do it enough."

"So I need to watch out for funny guys. Guess I got nothing to worry about with that Special."

The comment stiffens me. Light can see the connection between us. He thinks it's something more profound. If it is, how would I know? Can't really ask the boy that I'm supposed to be dating.

To keep him from noticing, I turn the conversation back on him. "You're gorgeous." He grins smugly. "You're nice to me. You're everything good that I've missed out on."

Light comes to my side of the bed and sits beside me, our legs touching. He wraps his arm over my shoulder to bring me closer. "I want to show you everything good in the world. So you forget about everything that's bad. Soon, you won't remember this time in your life. I'll make sure of it." He kisses my forehead and hugs me.

That's what I want. I want to see everything good. I don't want to remember the school. I don't want to think about it another day. Light, he has it in him to make the terrible memories fade. When I'm with him, I can see a brighter future.

But the problem with that is my family: Shakes, Mary, James, Brick, and Vapor, they aren't in that future. They are surrounded by darkness. The only way I can live in the light is to go separate ways. Could I do that? Could I live without my friends?

And if I could, do I want to?

We say goodbye after an hour and plan to meet in the morning. As we part, however, the intercom comes on. I stare at the circle on the wall. Part of me thinks Myers' voice will come on and greet us. If I wasn't positive he was dead, I'd be in a heap on the floor.

"Good Afternoon." The voice is a pleasant woman, and I visibly relax. "Starting tomorrow, the cafeteria will be open from 9 a.m. to 11 a.m. and 5 p.m. to 7 p.m. for all floors. Outside recreation for the female populace will be from 7 a.m. to 9 a.m. And for the male populace from 7 p.m. to 9 p.m. Please note safety is our priority. If any fighting or abuse takes place, these privileges will be withdrawn. Anyone seen with a weapon will be detained. We thank you for your patience and your cooperation."

Excited, I make my way to James' room. I hear the celebration, and several guys pass, holding up a hand. "Good job," someone says as they walk by. I'm wide-eyed until I remember telling Lisa. She must have told her clan, which, with the letters passing between floors, they told the boys. I didn't think they would use this system to talk about me. I don't want my name to be written anywhere.

"Thanks, Ember!"

"Way to go, Scream!"

I sneer, diving into James' room to escape. James' two roommates are resting in bed, and they wave, thanking me, but I rudely ignore it.

James stands in front of the window. He wears loose cotton pants low on his hips. His back is straight like a gun barrel, and he regards the height of the ground beneath him. I stand beside him, wondering the same thing he is: Could we survive the fall?

"I heard you an hour ago."

"Huh?"

He glances at me. "I heard your voice."

"Oh."

His eyes are on me, but I have no information for him. I'm not keeping Eric a secret, but I don't know what I should say otherwise. Light wouldn't like me hanging out with James.

'You know what Specials do, right?' Light asked me once. *'I'm not talking about killing or torture because I'm pretty sure you are aware of that. I'm talking about Spread; what Zack had them do? Why don't you ask him next time he feels like hugging you?'*

I am still trying to discover what James did in Zack's care. But I haven't been searching that hard.

For a subject change, I blurt out, "I want you to save your hand. I'll help take care of you."

James looks down at his hand tucked against his chest. He wants the easiest and quickest solution. And maybe logically, he's right; cutting it off would be easier. But that doesn't make it the best solution.

"Have you heard from the rest of the family?" I ask. "Brick and Vapor are still missing."

"Then let's find them."

James turns toward the exit. I latch onto his hand, trying to tell him it's not as easy as he makes it sound, but he slips out, continuing on. He's much more challenging to deal with than Light. He's bull-headed and aggravating. He's stressful and too intense for his own good. He needs to learn to relax. How could I make a guy like him smile if he's always looking for a fight?

James approaches the nurses' desk, to my confusion, so I stay out of sight. The woman looks up, and her face changes into a bright smile. "Glad to see you out of bed. I told you I'd find your girlfriend."

"Thank you, Grace." He bows his head pleasantly, and there is a delicate smile on his lips that pisses me off. Why the hell does *she* get a smile? "Your shift just started?"

"Six to six. I love the night shift. It's a lot less crazy."

"You must be very passionate about your work to take this job."

She bows her head, blushing. "I used to volunteer for mission trips to Africa, so when I heard about this, I couldn't pass it up. At least this pays."

"I won't take up much more of your time. I was wondering if you could help with one more favor."

"Sure thing, sweetie. What's up?"

"I am searching for my comrades. Their nicknames are Brick and Vapor, but their real names are Brian Taylor and Algeray Williams."

She sits in a chair and types on her computer. "There is a Brain Taylor in room six forty." She continues to type. "And Algeray Williams...he is in recovery. They don't do visitors, but he will also be in six forty later today." She pops her head up. "It's cool they are opening the cafeteria. I was told we weren't doing that. Tomorrow, you can reunite with your friends."

"Thank you again. Just knowing they are here and in the care of your associates is enough. Have a good evening."

She smiles tenderly, her cheeks reddening and she tucks a piece of stray hair behind her ear. I push off the side of the wall, and she quickly notices, our eyes meeting. Her lips tighten, and she flips away, grabbing papers from the desk and setting off.

I fasten after James, who returns to his room. "I thought you were going to cause trouble."

He climbs in bed. "Not everything requires strength. Some require finesse."

"Or flirtation," I mumble.

He smirks. "Whatever works. Will you stay with me again tonight? It's easier to sleep knowing where you are."

My stomach swirls, and I shift nervously. I bring up what I've been avoiding to place a barrier between us. "I'm supposed to meet Light in the morning."

James doesn't even flinch. "Does that affect where you sleep tonight?"

I pause and hate that he has a point. "No."

"Is there something you want to say directly?"

I rapidly shake my head. I'd have to admit to personal feelings, and I am not ready for that.

"Then will you come back?"

Sheepishly, I nod.

What trouble am I getting myself into now?

Chapter 8

Dream

Ember

I STAND IN FRONT of my windows, watching the sunset. So many colors ignite in the sky. I used to lay on the ground and watch dawn approached, the darkness fading as the sun rose. But it was never this type of beauty. This is magic.

It brings with it a familiarity. I've seen sunsets before. At least, I think I have, and they were over an ocean. If I reach for the memory daring enough, I could make out the waves and hear the sounds of the water.

But I'm scared, and I pull away from it harshly. It's an instinctual fear, like how you know it would hurt if you touched a thorn. I've had enough painful memories. What if the memory I've lost is even more terrible than the one I have?

James said once, '*You could break whatever wall you placed on yourself and find your past again if you didn't possess so much fear.*' And that thought follows me now. What if I'm the reason I can't remember? What if there's a part of me that is hiding on purpose?

Nothing could be worse than this.

I'd like to believe that, but I'm not as naive as I used to be. It could always get worse.

I change into more comfortable clothes, leggings and a long-sleeveless shirt. It's a better outfit if I find myself in a fight, but the flowers and the peace sign on the chest don't give the 'don't bother me' vibe that I prefer.

Lisa's standing outside my door, and I try to return to my room, but she follows me. I slump on the bed, hoping she feels how unwanted she is.

"Why do you always look like that? Can you smile or something?"

I force a fake grin, but even that falls flat after two seconds.

She crosses her arms in front of me. "You did good with the letters. With getting us access to the cafeteria. Made some friends today. Repairing all the damage you did as a Rat."

I sneer. "I could care less—"

"Are you and Eric dating?"

Light's real name is Eric. Everyone is slowly shedding their old identities except for me. I don't have any other identity beneath this.

The question catches me off guard, and my face heats up. "I.. uh...I don't know..."

"There's talk everywhere. I heard from Becky that Eric called you his girlfriend."

I hate that word. It's cringy.

Lisa chews the inside of her cheek before she asks, "Why am I hearing that you slept in the boy's dormitory with your Special friend?"

With the not-so-subtle accusation, I clench my teeth, remaining quiet. Lisa waits for an answer I'm not giving her. It's none of her damned business.

She caves with an exaggerated sigh. "Let me warn you because you're new to these things. The friends you made today won't be your friends by tomorrow. We're protective of our own. There's a reason we don't date outside our clans. What do you think happened between Tara and Shock?"

"We're not in school anymore, isn't that what you said?"

"That's right," she agrees. "All your protection has gone."

I despise her for pointing that out. Doesn't she think I know? Why do I have a knife in my pocket? Why do I lock my door? Why do I try to stay out of groups and make no attempt to make friends? I don't need her to remind me that Tobias is gone, Shakes is missing, and I am terribly alone.

Lisa sags on the bed beside me. I'm too busy focusing on my own problems to care, but when she sniffs and rubs her face, the room's tension becomes awkward, and I shift uncomfortably. I'm not the best person to confide in. Let her cry in front of someone who will care.

"Hail was my boyfriend. And he died trying to protect you. I resented you for a long time because I didn't believe in who you were. But now that we're out, I can't deny it anymore. It's a lot of effort, by the way, being around you. I hope you're worth the trouble."

Guilt weighs on me long after she left. I'm so busy concentrating on my own life, and problems that I never take the time to consider others. Lisa watched her boyfriend die because he believed I was Jennifer.

And I'm not.

Lisa doesn't know that, and I never want her to find out. I'm safer if she believes in the lie.

I stare at the floor as I mentally count how many people have died because of me. It's endless barrage of names.

Charles

Hail

Star

Tara

Tango

Tobias

Ash

Jet

Laura

And I know there are others, but they are shadows, unknown and unnamed.

My heart breaks, and I curl into myself. The self-hatred is so intense I'm sick like my very soul is drenched in poison. I think of Charles and how he deserved to live. He should be here, and I should be buried in the ground in a nameless grave somewhere. I can see every inch of his face. Hear his voice. His laughter. I curl in my pillow, my whole body shaking in horrible sobs. For a few seconds, I can't breathe. The pain is too much in my chest.

A knock on the door snaps me out of it, and I suck in a breath, sitting up, wiping my face.

"Ember?" Janice calls. "Are you alright? Do you want me to get a doctor?"

"I'm fine."

She tests the doorknob, but it's locked. "Can I come in? Let me check on you."

"I'm fine. Go away."

She pauses, and I use it to strengthen. I push myself up, clenching the bed sheets. "Okay. If you need anything..." Her shadow stays at the door for another minute before she drifts away.

I get up and continue as if nothing happened. Tears do nothing. They waste time. And though I know I'm a horrible person, and I'm not who Charles thought I was, I'll do whatever I can to make up for it. Destroying the school wasn't enough. Getting out wasn't enough. I don't know if anything will be. But I have to try.

I exit my room, and the same nurse calls my name, but I move toward the elevator unhindered. She's silly in her desperation. We are all kids of trauma. If she thinks the cops can come and pick us up and it's over, they're delusional. It's not over. It might not ever be over.

When I step out from behind the curtain, James takes one look at me and sits up. "What happened?"

I land roughly in the chair, curling my legs into my chest. "Nothing. Memories."

He eases back with a sigh. "Come here."

I clench my eyes tight, unwilling to give in. Lisa and her rumors, but the worst part is I'm wondering, too. What am I doing with James? Am I betraying Light by taking the comfort he is offering? Light could never comprehend my pain. He's lost nothing. He's lived as a clan member, safer than a clam in a clam shell. But James can understand me. We have both been through traumas that have made us who we are.

He shifts over, raising up his cast, making room beside him, and I foolishly dive into him. He clings to me, his injured arm resting on my back. His fingers brush through my hair causing an embarrassing shiver.

"What are you thinking about?"

"Charles."

He nods once. "He was a courageous little man."

James spent so many hours watching me, so it was inevitable that James had also watched over Charles. It warms me that someone else has memories of him. That James understands just how much he meant to me.

My walls are collapsing. Doors are opening, welcoming him in to see the damage. I'm comfortable here. Relaxed in his arms. "It was my fault."

"You like to blame yourself for things out of your control. Tobias enforced such emotional abuse. It was one of his few talents."

I smile against his skin. "You hated him."

"There was nothing to like."

I laugh. "I know. I love that you hate him as much as I do." Tobias floats in my head, killing all traces of happiness. He's everywhere, like mold, nearly impossible to dig out. Will I always feel damaged because of him? "Tobias did so many bad things," I whisper. "Will I ever get better?"

James is quiet, and I lift my head to look at him. He's staring at the ceiling and I wonder what kind of memories he has. He and I both had tormentors. It's another thing we share. "What was Zack like?"

His brows knit only a fraction, but he remains the same otherwise. I wouldn't have caught it if I hadn't been paying attention. Zack's name affects him, even when he doesn't want it to.

"Zack." He swallows and clears his throat, keeping his eyes away from me. "Despite his uncanny presence, took great concern in our education." His hand moves to the remote, and he clicks the TV on, searching for something to watch, a distraction from memories he doesn't want to think about. "From the time of initiation, we are taught twelve hours a day, seven days a week. American Literature, Chemistry, World History. As we improve, our classes change. Mannerism, table decorum, meditation. After puberty, we are removed from parties and placed in seclusion, where we undergo Spartan tutelage in various forms of combat. If we succeed, we live. In four years, only thirty-five have made it to the end."

I sit up, watching him. He clicks the remote repeatedly, a machine, mechanically speaking fact after fact. There is no emotion in his details. It doesn't mean there is nothing beneath the surface.

"As we get older, it moves on to the physical. The male and female form. The art of seduction. Bedroom etiquette."

Panicking, I latch onto the remote, turning off the TV. James quiets and the silence pounds in my ears. The conversation fell into information I don't know if I'm ready to hear. What did that mean, 'bedroom etiquette?' I thought I could handle it, but what if it's darker than even I have experienced?

Light's voice returns: *'You know what Specials do, right? I'm talking about Spread; what Zack had them do?'*

The void in James' gaze disappears, and he returns to himself, blinking. His brows knit, noticing the tears on my cheeks. I shake my head. "You don't have to talk about it."

He touches my skin, wiping the wetness away. "I thought if I displaced your thoughts, you wouldn't cry."

The gesture is sweet, but he doesn't understand that I care about him. "Perhaps next time, talk about...something simple. Like sunsets or something."

"Sunsets." He nods. "Alright." James gets out of bed and goes to the bathroom.

I remove my jacket and toss it on the chair. Pressing the button on the side of the bed, I stretch it out to lie down, positioning the pillows more comfortably, and tuck my legs under the blanket. I was freezing last night and woke up with a slight ache in my neck. Tonight, I'm not going to have that problem. I lay down watching TV, trying to ignore the twirling sensations in my stomach. I don't know why it's there. Usually, feeling like I am, I'd want to run, but James is safe. Despite being a guy, he's broken like me. Not a part of me fears him, and running is the last thing I want to do. James is attractive, and touching him is exciting when it shouldn't be. I like being with him. He's engaging and intelligent. I want to dig into his head and know everything about him. But that's wrong, isn't it? That's what I should be feeling about Light. Yet, I have to force myself to think about him.

James returns and pauses. My brows knit, looking down at myself, wondering what he sees. "What's wrong?"

He clicks the light off above our heads. "Nothing." He slips into the blanket with me. I'm careful with his broken hand, watching it slide under me before I lay down. We face each other. My hands curl up between us and our legs unavoidably touch on this narrow gurney.

"Good night." I twist my head away. It's awkward laying so close to his face.

James angles his head lower, resting his forehead against my temple. The move kickstarts my heart, and I swallow. James whispers, "Good night," as he slips his hand in with mine. He clenches my fingers to his chest.

How am I supposed to sleep like this? Not only are we in an intimate position, but he keeps causing me to feel things I shouldn't, and now I'm stuck here, unable to move, having to think about it all night.

"Ember," he whispers in the darkness.

"Hm."

Can he feel my quiver?

"Having you here, beside me, after everything—" His fingertips dance along mine, sending chills down my spine. "You are like a dream."

The words are a shock wave, repeating like an echo inside me. Everything about being with him is like a dream. Every time I'm with him, it's unreal; it's like the school never was, and I am without burden. He sees me unbroken, and I'm whole in his presence. It's like this is where I was always supposed to be, and I'm already *who* I am supposed to be.

He presses my knuckles against his cheek, nuzzling them, and my fingers flex, stretching over his skin instinctively. My palm shapes his jaw, and he kisses it. I observe his features in a way I wasn't bold enough to do before. He's beautiful, every inch of him. He leans against me, and I close my eyes, struggling to breathe. His lips grace the skin on my jaw, on my cheek and my breath hitches with every touch. He's slow and cautious, careful with each movement.

"Dream." His lips are at my ear. "That's what I want to call you." He kisses my cheek and my jaw. I tilt my head, meeting his eyes. His breath is fast, like mine. He shifts closer, something I didn't think he could. We melt together like one person.

In an effort to calm my pounding heart, I pull slightly away. "Do you remember the first time we spoke? You told Shakes that I was erratic and didn't follow directions–"

"I am truthful if nothing else."

I giggle, and humor glows on his face, easing whatever this tension is. It's an expression I have yet had the pleasure of seeing. And though I've seen him drop his guard a few times, it was always in a violent manner. This time, he drops his guard because he's content. "I told you, you knew nothing about me. But that's not true. You know me better than I know myself."

His fingertips glide along my hair, sending shivers down my spine.

"James." I tremble, but all because of the new daring thought that entered my head. "Kiss me."

There's a flinch in his brow, and he swallows hard to steady his breath. "I thought you had to meet Light in the morning."

The mention of Light doesn't faze me. There's nothing else I want to think about. His palm rests on my cheek, his thumb dancing over my lip. The anticipation is killing me, and I grip his shoulder, pulling him closer, but he keeps just an inch between our lips, never moving them closer.

And then he asks me, "Are you scared?"

Out of all the emotions that I'm feeling, fear is not among them. "No."

He licks his lips. "I am." With that admission, he presses his lips on mine. The impact stops my breath, and every muscle in my body tightens. I can't think, I don't want to think. His lips are soft and slow, almost hesitant. I break away to breathe before I find his lips again with more desperation, my nails digging into his bicep. He meets me with the same fervor, shifting slightly above me and pressing me into the pillow as our lips glide over each other. His fingers slip into my hair, encircling my neck, keeping me to him.

It's perfection. Everything about him.

James shifts closer, pressing his weight upon me, our legs twisting together. And here, feeling his body's heaviness, it reminds me of Tobias, and panic strikes me. I knock my arm against his chest, pushing him entirely off and I rush to escape, but he latches onto my wrist. I yank, but he refuses to let go. He doesn't pull me back; he simply keeps me from running further, and I bury my face in my legs. I sit like that, too ashamed, too embarrassed, to move.

I am *crazy.*

When he's sure I won't take off, James releases me. I stare at the floor, trying to regain my composure and whatever confidence I have. After several minutes of silence between us, I turn around to look at him. He's laid back down in the same position and waits for me to join him.

I throw myself down on the bed, facing the ceiling. If I tried to run, he'd stop me. It's one of the frustrating things about him. He's faster than me.

"Can I tell you something?" He breaks our record-breaking silence.

"Is it going to be weird and depressing?"

He half smiles. "Sort of."

I fling a hand, careless.

"That was the scariest thing I've done."

My brows knit. I've seen him do some pretty scary stuff. How could a kiss be frightening? "Really? Why?"

"To act on one's emotions is forbidden. We are taught better. Taught logic. Emotions are not logical. Eight years I've suppressed to kiss you."

I bury my face in my hands. "And I screwed it up."

He smiles fully. "No. You did what I expected you to do. I cannot erase your past any more than you can erase mine. I accept it as part of who you are. It simply means a physical manifestation will take longer than normal if we choose to continue. But I am content with our progress."

I wince at the awkward term' physical manifestation'. "Your directness is weird."

"Your shyness is weird."

I smile, and he mimics it. It lights up his whole face, and I'm hypnotized. "I love your smile."

"Then it's good that you seem to know how to make me smile."

I roll into him, and he wraps his arm around me, his broken hand going under my neck to tuck around my back. I snuggle into his chest, closing my eyes, returning to the calming bubble we've created.

"Do you like the name?"

It's the first name given to me by someone like him. Someone who knows me. "I love it." It is a name I can always be proud of. A name that will never be dragged into the mud. It will be a private name. A name only shared between us.

"I've wanted to kiss you for a while," he admits. "I did not think it would feel like that."

I hide the grin on my face. I can't believe he would confess something so personal. Every time we spoke since I joined Anarchy replays in my head and transforms those moments into butterfly-producing memories.

Tobias could see what I couldn't. *'She belongs to me, Special. Don't get any ideas.'*

While remembering, I'm realize something.

I have happy memories.

James shifts beside me and whispers, "Go to sleep. You need rest."

"I don't know if I can now. My heart is pounding."

"Should I talk about sunsets?"

I giggle, twisting to look at him. I stroke his cheek, too amazed I can do something so personal with someone else and not do it because I'm forced to.

"I should tell you I do not have much knowledge of sunsets. I haven't seen very many."

It's so quick how my heart clenches and tears build. It hurts that he's been inside those walls for so long. I snuggle my face deeper into his neck to hide any revealing sentiments on my face. Why does his past suffering bother me so much now? I want to erase it. To turn back time and undo everything that's ever been done to him.

"I have seen sunrises. My mother believed rising with the sun was the best way to ease tension and reduce stress. We would meditate in the garden as the sun rose each morning to the Buddha statue in the center of our garden."

"What's that word? Buddha?"

"It's a religion. My family's religion. They were Buddhist. I suppose I was at a time."

"I thought religion was something a person believed in. Not what a person is."

He pauses and thinks about my statement. After a short time, he digs my face out of his neck, and our noses touch and I bravely meet his eyes. I don't know what he wants to say, but the way his gaze flicks back and forth between mine, there's something more, but he can't find the words. "I want to kiss you again," he finally reveals.

I suppress a grin. "Okay."

"Why are you letting me?"

"Because I want you too." That admittance reddens my cheeks.

"I don't mean to embarrass you. I do not need any declaration of feeling. I simply want to ensure you aren't doing this because you feel indebted, obligated, or pressured. I do not-"

I kiss him, and he sucks in a sharp, surprised breath through his nose. His hand slips up my back, pulling me close, and I slide my own hand along his warm skin. Laying on our sides, I am less trapped and more in control. We part soon after, and I lay my head back on the pillow, burying my head. "Good night."

His fingers trace the back of my ear, tickling my hair and neck. He whispers the name with his lips near my forehead. Staring at his chest takes me a long time to get to sleep. His breath remains heavy, and I keep a hand on his pectoral, if only to feel his heart rate. I count the beating to help lure me to relax. I know he's doing the same. His fingertips are on my neck, resting on my pulse, waiting for me to sleep. I love how similar we are. How equally damaged we are. Our broken pieces fit perfectly together.

CHAPTER 9
Confusion

EMBER

I HEAR THE DOOR burst open, and instinct springs me to my feet. James doesn't miss a beat, clenching my arm and pulling me back against the wall, taking his place in front of me.

The curtain flies back, and Eric stands there with two friends at his sides. His face explodes in bewilderment as he looks us over and he pins his gaze on me, the betrayal knitting in his dark brows.

His friend nudges him in the back. "I told you."

James is prepared and slips a scalpel out of his cast. He bends his knees, ready to attack.

I grab his arm. "James, stop it."

Eric scoffs but puts his hands up anyway, refusing to back down. "Is that how it's going to be?"

"No!" I slip out, moving between them. "Let's talk. Put the knife away."

James eyes them over my shoulder. "They came looking for a fight. I will not disappoint."

I spin around. "Eric, send your friends away."

Eric shouldn't be dumb enough to challenge a Special, and I hope he realizes that. After a moment, he shifts his head, and though they disagree, they don't put up much of a fight. Getting beaten up isn't an ideal start to a brand-new day. They begrudgingly leave, sending daggers at us.

Eric pins his accusing gaze back on me, but then he unfurls his hand, holding them in surrender. "You know what? I don't even want to hear it." He backs away.

"Eric, wait."

Each step I take moves me further away from James. I glance behind me hoping he understands, but then he says, "Let him go."

"I can't." The admittance hurts him, but I take off after Eric anyway. "Eric! Just wait."

Eric stops in the center of the hall. There is a crowd watching from every direction like Eric's friends had spread enough gossip to bring them running in hopes of drama. Once more, there is a spotlight, and I fold in on myself, nervous.

Every muscle in Eric's body is tight, and his hands fist at his sides. A friend attempts to talk to him, but he doesn't listen, turning to me finally. "How could you sleep with him? He doesn't scare you, but I do?"

"Yes, I slept in the same bed, but it's not what you think. We're friends. We're family."

"That's not what the rumors are saying."

They are talking even now, whispering to each other. "Everybody needs to stay out of my damn business," I snap as if they are to blame for my unfaithfulness.

"Rumors usually have a little bit of truth in them. Why were you in bed with him?"

"I was with him, and I got tired. I just laid down."

"Did you kiss him?"

My mouth flutters, and I can't reply. How would he know that unless someone was peeking through the curtain? *Snitches.*

Disappointment drowns his face, and he shakes his head. "That's a screwed-up family." He turns to leave.

"Eric, Please."

"What?" He swings toward me, waiting.

I stutter on words. His anger intimidates me, and I want to clam up, but I know it's deserved. I know I screwed up. "I'm sorry. I don't know what I'm doing. You are everything that I want."

"Then why? I don't pressure you. I don't hurt you. I risked my clan for you. I gave up friendships for you. I nearly died to protect you. I...I want to take you with me when we leave here. Was that not in your plans? Were you playing with me?"

"No!"

"Then what?"

"I don't know." I struggle, holding my arms around myself. "I'm sorry, I don't know."

Eric looks behind me to James and with a proud back, he says, "He know we were making out in *my* room yesterday? That you told me you want to come home with me?"

I hang my head. It sounds so terrible, like something a clan member would do. Not me. I don't look at James. I'm too much of a coward to face him.

Eric steps in closer, whispering, "Do you know what he is, Ember? Do you know what he does? He is sick. You don't want to be with me, fine, but don't be with that freak."

He leaves and I don't know how to stop him. The fantastic night last night drowns in this morning of dejection. I don't hurt people. I don't like how it makes me feel, but I've hurt someone who's only been loyal to me, that's been wonderful since the day I met him. I could have done so many things differently, yet by avoiding it, it's blown up in my face.

With my head down, I turn around to face his judgement. But when his door shuts, I snap up. The lock is heard even from the distance. Pain pulses in my chest, the dejection worse than any punch to the face.

Whispers continue to circle around me, and I run to the elevator, refusing to appear weaker in front of my enemies. I press my face against the metal wall, wishing I could sink in and disappear. I've betrayed two people that mean something to me. I'm not different. I'm just like everyone else.

Crying over boys isn't exactly something I thought I would ever do. A week ago, kissing a boy would have been like touching a rattlesnake. Here I am, kissing two boys on the same day. Did I have no morals? It's not like I didn't know right from wrong. So why did I allow it? Why didn't I stop it and get control over the situation?

But it's an easy answer. I let things happen to me before I respond. It's been my method since I first arrived at school. Not having a memory makes it hard to know when bad things will happen. It makes me stupidly confident. It's the reason I stepped into the basement when Tobias took my hand. It's the reason I befriended Charles. And it's the reason I followed Shakes. If I thought like a normal person, I would not have done any of those things.

I attempt to hide in my room, but soon, an announcement sounds over the intercom, instructing all girls to line up for recreation. A nurse knocks on my door and ushers me out. Apparently, this recreational freedom is not an option. I file in line just as the last of us trickle out. Most are barely awake and struggling to put on shoes.

The air outside is cool and I hug myself. I know we aren't far from the school, but this world is so much different, so much livelier that I'm out of my element. There are soccer balls, basketballs, and footballs pile in a bin. A portable basketball net sits on the sidewalk, but it doesn't belong.

They did what they could in a limited time, but this space was meant for relaxing and meditation. The fountains spring upward through an Angel's arrow. Lush trees and vibrant flowers decorate the numerous paths. They weave through this man-made marvel. It is beautiful and well taken care of. But it is not meant for us as the girls chase each other through their bushes, knocking off petals and breaking branches.

The door opens, and Jose steps out. He smiles at the girls playing, waving his hand as if he's some mascot among them. He notices me against the wall and approaches. "Don't you want to play?"

Play. Like I'm an eight-year-old girl with a jump rope.

"No."

"It's still cool out. Feels great." He takes a breath in and lets it out with an exaggerated sigh.

This guy annoys me. I fold my arms, gaze darting to trees, searching for spying eyes. There are too many places to hide in this wilderness.

"Come by my office. I want to check on that list."

"I haven't made much progress."

"It's alright. We'll talk." He waves his hand. "Hey, Sara. Bianca. Kelly. Beautiful day, right?"

"Hey, Mr. Jose." Bianca approaches. "When are we getting out?"

"I have four sets of parents I'm interviewing today. I must make sure they are the right ones. Can't have anyone going home with the wrong mom, can I?" He laughs, but becomes nervous as more girls rally around him, hoping to hear a positive answer.

"I don't have a mom. Where am I going?"

"I'm not going to foster care!"

"Let us out!"

Jose struggles with their sudden serious concerns, and then he pops up with a grand speech. "Don't worry. I have two hundred people working on finding everyone a place. Six kids have already gone home. And we're only on day four. I think that's awesome."

Only on day four.

He acts like four days is nothing. Since I don't do this for a living, perhaps he's right. Maybe that's a great accomplishment.

He waves goodbye and rushes back inside.

"You plannin' on saving us from here too?"

It's a Coal Member named Cola. Black hair, black eyes, and tanned Spanish skin. She has thick thighs and a big butt. Cola wears her hair in a tight bun on the top of her head, showing off the gold jewelry dangling from her ears and neck. She may be a fighter, true enough, but one yank on an earring, and she won't be much of a problem.

"I never planned on saving any of *you*, to begin with," I bite back, eyeing her pack like the garbage they are.

"We never needed saving. Our life was perfect before you screwed it up. I ain't going home. And I'm gonna make damn sure you ain't goin' home either."

The girls comes closer and I bend my knees, ready to throw a punch. There are ten of them. I could take out two, perhaps three if given the right moments, but not ten. I have gotten pretty good at scrapping, but I'm not confident or dumb enough to take on their entire clan. My only choice is to run.

"Cola." Lisa walks toward us. Two dozen Boundary and Rain members follow. As she steps in front of me, I stare wide-eyed at the back of her head. I never expected her to come to my rescue. And I kind of hate that she does. It would mean I owe her, and that makes me ill.

Lisa has always had the air of a queen. She knows how to utilize her power. It gives her an ego I despise, yet I find myself unwillingly at her mercy. She stands in front of Cola with a soft smile. "Myers is dead. Ash is dead. She killed him. Do you really want to mess with her?"

A scoff jiggles Cola's long earrings. "She was too weak to kill him. Her dog did it. He'll get what's coming to him, too."

I push off the wall. "Don't you touch James."

Lisa silently shifts a hand, and I lean back, bowing down. "It's over. The school's gone. If you don't want to go home, fine, but don't mess this up for the rest of us. Our desperation might just be stronger than your need for revenge."

Cola steps up, meeting Lisa's face. "Such a fancy threat from a bloodless good girl. Every single one of us has put a bullet through someone's head. What are you going to do? Send us a gift basket?"

Lisa has never needed to fight. She has an army to do that for her. What I would give to be like her.

Cola looks over Lisa's shoulder, and says to me, "You won't always be lucky."

The Coal members slip through the line of defense and take an area to the left, all for themselves. Lisa turns to me and waits for everyone to disperse, the tension dying.

I refuse to look up, but I guess I have to show gratitude. "Thanks—"

"I warned you yesterday," Lisa hisses, and I snap my head up. "I told you to be careful. I can't protect you if you do stupid shit."

"What are you—"

"Eric!" she whispers, looking over her shoulder toward her clan mates. "It's only a matter of time before they all find out. Then what?"

Her panic confuses me. Why does my actions affect her?

I don't need her clan.

But even as the thought leaves my head, it's evident that I do if I want to survive. I screwed up deeper than I realized, and I don't know what to say. Lisa throws her hands up with an aggravated growl. "You're infuriating." She leaves, and I fall back against the wall.

Chapter 10

Reunion

EMBER

FOR THE FIRST TIME, we head to the cafeteria.

The chaos is overwhelming, and I'm glued to the wall. Girls and boys rush to meet their boyfriends and girlfriends. It's surprising how much excitement there is. I thought there would be killing and death. I never knew there was actually love inside the school. I didn't think it was possible for it to exist.

Has it always been there?

It's deafening as six hundred bodies pack a room meant for three hundred tops. But they squeeze in, making room at tables by sitting on each other's laps or simply standing behind one another. It's relaxing how happy everyone seems to be. They are like a family.

It makes me want to find my own.

James is easy to spot. He's tall for one thing, but he gives off an aura that makes everyone around him tense, and they keep a reasonable three feet distance. He stands in the food line, pushing his tray along the metal table and grabbing random items off the buffet. He's wearing a white collared T-shirt, black jeans, and bright white shoes. His hair is slicked back, and there is not a wrinkle on him. It's been a while since I've seen him like this; it throws me off. I'd forgotten how he used to be under Zack's care. Why does he choose to dress the same way?

Nervousness sets in. I haven't dealt with many people I care about being mad at me, especially for something I've intentionally done. Charles used to get upset with me, but this is somehow different. I doubt a fart joke would make James warm up to me.

"James," I call, and though he doesn't respond, I know he heard me. "Can I talk to you?"

"Talk," he continues walking down the line, keeping his back to me.

The crowd is obnoxiously shrill. I'm literally shouting, and we are inches apart. "Privately."

"No."

"Give me a chance to explain."

"Go ahead."

James holds out his wristband to the cashier, and the lady tags it with a laser gun before he lifts his tray. He heads for a table, and I'm desperately on his heels. "I... It's hard to explain, and I don't know how."

"Figure it out," he responds lamely and sits at a table.

I stare at his back. What does he want me to say? I'm not used to these emotions, and they are causing havoc inside me. How could he expect me to talk about them when I struggle to understand them?

"Hey, there she is."

Without realizing where he sat, I now look at the rest of the table. Brick, a giant red gorilla, rises from the table. I throw my arms around him. I'm not a hugger, if that's not clear by now, but relief overpowers rational thought. I'm ignorant of his injuries, until he groans. His shoulder is laced up in gauze. He holds onto me with one arm.

"How you doin, darlin'?" Brick murmurs softly. "You holding up okay?"

I throw random words of concern as I look him over, checking every inch of him. He shows off his wounds with pride, three bullet holes, and he's walking around like they were bee stings. He laughs and tells me he's fine and points to Vapor. I push out of Brick's arms and rush to Vapor, but he's in a wheelchair, and I don't know what to do, so I awkwardly hold his head, and he cackles, rubbing my arm. I sit down, asking him what happened, and he tells me about the shootout with Myers and Carbon's death. Part of a building landed on Vapor's leg, shattering his knee, but the surgery had gone well. I hold both their hands in mine. I feel like I've found pieces of my body. I can't stop the smile on my face.

"Hi," it's a tentative whisper, and I turn around to see Ink. He keeps his head down, with a hand on the back of his head. "I, uh, wanted to apologize."

Ink and I weren't close to start, and he did give me to Star, but he's a little boy, and I can't hold much against him. Especially since he reminds me of Charles. "Come sit," I tell him, and he smiles wide. Brick and Vapor pull him in, rubbing his black hair. He laughs and swats at them, but the grin on his face doesn't fade. He's back where he belongs.

Noise in the room begins to shut off, one by one, like someone going around taping mouths shut. It's nerve-racking, and we end our conversation abruptly if only to find out what's going on. Everyone is eyeballing the door.

Shakes stands in the doorway.

Holding Mary's hand, he looks bold, defiant, and proud. He wears jeans and T-shirt, and striking red shoes. I don't know when he shaved his head, but the Mohawk suits him. He's always been a little grunge looking and it fits his personality.

Shakes waits in the silence for backlash, for an attack, always prepared for violence. The crowd is quiet as if they don't believe he's here, like I don't believe it. I can barely breathe seeing him again for the first time.

It takes a bold person to step forward, and he holds out his hand. Shakes breaks his stern facade and grins, shaking his hand, laughing lightly. This action shatters the thick tension, and the crowd shifts toward him like he's the sun and his gravity is sucking us in.

I stand, and I get closer step by step before running toward him. I push and slip between the crowd. He notices the disruption, and he rushes forward to catch me. His arms surround me, and tears pour down my face. His fingers grip my hair, and his face is buried in my neck. I don't know what I mean to him, why he clings to me the way he does. I thought he'd be angry with me even though Mary told me he wasn't. I thought he'd cast me out the way he does everyone who disobeys him. But what I do know is what he means to me. Shakes is my Savior. He built me up from nothing, and he made me someone.

Just like he promised.

"Thank you, Ember," his voice breaks, and he sucks in a breath.

Thank you? What have I done but cause him problems?

I can only blurt out, "I'm sorry. I'm sorry."

He pulls back, his green eyes shining with unshed tears. "Don't be sorry. You did the right thing. I owe you everything. You...God, Ember, you did it all." He kisses my forehead and hugs me again.

Mary rubs my back. "You did so good, sweetheart."

Banging on a table interrupts, and then, a chant, "Shakes, Shakes, Shakes, Shakes. Shakes." A person pulls him, and he steps up onto a table. He's grinning and laughing, waving. The cafeteria is full of clapping and cheering. Shakes holds his hand for me, and I shake my head, but others push me forward, and I stumble upward. I hide behind his shoulder, and he nudges me. "It's for you, Ember."

Their chants transform. "Scream, Scream, Scream, Scream!"

For four months, I lived alone, unsure of everything around me. I lost more than I ever gained. I thought I deserved the Hell I lived in. And if it hadn't been for Charles, I might still be there, terrified of my shadow.

At this moment, there's a weird sense of gratitude bubbling about. If I hadn't struggled so badly, Charles wouldn't have befriended me. I wouldn't have lost him because I wouldn't have known him. I'm better off having known him. Look at where it's got me.

The celebration seems to be never-ending. It's overwhelming, and yet it's everything Shakes deserved. He should have a parade in his honor every day for what he's done for them.

Within all this exuberance and triumph, it's impossible not to notice the corner in the back. The one hundred members of Coal as they sit silent, scowling deathly in our direction. They are like a massive black cloud on this sunny day.

Vengeance is coming just as swiftly as fire consumes.

CHAPTER 11

Trouble

EMBER

SITTING DOWN AT OUR table, there's a tray of food in front of my seat. All the food James had gotten earlier.

"Aren't you eating?"

"No."

"You got all this for me?" It's all my favorites, down to the strawberries and a bowl of chocolate pudding.

James ignores the question, turning his attention to Brick to have a conversation. My cheeks heat up, and I bow my head. At least he isn't as mad as I thought he was. Now if only I could figure out how to explain my feelings.

The hour we spend at the table together is the best time since the morning of the rebellion. We are laughing and joking. Even James has a smile on his face from time to time. It is perfect. I couldn't have asked for a better reunion.

James gets up with a soft. "Stay out of trouble." I watch him, desperate for a little attention, but he gives me nothing. He leans into Shakes' ear, and when his green eyes shift toward me, I look away, cheeks heating up because I know James said something stupid about me. James leaves without looking back.

Shakes wipes his mouth with a napkin. "Ink, we're going to talk."

I flick my eyes back and forth, confused about what that means. Ink's dejection sinks his shoulders, but he gets up from the table and leaves. "What? Where's he's going?"

No one replies, keeping their heads bowed. Shakes begins, "I'm sure I wasn't the only one who noticed Coal."

Brick responds, "They are with us on the sixth floor. They've taken over the west wing, but we have guards watching their side, and someone is always watching Shakes' door."

Shakes rubs his lips, his thoughts swirling in a way I can never comprehend. "What's Jose going to do now that he knows who I am? I'm sure word will get back quickly about my arrival here today. They missed their chance while I was on the operating table." He lifts his shirt, exposing the bullet wound wrapped in gauze. "Anyone figure out who shot me?"

I break in, "Kevin knew. He tried to tell me. Jose said Kevin was taken into protective custody."

"Isn't that a nice coincidence? Too bad I don't believe in coincidences."

Mary whispers, "I told you we shouldn't have come."

"I'm not hiding anymore. I'm sick of hiding."

"What about Ember?" Vapor asks. "She's exposed too now."

Shakes agrees and reveals, "I have people keeping an eye on her. Lisa is trying to get back in my good graces." His green eyes land on me. "But you know not to go anywhere with anyone. Right?"

All this conversation is only making a jumbled mess in my brain. "I don't understand what's going on. We're safe here, right?"

Shakes changes the subject. "What's happening with Coal?"

"A lot of rumors," Brick tells him. I scoff loudly for once again being written off. Brick clears his throat. "Backlash is coming. They want you and Ember. I'm kind of scared of what they'll do."

"What about James?" Vapor wonders. "He killed Ash. Eye for an Eye."

Shakes pivots his head, and we follow his lead. There is a table off to the right. Twenty kids mimic James in their behavior: straight backs, stiff manners, and clean clothes. The rest of the Specials do not talk to each other despite sticking together. They eat quietly and chew as if the food is foreign. "We're working on it. For now, Blockade is watching for him. Keep your eyes open and your ears to the ground. It's not a matter of if they will attack. It's when and how and who first."

The intercom comes on to end breakfast. We hug each other, saying our goodbyes, and plan to meet in the same spot tonight. Shakes keeps me near. He holds an arm around my shoulder, walking me out. "What happened with Light?" he asks lightly.

Embarrassment floods my chest. I can barely talk about boys with other girls. There's no way I could have a conversation like this with a guy I see as my brother. "Um..I don't know."

"You have to be careful. Don't let your guard down."

"I know."

He chuckles, but it's clearly condescending.

"I do, I know."

"As one of the people who watched over you for the past four months, I don't know if I believe that. I wish I could stay with you."

I twist out of his arm, more determined to stand on my own. "I can take care of myself."

"Sure."

My hands turn to fists.

Shakes faces me. "About James. If my opinion means anything. I think Light's better for you. James—"

"I know James is different."

"He's not just different. He's... there's a lot to him that you don't know."

"I know enough." Aside from what James told me last night, I really don't know that much, but I'm defensive about James. He's been through trauma, and I won't have anyone judge him for it.

"What are you getting mad for? I'm trying to protect you."

"I'm not mad."

"You sound mad."

"I'm not. It's aggravating. I'm not a little girl."

"You have constantly gotten into trouble."

I growl, stomping my foot. "Tobias used to tell me that."

"Well, then, you know there is some truth to it."

Another odd grunt comes out of me.

"I just want you safe. So I can stop worrying about you."

And against my better judgment, I lash out, "Do you really care? I'm not Jennifer. I'm officially no one."

Shakes studies me, and I keep my head bowed. Jennifer is a sensitive topic. For months, the school believed I was this girl that was sent to save them, but they were wrong. Shakes was wrong. I transformed into someone else if only to be who he thought I was. I'm thankful for it because up until he told me I had the power to change, I didn't know I did. I thought I was always meant to be a Rat.

What he doesn't know is that Jennifer died weeks ago. And he killed her.

"I'm sorry I got it wrong," he manages. "I thought," Shakes sighs. "It doesn't matter what I thought. Or who I believed. Jennifer's dead."

I snap my head up. "How do you know?"

"Myers. He probably killed her the first day she came. While we were looking at you, he took her out of the game. This whole time, he was playing with us."

It's better if he believes that. I could never tell him the truth. It would hurt him too deeply and despite the trouble between us, I'd never want to cause him pain.

IIe slaps me on the arm. "Get to your room." Shakes waves, and continues up the stairs. The nurse waits impatiently, telling me to hurry as she holds the door to the girl's dormitory. She slams it shut after me and locks it, taking off down the hall. I lean against the wall, replaying our discussion.

It isn't the first time I got frustrated with Shakes. He's overbearing and overprotective. He thinks I'm utterly incapable of protecting myself. It drives me crazy. He's a control freak who wants me to fall in line and listen to his every command. But I don't need another person trying to control me. Tobias was enough. Whenever I spoke to anyone, Tobias had a problem with it. Rebelling became an automatic response. And that ache comes now, to do precisely the opposite of what Shakes says.

The quiet catches my attention, and I pop my head up, searching for anyone. It's then I realize I'm in Coal territory. "Shit," I whisper, pushing off the wall.

Slowly, I take a step. I don't make a noise, only the shuffling of my clothes, and even that, I attempt to control by moving lightly. My heart pounds in my ears. I can see the nurses' station up ahead, but all it would take is one quick girl to nab me and pull me into her room, and I'll never be heard from again.

That would be my luck. Just after Shakes tells me I'm constantly getting into trouble, and I'm in the middle of a bee's nest. It's not like I go looking for trouble, though. It just happens.

The moment I'm five feet away from a nurse who is so ignorant of my fear, I dash past her. Their conversation stops abruptly as they lean over the desk, no doubt confused. I slam the door to my room and take in a steady breath. I chuckle, feeling foolish. But at least Shakes doesn't have another thing to hold against me.

I can't make the same mistake twice.

The moment I step toward the bed, the air shifts, and the shadow in the bathroom suddenly moving.

I drop to my knee and turn, punching whoever it is in the stomach, hard and fully. A soft groan responds, and I look up. Cola flings herself at me. Rope spreads between her hands in her attempt to strangle me from behind. She drops her hands on my shoulders and spins the rope around my neck, but my hands come up, getting caught in between, making it difficult for her to tighten it. I drop to my back on the floor, pulling her with me, and she falls to her side, losing her grip. I fling the rope aside and flip on top of her, punching her in the face. Blood drips from her lip, and I grip her chin. "Get out."

I get off, huffing.

She kicks me in the knee, and I crash to the floor. Her heel hits me again in the face, and the world blacks out for a minute. She gets up and steps over me, snatching up the rope. "You're fucking weak. You should have killed me." Cola knocks my hands from my face and slips the rope around my neck. It tightens against my larynx, cutting off air supply, and panic clicks on. She grins. "Aren't you gonna scream, Scream?"

I slam the heel of my palm into the side of her knee, and she jolts just enough to loosen her hold. I yank back hard, pulling my knees up to my chest to shove my feet against her stomach, sending her flying. The back of her head hits the corner of the wall, and she falls to the floor, unmoving.

I tug the rope off me and scramble away, pushing against the wall preparing for more. But seconds pass, and Cola doesn't get up.

A nurse knocks on my door. "Ember, are you alright?"

When I don't respond, she tries the door again. "Ember?"

I crawl over to the door and unlock it, sitting back. The nurse enters and fright blares on her face as she kneels beside me, but she notices where my eyes are. The moment she sees the body, she races toward her, pressing an emergency button on her necklace. An alarm blares through the hospital with bright red lights rolling along the hallway. "In here!" she calls.

I hide my head and pretend I'm invisible.

CHAPTER 12

Target

SHAKES

BRICK AND VAPOR CAN'T take a hint. There's a time when a guy and girl want to be alone and do 'alone' things. I don't know how to make that known without being obvious and without being a jerk. In their defense, it is noon, but Mary and I haven't had much privacy in—years, pretty much. Just this morning, the doctor told me as long as I'm careful, there shouldn't be a problem with a 'romantic partnership,' as he put it. I just can't understand how they don't notice. I'm so obviously nervous. I haven't sat down in an hour. I'm pacing. I can't form a freaking sentence, and my face is as red as a cherry tomato.

Mary keeps laughing out of nowhere. She's noticed if only to make my humiliation worse. It is pretty funny, and if I didn't know any better, I'd start to think they were doing it on purpose.

But the reality is, Brick and Vapor know my life is in danger. Coal wants to kill me, but how is this new? I've lived every day in school with that terminal intimidation hanging over me. It does little to rattle my nerves. That isn't to say I don't believe they won't try and can't succeed. But I'm prepared at every minute of the day. It's like putting on clothes, it's natural, I don't even think about it anymore.

When a knock on the door interrupts us, I roll my head back. Who else wants to join this cock-blocking fest? Mary rubs my back, giggling into my neck. I love her sense of humor, but not when it's at my expense.

"Adam."

Leaning around her, a nurse stands at the doorway, and all thoughts dissipate. I've been wondering when they would come for me.

"Detective Jose would like to meet you."

Mary clenches my hand, and I whisper words of comfort into her ear. "They aren't going to kill me," I say while withholding the words, 'not yet.' She doesn't let me go. With a glance towards

Brick, he wraps his arms around her, holding back. I listen to her cries even as I walk out of the room. I want to believe that this detective won't kill me so blatantly. But the sad truth is, I know nothing about him. Myers told me he was the nice one, and I somehow think he was being honest.

I mark the path we take in case I need to make a quick escape. I don't understand what this hospital is, but I know it's unsafe. Nothing from the government can be trusted. The nurses and doctors are ignorant. They may even be captive themselves and not know it. From the details I've received, they have all joined this assignment with a sign-up bonus of five thousand dollars. What gains my interest is the fact the location was kept secret. Nurses and doctors aren't going home after their shift. They live next door, above the parking garage in group settings. Males on one floor, girls on the next. It's cramped from the numerous overheard complaints. And some aren't as clean as others.

One month, the doctors and nurses were told. One month to get us all healthy enough to go back home.

I will admit it seems real. The nurses and doctors are kind and caring. The food is plentiful. The free clothes and the bedrooms are gifts. If I were anyone else, I might believe this was actual freedom. I'd celebrate like the crowd had at lunch. I'd stop fighting and try to be a normal teenager. I'd begin planning my trip to Florida and even think about where Mary and I will get married.

But Myers stole my childhood and now at eighteen, I'm not pathetically gullible. *No one gives things away for free.*

There aren't any people on the first floor, or they may be behind closed doors. We pass six different rooms that are unmarked. Any number of people could be lurking behind them. The nurse opens the door, and boldly, I step in.

The first thing I notice is the glass wall, and on the other side is Ember. She sits on a metal chair in the center of the room with her head down. Her long, messy brown hair encases her face, and an ice pack rests lazily in her hand on her lap. The way she sits is what stands out: defeated.

I rush up to the glass, pounding it and calling her name. She either can't hear me or chooses to ignore me.

"The infamous Shakes."

Behind me, Jose leans against the wall: a Spanish young business-looking dude. He doesn't smile, but he isn't glaring either. He's sizing me up as if I'm competition. I strengthen my stance, fisting my hands. He's taking into account I'm not a small kid that he can bully. He was probably hoping I was a scrawny little pup barely passed puberty, instead he finds a fully grown wolf. "What did you do to her?"

"Me?" he asks incredulously. "Why would I hurt any of you?" He approaches, slipping his hands in his pockets casually. "No, she got into a fight with a Coal member, *bendito*. Though we aren't sure on the details, she's not talking."

"What about the coal member?"

"Cola. Also known as Danielle Wilson. Dead."

Sadness billows in my chest, and I move for Ember.

"Before that—" He stops me and a warning triggers in my chest. Jose spins on his foot and rests back against the mirror, crossing his arms, trying to appear less of a threat. "I'm Detective Jose. I'm sure you know that." He watches my face for any giveaway signs. He wants to know how good my intel is. I'm not about to reveal my secrets or let him know I know his. "I've been looking for you, and Scream-"

"She doesn't like that name."

"Ember," he politely corrects. "Because I wanted to offer my protection."

"We're fine."

"Oh?" He glances behind him.

The fact that Ember was almost killed because of misplaced trust eats at me. Lisa failed to come through. "It won't happen again."

"I can get you someplace safe. I already took a few people because they asked. Kevin knew who shot you."

"I don't suppose you are going to tell me."

"And allow your acts of vengeance? I know the clan creed: an eye for an eye. I know everything about the clans. Even Anarchy."

"I doubt that."

Jose ignores me. "I won't have any disruptions here. Keep your violent tendencies to yourself while I work on getting you home."

"Just let us go," I counter. "We can find our own way."

He smirks. "Isn't finding your own way what got you in that school in the first place?" He holds up his hands. "Cheap shot, I'm sorry. Listen, Shakes—I'm going to call you Adam. We can help each other. I'm putting together a list of kids needing more help before returning to society." He walks over to the desk in the corner and picks up the file. "Look it over, let me know if anything needs adjusting, and maybe you and I can come to an understanding. I do something for you. You do something for me. Right now, what I want is a confession. Easy breezy."

"A confession? About what?"

He looks at Ember. "From our analysis so far, Danielle was waiting in Ember's room, hiding in her bathroom, and when Ember returned from lunch, she sprung out from behind and attempted to strangle her. That's the line of bruising on her neck. From there, Ember fought; she got hit in the face rather hard. We will take her for an x-ray soon to ensure her cheekbone isn't broken. After that, whether on purpose or by accident, Danielle hit the back of her head on a corner wall, shattering a piece of her skull, killing her instantly."

"It was an accident," I reinforce. "Ember doesn't hurt on purpose. She fights to protect herself."

"Considering she blew up a school, I don't agree with that assessment. Plus, I hear rumor she killed Ash. So, right now, she's on my list. Get me a confession, and I'll take her off."

"Why does that seem like it's a win for me? Why don't you just cut the shit and tell me what's really going on?"

"*Bendito*," he murmurs softly. "So broken you are. I'm not here to hurt you, Adam. I'm very religious. I took this job to do right by God. But if that's not enough for you, if we wanted to hurt any of you, why would we spend so much money on your surgeries and your health? Twenty-three kids with gunshot wounds. Ten others were crushed by falling debris. One amputation. Twelve in body bags caused by your revolt. The state of Oklahoma wants you well when we find you a new home. Trust in us. It won't be long, I promise."

A new home, he says. Not the home we belong to.

"Myers was religious too," I point out.

He shifts uncomfortably and changes direction. "This will be our foundation of trust, and we'll go from there." Jose gestures toward the door to the interrogation room, and though I'm hesitant, I can't stop my feet.

I kneel in front of Ember, grabbing her hand. Her blue eyes are distant, not responding as I call her name. The swelling is massive, nearly shutting her entire eye. I guide her to place the ice pack on it and she robotically obeys. The guilt swallows me. Not an hour after I left her, she was already hurt. What happened with Lisa? Why did she fail me? She was the one who wanted my forgiveness. If she wants to keep leadership of her clan, then she'll need me to back her up, but she has a lot to make up for. I expected my debt to be fulfilled. But I can't let this slide. I must protect my family.

This man Jose is not on my side. He wants me to be a snitch, and snitches don't live long in our world. I can't turn on my own kind. Even if I hate half of them, even if most of them betrayed me at some point, or turned their back on me, or closed a door in my face. I can't turn them in. We are all the same. We all have blood on our hands and evil in our hearts. Jose wants me to pick out the most dangerous.

How ironic he's talking to one.

Jose is at the table. "Let me say again, violence will not be tolerated here. This is a government facility. Every action will have repercussions."

I clench my teeth, searching for lies. *'Government facility,'* he said. Myers' words, **'Government-owned, government-funded,'** echo in the shadow of Jose's. He's part of Myers. I have no doubt.

"Sarah, our guidance Counselor, has compiled a list of students with certain tendencies we see in serial killers. We are hoping to help rehabilitate the worst of you. In the meantime, get your girl to talk." He points to the camera. "No coercing either." He winks and leaves out a different door. I glance toward the mirror, toward the open door to the viewing room, wondering if someone is watching us now.

I stare at the folder. Every time I open one of these up, I learn things I don't want to know. I flick back the cover and scan the list. My fist pounds the metal, and I fling backward, pacing the ground. He didn't have the balls to stay; he knew I'd punch him in the throat.

I bring myself back to the folder, and the names pop out like streetlights in the night. My entire family is on here.

Mary, Vapor, Brick, James, and Ink are among them, including several members of Anarchy. Coal Members, Rain members, Boundary members, and every single Special. He's got a list of a hundred he will take away. He'd put me on here, too, if he wasn't trying to keep me cooperative. Unlike Myers, he doesn't underestimate my ability to move mountains.

This is a threat. He is acknowledging my strength, my dominance over the masses. However, he is exposing that he knows our secrets. He may even have evidence to our past misdeeds that could have us imprisoned if convicted. He is using a form of legality that I'm not privy to.

I always assumed that my actions would be forgiven when I was out of school. I thought that's how it would work. How could anyone blame a victim for killing the villain? But I had to do a lot more than that to survive. Five years of fighting, and sometimes I've lost sight of who the bad guys were.

That's why Ember is so important to me. She hasn't forgotten. She reminds me that we are innocent despite our fight for survival. That day of the rebellion, I would have killed us all if it meant never to be trapped again. Carbon's death clouded my rationality. I wanted nothing more than to join every brother and sister I've lost. I shouldn't be alive when they're not. My blood should be with theirs, in that school.

That's the misery talking. The irrational part of me.

But when I'm around Ember, she makes me think forgiveness is possible. Hope springs back to life, and all I want is that wedding on the beach with Mary and maybe even a kid or two. I can see a future that isn't tainted by blood.

And now Jose is threatening that future.

He just became my next target.

CHAPTER 13

Trust

SHAKES

I GRAB A CHAIR and set it in front of Ember. With
my elbows on my knees and my hands in hers, I
try to gain her gaze. Guilt is like a gas pain. It
makes me angry. I put trust in the wrong people
because I didn't have much choice, and look at
what happened? Ember killed someone trying to
protect herself, something I never wanted her to
have to do. I've kept her hands clean for months,
and a single slip has put us here.

There's a reason I have a system. I shouldn't have
needed a reminder.

"Ember."

"I didn't let my guard down." Her voice is dull
and a tear drips on her hand.

I try to smile, but her misery ruins it. "You did good, Ember. Can you tell me what happened?"

She sets the ice pack down, revealing full view of her face. Her eye is half swollen by the swelling of her cheek. Black bruising has already expanded from underneath her eye. It's difficult for her to talk, trying to keep her jaw closed. "She was already there, waiting. I felt her." Her fingers play with the plastic, and I don't know what else to do but listen. "We fought, and I thought I won. I let her go..." She drops her head upward to stare at the ceiling, swallowing. I now see the thick line across her neck where she was strangled. I clench the chair in a rage. "She wouldn't give up. I pushed her, and she fell."

"It was an accident."

She nods, lowering her head as tears begin to fall. "I didn't want her to die, Shakes." I get out of the chair and wrap her up in my arms as she combusts. "I'm sorry. I'm sorry. What about her mom? Her family? Her friends? All the people that loved her? She made it so far, and she was so close. How could I... How could she just—" Ember can barely breathe as a full-on anxiety attack envelopes her.

She sucks in the air with deep gulps, but it doesn't seem to do anything. She looks at me for help.

I grip the side of her face. "Focus on my eyes. You have to calm down. Think about Charles, Ember. Think about Charles. What was the best thing about Charles? Can you remember? What did you love most about him?"

"His eyes," she breathlessly replies after a moment. "Your eyes."

Exhausted, she drops against me. I hold her close, letting her rest. Her fingers cling to my skin. I never met Charles. I knew he was trying to get into Anarchy, but I was afraid of his relationship with Ember. I wish I hadn't let fear stop me. It's so clear that she is innocent in all of this. She and Charles were the kids I had initially set out to protect. I took on the role of leader to help those like her. When did fear envelop me so deeply I forgot that? I became too cruel to those I didn't know. I didn't even give them a chance.

"Ember, listen to me. It wasn't your fault."

"But—"

"If you want to take the blame for something, there are plenty of things that are your fault. Okay? Blowing up a school? Totally your fault."

She snorts, and I smile. "Kissing Light and James, your fault." She chokes on a laugh. Encouraged by her humor, I make another joke. "Wearing leggings with your ass—"

She shoves me away. I wonder if I took it too far, but she's hiding an annoyed smile. Ember looks behind her, trying to see, and I stifle a laugh. "I've never worn leggings before. I didn't know how revealing they were."

I latch onto the ice pack and delicately press it against her cheek. "This was an accident, Ember. I'm proud of you. I'm really thankful, too." She searches my face for the truth. She thinks I'm mad at her for standing up to me in front of the police and no amount of reassurance has yet gotten through. "I don't know what I'd do without you." Her eyes water and her lips press together in an effort to hold back. She is one of the strongest people I know and she doesn't even realize it.

"Probably have less to worry about."

I smirk. "Where's the fun in that?" Her weak smile eases me. "Let's get you an x-ray." I grip her hand to help her stand. The door opens. "Don't worry, Jose, I got your confess—"

Closing the door behind her, the woman stands with a bowed head and her hands tucked behind her back. She wears black-rimmed glasses, a purple pantsuit, a gold necklace dipping into her bustline. Her blond hair clips in a bun to the back of her head. She appears like a corporate office manager or some other type of business executive. But I'm not fooled. A year can change us, but not enough. Not enough for me to forget.

Ember calls my name as I begin to step backward. She stumbles, but I steady her, a hand on her arm and I push us near the glass wall, placing the metal table between us. It's not enough space. A world isn't enough space. Death isn't enough space. I'm searching for a weapon, a distraction, and a way to get away.

"This is Sarah, Shakes," Ember tries to assure. "It's okay, she works here."

'Sarah' reaches up above the door and unplugs the video camera.

My body trembles. "Her name isn't Sarah."

She lifts her fake green eyes and meets mine.

All my control vanishes, and I snatch up the chair and jump the table. My feet hit the floor, and I swing it over my head and slam the feet of the

151

chair to the wall with her trapped beneath. Fear is present in her face, but I want more. I want pain to reflect. I want to inflict as much torment on her as she's done to me. I press my entire weight against the chair, but she can't feel it.

God, I want her to feel it.

A tear falls down her cheek. "Shakes—"

"No," I cut her off. My whole body trembles. "Don't talk. Don't say anything. Ember, get out."

She whimpers, "Please—"

"I said!" My voice echoes in a violent scream, and it scares even me. "Don't. Talk." I glance at Ember. "Go."

Ember rushes to the door and slips through it. She holds it open for me, but I can't move. I can't take my attention away from this ghost. From a girl that betrayed me, shot me, destroyed me. I had to rebuild every piece of who I was and what was left over was barely human.

"If you come near any of my family, Memory," I bite through clenched teeth. She shakes her head, her lips trembling. "I'll slit your throat and watch you choke on your own blood. Do you understand?"

"I need to—"

Tears drip down her cheeks, but they mean nothing to me. "DO YOU...understand me?"

With a sudden force, Memory throws out, "I know why the bombs didn't go off. Dust was killed by a Special. Zack stopped us."

I tell myself I don't care. I tell myself it doesn't matter. She's lying like she always does. She would know this failure would bother me. She would know how to get to me, how to earn my trust back.

And I despise how it works.

Which Special ruined the rebellion? Was it James?

Ember touches my shoulder. She's an anchor, pulling me away, and I latch onto her, grabbing Ember's hand and allowing her to pull me away. The chair drops with a crash, and Memory slides to the floor, panting and crying. It pisses me off more that she has the audacity to be weak in front of me. I lean down to whisper in her ear, "I'm going to make you regret showing yourself, Memory. You should have killed me when you had the chance."

I yank Ember away as fast as our feet will carry us. She stumbles, trying to keep up in my rush. I know she talks, but I can't hear her. The pain in my chest, in my head, in my gut, is crushing me. I can't breathe. My whole body is shaking. I want to kill her. Every ounce of me wants to go back and put a bullet through Memory's skull.

Ember pulls me. "Shakes, what's going on?"

"Leave it alone." I let go of her, slapping the elevator button. All I can see is Memory as she raises her gun and shoots me. 'I'm sorry'. It was all she said. No reason. No excuse. Just a stupid-ass, lame apology that meant nothing. That helped me understand nothing.

We're in the elevator, and I'm pacing back and forth. I punch the wall once, twice. The metal bounces off my hit. Little dents that give me no relief.

"You're scaring me."

Ember's timid voice breaks it. It breaks the overwhelming killing intent. Ember stands in the corner as small as possible with a huge bruise on the side of her face, and I'd forgotten about going to get her an x-ray. My need to care for her takes reign and drowns the sickness in my gut, and I can breathe again. I approach tentatively and tap her under the chin. "Heads up."

She tries to smile with a swollen cheek. I hug her, apologizing, and with her head resting against my shoulder, I can find myself again.

"That was Memory? I'm sorry, Shakes."

The elevator door opens back on the first floor, and we exit. I'm timid, walking back toward the room. I don't want to see Memory again. I don't know how it will break me.

Sensing my hesitation, Ember stops. "Go back. It's okay. I can go by myself."

"No, never."

"I'm safe down here." She points to Jose when he walks out of a room with a nurse on his side. "There's Jose. He'll take me." She pushes me back in the elevator. "I can protect you too." She waves her wristband against the panel and hits the sixth floor before she backs out. "I'll see you when I'm done." I don't put up much of a fight, and the doors close before I bring myself to reach for her.

I fall back against the wall. My hand crawls up the inside of my shirt and rests on the bullet hole beneath my left pectoral. Inside the school, medicine was hard to come by. Pain pills were rare. Any injury we were supposed to go to the nurses, but they reported to the teachers. I couldn't go, or I'd be killed. Jared was our only medical student, and he was fifteen then. He was good at burns and cuts. He could stitch like a pro, but bullet wounds were beyond his scope. I think I only survived because of what I needed to do. My purpose wasn't finished, and my body couldn't give out until it was done.

'*Zack stopped us,*' Memory said.

If Zack stopped us, then James would have been a part of it. Memory is trying to dismantle my faith in my friends and strengthen my trust in her. It's a common tactic.

I press the fifth floor, a sudden need I can't stop. Memory is already getting to me, and I curse myself when the doors open. I pause, telling myself she's lying, but I can't shake the awful thought developing in my head.

Guys glance at me as I pass them in the halls. If they didn't know who I was before the rebellion, there is no question now. They whisper my name to each other, pointing and calling to their friends. When I ask one of them where James is, they stutter, unsure how to respond before someone finally points a finger.

I enter the room. James is sleeping having just returned from surgery, but his eyes pop open when

I close the door. "Shakes." He shifts, attempting to get up, but I put a hand up, and he stays lying down but stiff and alert.

I don't want to ask. I don't want to believe Memory, but more importantly, I don't want to lose James. Though I barely know him personally, he has become someone I trust fully, and that's a rare quality in my life. He's important to me and everything I'm trying to do. He has done everything I've asked of him and more. His friendship is valuable.

But I can't stop the question from forming, "Where were you on the day of the Grounding?"

There's a flinch on his brow. Usually, such a reaction would be the only answer I would need, but I have to hear him say it. There can be no doubt.

Clearing his throat, he responds, cold and direct. "I was ordered to kill someone."

"Who?"

"I don't know his name. I was told the location."

"What was the location?"

"A Rat apartment adjacent to the school."

My hands fist at my sides. It's still not enough. I need everything. "Was it because of you the Grounding failed?"

"There were many reasons the Grounding failed–"

"Was it because of you the bombs didn't go off?"

"Yes."

My face twists, and I drop my head, trying to hide it, but the mohawk does nothing to shield my expression. My hands curl at my side, eager for a gun to extract instant revenge. It's all I've known, it's all I'm used to. "Did you think I would never find out?"

"I knew you would. I hoped by then you would give me the benefit of the doubt."

I scoff at the hilarity of such a statement. He must not know me as well as he thinks he does. "Why would I do that?"

"Because I have made up for it," he snaps harshly full of desperation and fear. It's uncharacteristic, but I know why he does. He knows there is no 'making up for it.' I give people one chance to show me what kind of person they are. I can't afford to second guess. And this reveals what I've been missing. James can't be trusted.

"Shakes-"

"You're done. Next time I see you, I'll kill you."

CHAPTER 14
Another One

SHAKES

WHEN I RETURN TO my room, all the rage, fear, and misery cascade into an avalanche. Mary is pacing, waiting for me, and as soon as I walk in, she rushes into my arms. I'm numb. I'm left with nothing but a hole. Mary tries to get words from me, but I can't speak. I can only hold onto her, a way to stop myself from drowning in despair. I'm shaking, and it scares her. She attempts to break away to find out if I'm okay, but I don't let go. I can't let go. I need her to keep me from slipping. I'm three feet away from breaking down. Tears burn, and the harder I wrap my arms around her, the more water builds, and I can't seem to stop it.

Memory is here, and James was the reason the bombs failed. How am I supposed to be okay?

"No one's dead, right?" Mary questions. "Tell me everyone's okay."

I nod into her neck.

She pulls at my arms, and when she sees the wetness on my cheeks, her lips touch them, over my chin, my eyes, my lips. "What's happened to you, honey? You're breaking my heart."

I grip her cheeks and press my lips against her, and though she keeps talking, trying to get words out of me, I don't want to talk about it anymore. I want to forget it. "Shh," I tell her after several attempts, and she laughs into my kiss and finally responds with the same vigor.

There are so many things I wanted different for Mary and I. When I proposed two months ago, it was unthoughtful and offhand. I was simply daydreaming and talking out loud when she heard me say the word married. 'You want to marry me?' She wondered with bewilderment, like it was the biggest shock she'd ever experienced. To me, it was a natural thing. Of course, I'd marry her. That's what you do when you're in love, and no matter how many times I said the words to her before, it was like she finally believed me. I didn't have a ring. I was still trying to procure one through bargains and trades. The problem was I didn't want just any ring. So, whenever I came into contact with one, I turned it down.

We winded up on the floor taking the mattresses from both beds because one single gurney was not big enough to hold both of us. Under the blankets, Mary's giggles are infectious, and I can't stop smiling, squeezing her naked body against mine. "Stop it." She swats me away. "You're bleeding on me." Mary snatches my shirt and presses it to my stomach.

"Guess we weren't as gentle as we should have been," I nibble on her ear, enraptured by her. I've always been amazed by her beauty. She's the kind of girl that doesn't know how beautiful she is. Her weight makes her unconfident. Which is good for me because if she did know, she'd realize she's too good for me.

My hand shifts down her leg and she squeals. "Get!" I relinquish my hold so she can go to the bathroom, and I lay on my back.

I don't care about my stitches. I'm euphoric and light-headed, and nothing matters right now. Right now, I'm a regular teenager with typical teenage thoughts. We didn't use a condom, and I hope that doesn't cause a situation in the future. But I don't know how I'd feel if it did. Is it silly of me to become excited at the idea of her carrying my kid? We never talked about kids for obvious reasons. The school forced contraception on the girls before they were even brought in. Here, removing the implant was the first thing they did. It's a possibility now, and it opens the door to a whole new future I didn't think I'd ever have.

I'm only eighteen. There's a thousand things I want to do. But life is too unpredictable to wait around.

My smile is fading as thoughts come barreling through like weeds in a garden. No matter how fast I pull them, more take their place.

Mary returns, redressed, much to my disappointment, and lays down beside me. I am hoping for round two, but she points out my stitches, and I give up. "So tell me. What happened?"

I stare at the ceiling. I don't know what to say or how to tell her. I don't want her to be afraid, but I can't keep a secret from her. Especially one like this. "Memory's here."

She sits up, and I can tell she doesn't understand.

I grab and kiss her fingers before holding them to my chest over the bullet hole. "She's alive. And she's here."

"You...You saw her..."

"She tried to talk to me."

"She— That damn girl. I told her—" Mary cuts herself off as every muscle in my body tenses. I sit up, releasing her hand. After losing James, I'm unprepared for this. Mary has supported me for years. To betray me like this, hurts in a different way. I'm not angry and reaching for a weapon. I'm in pain.

"You knew?"

Shame builds on her face, but I can't look at it. I get to my feet, grabbing my pants.

"The first day we were here, I saw her." She speaks rushed and chaotic, but blood is pounding in my ears. "I thought it was my imagination. You were in surgery, and she was walking by. I didn't know if you were going to live. I didn't go after her. I couldn't leave you."

I keep moving, slipping a shirt over my head. Her words are under water and I don't try to focus on them.

"She came to me two days ago, begging me to talk to her, but I wouldn't. I told her to get out, to leave, to never show her face. I didn't want her to hurt you. I didn't want that pain for you. It was to protect you because I love you, please, please just stop."

I have my hand on the door when Mary grabs my arm. The touch is like fire. Even if it's painful, I allow it because I'm going to let her again.

"Where are you going?"

I don't look back at her. "What was the one thing I said never to do, Mary?"

She stutters, terrified. "I. I didn't. I didn't betray you, Adam."

The fact that she can't see it only proves I'm right to leave. "We're done." I step out the door, surprised she doesn't fight it. She lets me go. She knows me too well. Memory made sure that my heart made no decisions for me.

In the hallway, my chest is in agony, but I'm still aware of those watching me. They slink behind corners and in doorways. Coal is everywhere, spread out like snipers on a rooftop. All their little lasers aimed at my chest. I enter Brick's room, and he and Vapor both become alert at the sight of me.

I throw my bag down. "I broke up with Mary." I fling myself in the chair and hide my face.

They don't ask. Guys don't ask. Brick hands me a soda as if that could cure me.

After a half hour, the grief is bearable, and I can form rational thoughts again. "Coal attacked Ember," I announce, and they snap off the TV, wondering what we're going to do in response. "Cola's dead. Jose is watching us, figuring out who I work with and how I work. It makes revenge difficult."

"With Jet and Ash dead, Peat and Noah have taken over. Crazy enough, Noah happened to be dating a girl named Cola."

"Coincidence?" I scoff, hating that I'm learning this too late. "He's gonna be wanting retribution. Send Blink to protect Ember. Lisa failed, and I'm sure it was on purpose. I want to know why before I kill one of her friends."

"Ink can-"

"Don't bring up Ink again. I told you, he's out. He better not be who you've been using so far."

They shift uncomfortably. I hadn't intended to be brisk, but it's aggravating having to repeat myself over and over again. I get it, Ink was great at getting information and passing the word around. He was a good little sidekick. But he screwed up. No one's more upset about losing family than I am.

"I'll get it done, boss."

"James is out too. We don't need him." Vapor taps Brick, nudging him, and I get fed up with the lack of confidence. "What?"

"Why aren't we telling everybody about what Myers said?" Brick asks. "This place is wrong, and we know it. We need to be getting the clans together and taking this place down. We are worse off than in school. We have no weapons. No friends on the outside or the inside even. We're sitting ducks here. I don't like it, boss. I'm sorry. I just don't."

I pick at the gauze on my hand. I knew he felt like this. I saw the irritation on his brow the last time we spoke. He finally had the guts to say something. "Until we know for sure, we can't go around making ourselves a target. We have to pretend like everyone else. Jose is looking for a reason to get rid of us."

Vapor murmurs, "Then we need to do it in secret. But I think we need to work fast, boss. I don't think anyone that's left here has actually gone home."

I nod, agreeing, but unsure what I'm supposed to do about it. Why do I have to be in charge of it? Can't someone else do it?

"Memory's here," I find myself saying. It's stupid. It's not like she's gonna help. It's not like I'd let her. "She's posing as a counselor named Sarah. She wanted to talk to me. The bitch wanted to talk to me." I scoff, dropping my head in my hand.

It's silent for a while. Neither Brick nor Vapor knew Memory as well as I did. They were simply members of Anarchy back then. They didn't talk to her or trust in her. They didn't put all their hope in her like I had. Her betrayal had only affected me and the others who were dead. Carbon, Star, Nail, and Hail. Everyone who knew her, tied their lives around her, was dead, and it was her fault they didn't make it. They would have made it. They were all alive a year ago. They would have made it.

Brick is the one to speak first. "Don't you want to know what she has to say?"

"No!" I get to my feet. "What the fuck could she say? She betrayed me. She shot me. She set us up and got everyone killed. Nothing, absolutely nothing, could make what she did forgivable. I can't stand the thought of her. And she's in here in this goddamned building. I can't."

Vapor points to the blood on my shirt. "Boss, you're bleeding. Let me get a doctor."

I sit back down, holding my head.

"We have to kill her. Before she kills one of us."

Vapor tentatively mutters, "We can't go around killing anymore, Shakes. It doesn't work like that in the real world."

"What real world? This is the world."

CHAPTER 15

Say

EMBER

I'VE BEEN LYING HERE in and out of consciousness, staring at my wall. There is a dark, dry spot of blood where Cola hit. But otherwise, there is no evidence that we fought. The x-ray revealed a slight fracture, but there was nothing the doctors could do except give me pain pills and ice packs. Their high-dose pain medication knocked me out longer than I wanted. It wasn't until the intercom came on that I woke up. The ice pack I had is nothing more than warm water. My cheek throbs, and I get up and look in the mirror. It's not too bad yet, but bruises like discolored flowers sometimes take a day or two to bloom.

After getting ready for the day, wearing a weird combo of leggings and a long shirt that annoyingly says 'happiness' on it, I snap open my door to find two girls hanging on the outside. Blink is a lanky girl, a half foot taller than me, and meant for the WNBA. She's part of Shakes' assassin team.

On the other side is Lisa. The two of them glare at each other, silently fuming as if my arrival cut off their bickering.

"What's going on?"

Blink answers, "Shakes wants me to stay with you."

"You can tell him we're doing just fine," Lisa bites.

"And as I just told you, you're fired."

I shove past both of them and head for the stairs. Lisa is on my heels. "Okay, look. You hurt Light. I told you that wasn't a good idea. But we're even now. I'll protect you like I'm supposed to. There's no need for further problems. Right? Tell Starbright here to go away."

Blink replies under her breath, and I can't hear it. Probably full of curses.

"Ember?" Lisa tries again. "Please. I can't control everything. I need us to be good. I don't want another war. We're getting out of here soon. Let's all get out alive."

She's so obviously desperate; it's sad. My big brother must be very scary. I stop in the hall and turn to her. "Look at my face. My neck. Cola tried to kill me. She almost did. Did you know she was in my room?" The hesitation is enough for me. "Stay away from me."

Lisa latches onto my arm, and I knock her hand off violently, ready to throw her on the floor. She steps back with her hands up. "You don't understand the clans. It's tit for tat. You do something to us; we do something to you. By neglecting to protect you, we are even. It can stop here. If Shakes lets it. If you let it. Talk to him, please."

Her alarm is overwhelming, and though she doesn't deserve my pity, I say, "Relax, he's not a monster. You are acting like—"

"Listen. You don't know Shakes like I do. He's a great person but does bad things to those who betray him and his family. I'm asking you as a friend to tell him that we're okay. I don't want anyone else to die. Do you?"

"He wouldn't—"

"Do you truly believe that? After everything you've seen?"

Her brown eyes are wide and desperate. For a moment, I can't say exactly what Shakes would or wouldn't do. I remember how he was about to start a fight with the police. He had a gun in his hand, prepared for war. Lisa said something similar then, too. *'Shakes doesn't know good from bad anymore. Help us. Help him.'*

"I'm begging you, before someone gets hurt, stop him."

I stand there, unable to move. I stood before those police because I knew Shakes would harm them. Now, here I am, acting like he wouldn't kill someone for something as minor as failing to protect me. But he would, wouldn't he?

Blink remains quiet, staring straight ahead even though she feels the weight of my stare. How many people has Shakes sent her to assassinate because of petty revenge?

Outside for our 'forced recreation,' I sit against the wall with my arms around my knees, watching the others talk and play. Coal is distant, and a few of them glance my way, but I don't dare to look. Blink doesn't leave my side, and Lisa stands a couple feet ahead with her clan members, like a wall of protection.

But neither of them save me from the images in my head. Cola tortures me in the silence. I never met her before yesterday. I don't know why she hated me enough to try to kill me. I blew up the school but was that really a just cause to take my life? Why come at me as she had? Do other people hate me?

I don't go to breakfast even though I'm starving, having missed dinner the night before. I have a little nest of granola bars on my nightstand, but chewing hurts. When the day nurse tries to give me pain medicine, I deny it. I'm not sleeping the day away again. But I lie in bed and stare at the spot where Cola fell and torture myself for everything I could have done differently.

I could have yelled for help.

The thought is so strange because for so long, I knew no one would come. It's why I never screamed. But now, I have people that care for me. I can rely on them. Blink falls asleep in the chair beside my bed. She's not very talkative, but I don't mind her as much as I thought I would.

No matter how I avoid it, I want to be with James. We haven't talked since yesterday. I hope he hasn't learned what's happened. He's probably biting at the bit to talk to me.

James wants me to explain what I feel for him, and I don't know what I can say. But I don't want to ignore him anymore. I need to confront him and stop running. I just hope when he sees my face, he won't want revenge, too.

I force myself up when evening recreation is over. I'm not tired after sleeping all day, but for some reason I'm weak. Maybe because I'm crazy hungry, but I'm used to such a feeling. Blink eats a burrito, and I stare at her, envious, but she doesn't seem to care.

We head up to the boys' dormitory, but I slow down as I approach James' open door. I'm scared he'll take one look at my face and want a fight.

Blockade walks up. "Your boy has been antsy as hell. Got him a private room down the hall." He points, walking beside me. Blockade and I are new to talking, this being our fourth time, but I'm calm in his presence. He's been respectful and given me no reason to fear him.

This is a new improvement. Just being a guy would have put him on my enemy's list.

"How you holdin' up?" He points to his face, indicating my own.

"Fine."

"I heard about it at lunch. You're really an impressive fighter."

Little does he know none of it is skill.

He glances back at Blink before he points to the guys in the hall. "We got you covered up here. Rest easy."

I turn to Blink. "Why don't you get some sleep?"

She hesitates, but Blockade works for Shakes. She eventually concedes, promising to be back in a few hours.

I take a deep breath, forcing fake courage. I step into James' new room. It's a single bed with a window on the back wall overlooking the recreation area of the hospital, but the curtains are closed, leaving the room in a soft haze of light. James is sitting up, awake, and back to being shirtless. But sitting beside him is the nurse, Grace. The phone light illuminates her smile, and the red shade of her cheeks. And as she hands him the phone, their fingers touch.

I want to stab her in her pretty face.

James notices movement first and pops his head up. Grace takes back her phone and stands. "I'll come back for your vitals." She slips past me and greets, "Hi, Ember." She smiles forcefully, saying nothing about my obvious bruise as she rushes past.

I don't move any closer. I'm angry, and I don't know why. Staying in the shadows keeps my emotions from being revealed, and I also can hide my injuries. But James lifts his hand above his bed and flips on a switch. It lights up the entire room and me.

James' eyes widen.

"I'm fine."

"You don't look fine."

"I'm fine," I say again and for some reason, it doesn't sound as convincing as the first time.

"Come here." I take one step closer, but I don't want him to see any further. Aggravation builds on his black brows. "I had surgery again."

I glance down, noticing his arm resting on a pillow. There is an ice pack surrounding it.

I'm relieved to see his fingers through the cast. "I thought you were going to get it removed?"

"I thought you asked me not to."

There he goes, just acting like my words are important and the things I want matter.

"They advise me to rest. But if you do not come closer, I will come get you."

With a bowed head, I step to the bed until I'm close enough for him to snatch my arm and pull me. He touches my chin, raising my head to analyze the bruising on my neck.

"Who did this?"

"It doesn't matter."

"I did not ask if it mattered. Answer my question. Who did it?"

"It doesn't matter—"

"I will not let this happen again—"

"It doesn't matter because they're dead!"

Tears drip down my cheeks, but I don't want to think about it. I focus on the stupid scene that I saw when I came in simply to drown out my guilt. I'd much rather feel anger than sadness. I'd much rather feel jealousy than remorse.

I toe the ground, refusing to speak. I'm stupid for being jealous because we haven't talked about what we are. And with me and Light, he has every right to talk to other girls. I am being insecure for stupid reasons. But being insecure is who I am.

Compared to Grace, a grown, confident woman with whom I have nothing in common, I am far removed from competition.

"What happened?"

"I don't want to talk about it," I snap unnecessarily, curling into myself, guilt pecking at me.

"You have something to say, then say it."

Taking the dare, I lash out, "Grace likes you."

"What's your point?"

"She's pretty."

"You have always been observant. What are you implying?"

"You know what I'm implying."

"Perhaps I refuse to believe you would insinuate a pretty face would affect me."

"I hurt you," I say, despising myself for pointing out the obvious. "Isn't that how it works? You hurt me back? We're even then?"

"You have not hurt me. I am a Special. It will take much more than words to reach me."

My eyes drop. James' harshness makes me wonder what emotions he can actually have.

James clears his throat and there is silence between us before he takes a deep breath. "I am confused. If Light is everything you want, then why kiss me?"

I shrug. "I don't know."

"That's not an answer."

Frustrated, I lash out, "I don't know what you want me to say. I don't know what *to* say. I don't know what it is you make me feel. I just know it's different. It's not like Charles, or Shakes, or Tobias, or Light. It's not like any of them. All I know is it's consuming, and it's overwhelming, and it won't go away, and I can't stop it. I can't get you out of my head. And I want to be with you even when I'm mad at you. Even when you frustrate the crap out of me. Even when you scare me sometimes with how inhuman you are. But you fascinate me when you smile. I see emotion in your eyes when you look at me and I want to make you happy and I want to show you the way Charles made the world because there is good out there. I want to see it with you. But I don't know what you want me to say. I do know that I don't want to lose you even if you don't want to be with me. I just want to stay with you even if you're mad at me or you like that other girl. I don't care." I chew the inside of my cheek, nervous, afraid it's not good enough. "I don't know what you want me to say."

He smiles, a full-fledged smile, and with the lights shining, he looks nearly angelic. "That's good."

Relief pours over me, and tears pour out this time because of relief. I drop my head on his chest and curl into him. He kisses my hair, hugging me tight. "I was good at half of that," he admits, chuckling as he touches my chin, leaning me back, and kisses my lips. I wince, however, pulling away. He analyzes my face and removes the ice pack off his wrist and presses it to my face.

"No, you need it more than I do."

"I'll get another one. What are you taking?"

"Nothing."

He presses the button on his remote, and a voice comes over the intercom. He asks for another ice pack and hydrocodone. I explain my reason for not wanting anything. I can't be under the influence of any drug if I need to fight. But his reply makes me give in. "That's why I'm here."

I want to disagree, considering he just had surgery, but I can't. Even in the state he is in, I'm safe. And there are always the bodyguards outside the door.

Grace appears in the doorway with her cart. "Got to do your vitals one more time before bed. Do you want me to get you a chair, Ember?"

"No," James answers for me. "She's sleeping with me."

Grace bows her head and continues on her work as I stand in a corner smiling. James smirks back, never taking his eyes off me. Grace rushes through and hurries out, closing the door behind her.

I crack up laughing, sitting on the bed. "That was cruel."

"But subtle."

"No."

"Perhaps not."

CHAPTER 16
Brother

EMBER

COLA FOUND ME IN my dreams.

She pulls the rope around my neck and tightens it. I choke. My heartbeat slows. And then her face transforms into Myers. His beady eyes overtake her face. His fat cheeks, his double chin, and the hate billowing in his face. He squeezes my neck, and his skin shakes. "I know your name," he laughs. In his other hand he holds a folder and the tip of it ignites.

I reach for it. The folder curls in black smoke and flame, and I still grab it, my hands burning in a fire. My skin is melting.

I scream, waking, nearly falling from the gurney. James catches me, but I'm staring at my hands, touching my neck. The pain lingers, tingling. James calls my name, whispering words of comfort, telling me it isn't real. But it is all real, isn't it? That's the problem. It is all real.

James lays me next to him. I stare off, their faces like shadows on the wall. Will they ever go away?

James traces his fingers along my hair, and the sensations are enough of a distraction. A man's touch has never been so gentle. I didn't think they knew how to be delicate. Tobias hurt me whenever he touched me. But James is soothing, and I sink further, away from haunting memories. It spurs an ache in my gut I can't explain.

His breathing is oddly heavy, and I fear he's in pain or has a fever. I shift my head to look at him. "I can..." James hides his face against my neck. "I can help you forget."

"What do you mean? How?"

James keeps his head buried as if he's embarrassed or ashamed. It's such an odd thing for him to do because he's prideful. It's one of the first things I learned about him.

He swallows hard before he whispers, "I know things. I can..I can make you feel good." His fingers trace along my arm, making his insinuations clear. "Get your mind off things."

The sensations spark fear. The movement is too similar to Tobias. He would run his fingers along my jaw, a gentle caress before he'd choke me. I yank back, but James clenches onto me, keeping me close. I almost panic before he pleads, "Stay. I won't hurt you."

I'm stiff, laying there. James continues to hide his face while his fingers slowly trace my spine. The sensations that I thought were frightening aren't. If I allow myself to, it might be enjoyable.

Could I enjoy being touched?

It's not something I'm ready to explore right now.

"Can you run your fingers through my hair again?"

James pulls back, and I touch his cheek, relieved to see his eyes. They are the most expressive thing about him, and without them in my view, I'm blind. There's confusion reflecting inside him and I whisper, "This is enough for me. You holding me is enough. Is that okay?"

His eyes water and his cheeks flex as he clenches his teeth. There is so much he reveals, but none of it I understand. James nods and lays back down, staring at the ceiling. His fingers dance in my hair again, but I now stare out, concerned why my response brought unhindered emotion to him when so many other things don't. I'm missing a crucial part of James, and I fear it's the part I stopped him talking about yesterday.

'Bedroom etiquette.'

I know all I have to do is ask him, and he'll tell me, but the words clog in my throat. We fall asleep, but it's not peaceful.

• • • • • • • • • •

A knock wakes us. It's still dark when a Special comes to the side of the bed to whisper in James' ear. Even this close to them, I still can't hear what's being said. But soon enough, James sits us up. "We have to go."

I slip on my shoes and attempt to help him put on a shirt. He doesn't like the aid but stays quiet and puts his hand through the sleeve. He shouldn't be out of bed for so many reasons, but I'm not about to tell him how to do anything. James is stubborn and resilient. He's been fighting a war much longer than I have and has lasted through hell. He knows what he can and cannot do.

Blink is absent when we step into the hall, but three Specials wait for James' order. Members of Boundary have fallen asleep curled on the floor.

So much for their protection.

James looks down at me. "We have to split up." When I'm about to protest, he explains, "Shakes doesn't want to see me, and hopefully, he'll listen to you."

"This is about Shakes?"

"He's gathering team Black to take out a member of Rain. I can only assume it's backlash for Lisa failing to protect you."

Disappointment douses me. "Backlash? Lisa was right? He's going to hurt someone?"

"Room 640." He nods to two members and turns the opposite way.

"Wait, where are you going?"

He throws over his shoulder. "Mary and Shakes broke up. She was seen heading to the first floor. Whatever she's doing, I have to protect her."

How does he know all this?

James and Shakes have a thought process so much different than mine. I'm entirely focused on myself, struggling with the memories in my head, watching all the trauma repeatedly while James and Shakes move like machines. I don't know if it's me or them. Is it better to live without a conscience? Or suffer because of one?

I bounce in the elevator, full of fear and adrenaline. It sparks a light in me that I hate enjoying. The action gets my brain to quiet. If I could keep moving, I'd never have to think about all the deaths I've witnessed.

We race to room 640, and I knock once before entering. Just like James said, all of Black have gathered. Blink sits on the window sill.

Shakes stands in the center of the room. He stalls in his speech, shocked to see me. "What are you doing here?"

I step in. "Are you planning on killing someone?"

"How do you know that? Who are you talking to?" His green eyes blaze past me to the Special that lingers in the doorway. He narrows his gaze, growling, "James. He's spying on me." Shakes ruefully rushes over and slams the door in the kid's face.

"He doesn't want you to do anything stupid. You know, like *kill* someone," I sneer.

"Stupid was trusting a Special. I won't make the same mistake twice. Get out." He latches onto my arm and pulls me to the door.

I slam my heel into his toe and shove him off. He should know by now not to be aggressive with me. He hops on his foot and it's pathetic. "What are you doing? Revenge killing? Who are you?"

Leaning against the wall, he bites back, "I'm the guy that's kept you alive. I do what I have to do."

"You don't *have* to do this," I point out. "You're doing it to prove a point. To prove you're stronger, better. But who are you trying to prove that too? Myers is dead, Shakes. You don't have to fight anymore."

He scoffs, sneering at me. "You think life is just going to be perfect now? You and James are gonna go off and live happily? That's not reality. There will always be a fight. There will always be evil people."

"You can't fight them all. You get that, don't you? Sometimes, it's not your fight."

"This is who I am now." Shakes straightens, approaching me. "I can't go back to what I was. I was weak. I was stupid and gullible, and people died because I was forgiving. But not anymore. Rain failed you. Rain will be punished."

I know there's more to it. Despite not being tortured as I was, Memory is his Tobias. She's the voice in his head, taunting him. "It's because of her, isn't it? Because of Memory. You want her to see how you've changed?"

"Shut up and get out."

"Is that where Mary's going? She's going after her."

Shakes stops moving. "Mary? What are you talking about?" He looks back at Brick. "Who's watching Mary?"

Brick stumbles over a response. "Um..You... didn't tell me to put anyone on her."

Shakes rushes by me and runs down the hallway. Before leaving the room, I point a steady finger. "No killing." And though it seems silly, I hope they listen. Brick and I go after Shakes with the Special following us. He's diving into the bathroom, calling her name, but it's empty and he runs a hand through his hair as he spins around in the center of the room, completely thrown off guard by her sudden disappearance. I stay back, unsure of his temper. "James went after her. He'll stop her."

"I don't trust James," he snaps.

"Why? What's changed?"

Shakes sits on a metal gurney and buries his face in his hands. I don't know why the mattresses are on the floor, but I don't think now is the time to bring it up. I sit next to him nervously, my feet swaying. Brick pushes the others out the door and gives me a thumbs-up before he shuts it softly. I chew my lip. The last person I comforted was Charles. He's younger, naive, and so easy. It came naturally with him.

"Why'd you break up with Mary?"

Shakes keeps his head low and speaks to the floor, "She kept a secret from me."

"What secret?"

He glances at me but turns away. "I don't want to talk about this."

"You're acting like a jerk."

Shakes snorts, a smirk pulling at his lips, but it's gone quickly. "I don't know if that's confidence or attitude." He tears at the shredding fabric of the gauze on his hand. "She knew about Memory. She didn't tell me."

"That's not that big." He sends a quick glare, and I quickly dig myself out of the hole. "She cares about you."

"Three days, she knew. For three days we were living here, and my family was in danger. I wouldn't have been unprepared when I saw her again. I would have been able to...to...speak...to think...to kill her...or something other than running like a little punk. I ran from her."

"Hey, sometimes running is the best option."

He chuckles, and his bad mood begins to shift.

I weasel my speech in now. "You don't have to delete people from your life when they upset you, Shakes. Soon, you're not gonna have anybody left. Ink. James...They cherish you. They want to be with you. James followed you into the Coal building. He's out there now, going after Mary, simply for you. Those aren't friendships to throw away. And I...I went against you in front of the whole school....I was terrified you'd... I don't think I could live without you in my life."

He looks at me. His eyes are soft and warm. It's a rare moment I can see Charles reflecting inside of him. It reminds me that despite everything he's done, he used to be a little boy with the same innocence and ambition. He's not far from it despite the atrocities he's been through.

We sit staring at the door, waiting for Mary and James. It's a terrible feeling sitting and doing nothing, but that's where trust comes in. James doesn't fail. It's who he is. It's one of the things I admire about him.

"Shakes. You love Mary."

"More than anything."

"What does it feel like?"

He shifts away, looking at me. He's sad, and he brushes his hand through my hair. "I don't understand why you don't have your memory yet. Something must have happened." He drops his hand, leaning back against the footboard. "I'm guessing this is about James?" He smiles warmly. "What do you feel?"

"Nervous."

He laughs, his face heating up. "I guess that's part of it." He pauses, searching the ground for words. "It's consuming. Overpowering. It's happiness. There's a bunch of feelings. But I think most of the reason I want out so badly is for Mary. I want...need her to be safe...to be happy...to fulfill every one of her dreams. It's almost an instinct. I have to make life better for her. I won't be satisfied until it is." His green eyes slip to me. "Was that the answer you were looking for?"

I throw myself back on the gurney, staring at the ceiling. "I don't know. I've been afraid of men since I came to this school. And then you happened, and I realized they aren't all bad. I lost a lot of my fear. James...is not scary to me. He should be. I've seen him kill. But I feel like... I'm safe. He makes me feel...a crazy amount of stuff. And when we kiss, I'm...excited—"

"I got to stop you." He folds his arms, discontented. "First, you guys are new to this whole thing. I'm pretty sure you're his first girlfriend, and he's your first boyfriend. This is the time to get to know each other. Talk to each other. No need for anything...physical."

"No, I don't want to—so boyfriends and girlfriends don't do physical things?"

He glances back to the mattresses on the floor. "Not really."

I found that odd. "Tobias always touched me and called me his girlfriend."

"Tobias—" Shakes stalls, blowing out air. "wasn't a boyfriend, and you weren't a girlfriend.

He was a giant abuser. You never deserved what he did to you and I'm sorry I let it go on for so long. But do yourself a favor and forget what he taught you. That being said, James isn't relationship material, and I don't think he's good for you."

Shakes goes from one end of the spectrum to another. I felt happy hearing him talk about Tobias. Shakes is like my big brother and hearing the protectiveness in his voice makes me feel special and cared for. But then he goes to the radical end. How can he hate on James after everything he's done for him? "Why?"

Shakes doesn't answer, crossing his arms with a weight on his shoulder he isn't sharing. He knows something I don't and though I want to trust in him and respect his request, the rebellious part of me devours it. I'm not going to stop seeing James.

"Is this about what's going with you guys or because of what I'm hearing about Zack?"

"Both. It's not my place to tell you about Zack, but believe me, you should go back to Light. In fact, I'm asking you too."

Brick snaps the door open. "They're here."

Our conversation is forgotten as Shakes stands up, but I'm left raw, like an open sore. He's asking for something I don't think I can do. But I realize, he does that often, and it's perhaps the reason I am constantly going against him. He wants me to obey without question and I don't know how to do that.

Brick comes forward with his hands out. "You aren't going to like this." Before Shakes can question it, Brick pushes him to the back wall, ignoring Shakes' struggles.

Mary enters first, and Shakes attempts to break away, but Brick has his arm braced tight, and no amount of pushing could break his inhuman strength. "Would you stop it, you freaking giant? Mary?" Shakes complains.

James enters the room. "It's for your own good."

I relax, and our eyes meet momentarily, a assuring moment on both our parts that we are safe. James turns to the door, holding it wide open.

Memory slides into view.

Chapter 17
Temper

Ember

MEMORY HOLDS ONTO THE edge of the doorway. She has taken off her costume: no glasses, necklace, or earrings. She replaced it with jeans and a hoodie to hide her face, and her blond straight hair hangs over her shoulders. Her blue eyes are prominent, much like mine, and I despise her for it. It was because of those eyes I was targeted.

Shakes doesn't move. Not for an entire minute, and I hold my breath, terrified of what he will do.

He slams his fist into Bricks' armpit, and the giant breaks his barrier. Shakes slaps a drawer open on the nightstand, and pulls out a gun. He aims it right for her heart.

We all move, but James gets there before anyone, and takes a stance in front of her.

It doesn't deter Shakes. "I'll take you out too."

Why would Shakes threaten James? What happened between them? I step in front of James.

Shakes gets annoyed. "Get out of the way."

"Don't run," I tell him, hoping he can find the confidence I admire. "Face her."

Indecision rolls through him, but soon, Shakes drops the weapon back in the drawer and slams it shut, turning his back on us. Mary approaches, whispering sweet, assuring words, and he wraps an arm around her blindly and kisses her forehead.

"Go ahead, Memory," Shakes says and finally turns around to face her. "Everyone wants to hear your excuses for betraying us and getting a hundred and sixty kids killed. It's a shame they don't know you like I do. How good you are at manipulation. How believable you are. Then they'd be smart enough not to trust a single word you say."

"Adam."

His name on her lips causes an unknown pain. He turns his back and presses his hands against the wall. I begin to understand why Mary kept her a secret. I don't want him in pain. I want to protect him from her as if she's the devil grasping for his soul.

Memory steps only a foot closer, keeping small. She isn't very big to begin with, much like me. But for sisters, I don't see similarities. She's blond, light-skinned, and lightly freckled. We're opposites in everything but our eyes.

"I didn't plan it," she begins.

"Yeah-fucking-right."

"Let her speak," James orders.

"You are as much to blame as her." Shakes glares at him. "Don't push me, James."

James fastens around the bed, and pulls open the drawer. He takes out the gun and holds it out, the handle toward Shakes. "Then be done with it. I won't stop you. I will not waste my life wallowing in my sins. If you cannot get through it, then get your revenge."

Shakes doesn't turn to take it. He hangs his head instead. "We'll be separated soon enough. I won't have to see you again, and I can forget you ever existed."

Why are they talking like this? We are a family. We are supposed to get out together and live together. Shakes is my brother. James is my...something else. They can't hate each other. But what did James do to be kicked from the family?

James drops it back in the drawer and slams it shut, returning to his spot by the door, ignoring my inquiring gaze.

Memory starts again. "I didn't plan it, Adam. But I knew it wouldn't be perfect. It was improbable that our plans would go without a hitch. So I began to think of alternatives. How to live beyond the rebellion? When the bombs did not go off, there were factors that were put into place instantaneously. Tobias' location. Your involvement. Carbon's whereabouts. Star's position. My own. And Hail's. We would all die, and the rebellion would end. I could not allow this. There needed to be survivors. Leaders left to strike up what we started. But first, I had to make a decision."

"To kill me."

A pause before Memory whispered, "Yes."

"You know what?" Shakes paces, holding up a hand. "I'm good. I don't want to hear your self-sacrificing speech. Let's skip, pretend we believe you, and move on. What are you doing here?"

She is aggravated by this and doesn't reply. They stare each other down, and I'm entirely out of place. I chew my bottom lip and glance towards

Brick. He is uncomfortable like I am, staring awkwardly at the ceiling.

Memory grounds out, "I hope you realized by now, you were simply transferred to a different location. You are still inside the trafficking ring."

She pauses like that was supposed to mean something. I look around to the others, trying to understand.

"Myers knew the tensions were escalating, and your strength had gained far past his ability to control. Jose was his partner, and they began their plans the week after I escaped. This was a way to de-weaponize you, make you vulnerable, separate you, weaken you. Jose is in control here. One by one, he is selling off the ones that know him. I believe he is currently making a list to find the ones that need to be sold off first. By the time the kids figure out what he is doing, it will be too late. He's finishing up with automatic locks on all the doors and video cameras in all the rooms. You will be inmates in this adopted hospital."

I stand there comatose. The words reverberated in my head. I repeat them and reword them. Inmates-**prisoners**. Automatic locks-**cells**. Myers and Jose, **partners**.

Trapped.

This is my fault. I did this. I brought us here.

I turn to Shakes, desperate to see him deny it. I need him to tell me she's lying. But he stands there with his head bowed. His hair can't hide the acceptance on his face. He knew it. Somehow, back at school, when the cops came, he knew what they were. He wasn't fighting because of grief. He was fighting because of fear.

I curl into myself.

I've killed us. I single-handedly killed us all.

James' feet come into view. I lift my head to look at him. Does he know? Does he realize? His knuckle rubs against my cheek, smearing my silent tears. I dart for the door, but he snatches my wrist.

"Sit down, Ember," Shakes orders, and I slam my back against the wall, falling on my butt to drop my head into my knees. I shouldn't be here. I'm a piece of shit.

"What about the cops?" Brick continues, unconvinced.

Memory has a readied answer. "Some were real. Jose used to be a cop when he was younger. That's how he learned about the G.O.D.S. The Guardians of Daughters and Sons, a worldwide human trafficking ring. He became a real investor at twenty-eight and is now known as a Shepherd. Myers was also a Shepard. There are countless of them. The bigger their flock, the more money they have, the more teachers they have under their wing, and the bigger their territory is. Myers owned the whole southern half of the United States. But when I escaped, Jose saw an opportunity and brought up this idea to move the students to a more confined location, to end the uprising and gain back control."

"How do you know all this?"

"I tried to tell you my story, and you didn't want to hear it. Perhaps now you see a relevance."

Shakes scoffs. "Your arrogance hasn't diminished any."

"Neither has your impatience."

"I think I have a bottomless well of patience. You're still alive, aren't you?"

"Typical Shakes. Threaten, maim, forget human decency."

"Typical? Typical? I was the last one out of all of us to kill. I learned everything from you. Talk of decency. You were in love with a psychopath. Do you know what he did to her? Ember, show her your back." The two of them step toward each other. "Don't act like you know a shitin' thing about me anymore. About any of us. You betrayed all of us, Memory. And I don't need to hear your bullshit story, you know why? Because Carbon can't hear it. Star can't hear it. Hail can't hear it. Tara can't hear it. Tobias sure as hell can't hear it. And I am not going to let you clear your conscience through me."

A single tear is rolling down Memory's cheek, but she swipes it away. Aside from anger, I can't see one bit of sadness. She is strong, just as I always imagined her to be. No wonder Shakes idealized her. Maybe he still does.

"I'm working with someone." She says, backing away, backing down. "The team has been following the G.O.D.S for a few years. They want the leader, but she's untouchable. She calls herself Faith. Her religious organization stretches across the world. She's been evading the FBI for years. Partly because many FBI Agents are in her control. I'm telling you this is deeper than you can understand. The five other schools–"

"Other schools?" James questions.

"They are all under her jurisdiction. She created them."

"Boss," Brick whispers. "Myers said the same thing."

Mary looks at Shakes. "What is he talking about, Adam? Did you know about this?"

I stare up at Shakes as he stands above me. His green eyes are dark, tired, and dead. Water blurs my vision. Of course, he knew about the other schools. Why else would he stand against a parade of police that were sent to save us if he didn't? And I got in his way.

Memory continues, "Myers' school was a trial run. He got greedy and failed to pay attention. Before I got out, Faith was going to attend to shut him down, but our rebellion brought in the ratings. More cameras were added and Myers was allowed to do whatever he could to bring in more customers." She pauses and waits for a response but when she receives nothing, Memory continues. "After I escaped, a team of FBI agents were scouting nearby, waiting for Faith. I stumbled upon them dehydrated, traumatized, and insane after I killed my best friend and betrayed my boyfriend." There is a pause before Memory steps forward, suddenly desperate. "I went seven months think-ing I killed you, Adam. I have a photographic mem-ory. I see it over and over and over again. Your face. The feel of the gun. The way you fell. Every day, I relive it. Tobias—how he couldn't understand." Her tears flow freely now, and she cups a hand around her mouth. "I couldn't even tell him why. He died thinking I hated him." She drops to her knees, her body convulsing in sobs.

No one attempts to comfort her. Shakes doesn't even look down at her. He steps around the bed, sitting on the gurney with his back to her as if her cries mean nothing.

That's your sister, I want to yell at him. *Why do you let me stay, but you've done away with her?*

I push myself up to my feet and kneel in front of Memory, wrapping my arms around her shoul-ders. She's stiff and unsure, but I hold on to her. Soon, her head rests on my shoulder, and she cries harshly, her fingers clenching my skin.

Mary engulfs us in her embrace, and we both giggle as she gives us a shake. She takes Memory's face in her hands. "Tobias believed in you even in the end, Becca. He never stopped loving you." Her brows knit, but she nods, whispering a soft 'thank you'.

James holds his hand for me, and I get to my feet, resting my forehead against his chest. He wraps his arm around my shoulders, keeping me to him. I simply breathe in his scent. I want to return to bed, where only he and I exist. All of this information is too much. Too many emotions drowning me. But for a moment, right here, I'm calm.

"I should go," Memory murmurs, cleaning her face. I twist my head to watch her. She recovers from her breakdown so quickly, almost inhumanly. Her blue gaze flicks over James and me with an odd expression, noticing the way he holds me. As she reaches for the door, she pauses and reveals, "I've disabled your camera. Don't let any stranger in the room." There's more on her lips, but she's hesitant. "I'm afraid to ask, but have you seen Jennifer? I can't find her."

None of us reply and the answer sags her shoulders a little.

"I figured after she failed to contact us, I just...had hope."

The reaction is odd to me. Losing a sister should be like losing a limb. There should be tears or at least some sign of melancholy. She had tears for Tobias and for Shakes, but none of her own flesh and blood?

Memory steps out the door, but looks over her shoulder. "The changes should be occurring in a few days. Don't fight it. I won't fail you again. I'll get you out."

With a sudden turn, Shakes hollers, "We're not trusting you!" He laughs bitterly. "Haven't you been paying attention?"

Her light brows tighten. "I'm your only chance."

"No." Shakes grits his teeth. "You *were* our only chance. You are nothing now. Don't come back, Memory. Or I'll shoot you."

"You have to keep your hand still long enough to aim," she taunts like an aggravated older sibling, slamming the door.

"You should have *aimed* better!" he hollers after her.

I don't like who Shakes becomes in front of Memory. He loses himself. He's crude and unforgivable. My brother lost his humanity the moment she walked in the door. He stares after her, void of feeling, with his hands shaking at his sides. He looks so lost now that she's gone.

Mary is the first to move, picking up a mattress and flinging it on the bed. "That was ridiculous. Are you two little five-year-olds? You two used to agree on everything. She's still the same girl, Adam. Nothing's changed." Mary snatches up the blankets, spreading them out. "But you've got this ball of hate-"

"Yeah, I wonder why that is."

"Oh, get over it. I'm sick of it."

Shakes advances on her, and she ignores it till he grabs her arm. "Get over it?" She snatches it away, taking a step back against the wall.

I twitch to intervene, but James keeps a hold of me. "He won't hurt her," James assures, but it doesn't look that way, and my heart is pumping madly. Shakes is confronting her like a pit bull, and she glares back. It's how I typically ended up with a black eye with Tobias.

"You have always been on her side," Shakes accuses. "Since day fucking one. She doesn't need you, Mary. I do."

"I *am* on your side."

"You kept her from me. You know how stupid you made me look?"

James pushes me toward the door, and Brick slips past them on his tiptoes, wide-eyed and uncomfortable. I wiggle away from him, however. I'm not about to leave Mary in the presence of an angered man. I've never seen Mary throw a punch. Does she even know how to fight?

Mary seems oblivious to the danger. "Can't you see what it's doing to you? It's consuming you. You can't sleep. You have nightmares when you do. Your temper has gotten ridiculous. I can't stand back and do nothing anymore. I love you, and I'm losing you. You need to forgive her, Adam. It's killing you."

Shakes throws himself backward, running his hands through his hair, and then he notices we are still in the room. "Can you guys go? Please?" We flip around for the door.

"No," Mary calls. "They're your family. Don't push them out."

"I'm not pushing anyone out. You aren't losing me. You're twisting this into something stupid." He sees us staring. "Guys, get out!"

"Ask them," Mary prods. "I'm not the only one who thinks this."

His attention pins us where we stand. "Well?"

I stutter. I hadn't expected them to turn their conversation on us. Brick makes odd noises, and James attempts to speak, but they aren't whole sentences, and we all just eventually fade into silence.

Mary points. "Look, they're terrified of your temper."

Brick bows his head, toeing the ground. "I'm not *terrified,*" he whispers barely above his own hearing.

Shakes throws his hands up and sits on the bed. "This is dumb. I'm done."

"That's it, Adam decided, it's over." Mary stomps around the bed and goes by us. "Let's go, let him pout by himself." Shakes narrows his eyes on her as she leaves the room. He scoffs in exasperation, throwing himself back on the bed to stare at the ceiling.

James and Brick both follow her, but I struggle to pick a side. I'm obligated to go after Mary, but I don't want to leave Shakes. James calls me, and I force myself out. We stand in the hallway, lost on what to do next. Brick nervously chuckles. "This is what it feels like when my mom and dad fight." We observe Mary, who lingers further down the hall, pacing and talking to herself. "You should go talk to her."

It's then I realize he's talking to me. "Me? Why?"

"You're a girl."

"What does that have to do with anything? I don't know anything about relationships." James shakes his head, agreeing with me.

Brick gets behind me, resting his hands on my shoulders. "Just listen. Girls like to be listened to." He pushes me forward, and awkwardly, I approach. She rests her forehead against the wall, and I realize she's crying. Her tears drip down her nose and hit the tiled white floor silently. I rub her shoulder and snuggle into her side. She giggles at me.

Shakes pops his head out and calls the boys back inside, glancing at us. His brows knit, noticing that she's crying, but he shuts the door regardless.

CHAPTER 18
Knife Fight

EMBER

I HOLD MY KNEES to my chest, staring at the tiled floor. Mary sits next to me, jabbering about Shakes and everything he does that annoys her. It's cold in here, but not as cold as it is in my chest.

Memory gave too much information, so I concentrate on what I can understand.

This hospital is a school. They will lock us in here and sell us off. And I'm the one that put us here.

Then I have to be the one to get us out.

But how?

"What are you girls doing out in the boys' ward?"

Mary and I ogle the male nurse standing in front of us. He has his hands on his hips as he looks us over. Mary holds up her wrist to expose the band. "I'm staying with Adam Bryant."

He latches onto it with a skeptical look, scrunching up his lips. "Hm. And you?"

I hold up my own wrist. "I was just visiting."

"Um, hm." He glances over the name. "Ember. That's a pretty little name. Don't know if it fits exactly."

I narrow my eyes and bite, "My other name is Scream. Is that any better?"

"A little," he admits. "Now come with me."

"What? Why?"

He looks down his nose in contempt. "I have to call it in and confirm your stories. Kids have the tendency to lie. And if either of you girls got hurt while you were up here, it would be my job. So get up and follow me."

I help Mary to her feet, and we uneasily follow behind, asking question after question. Why have wristbands if they don't mean anything? Mary looks for her as we pass the Nursing station, but no one is there. She whispers in my ear that something doesn't feel right. Her fear escalates with every step. "He's taking us too close to Coal. We need to turn around."

I don't need to be told twice. I grip her arm and turn, but it's too late. Our path is blocked by three strangers. We whip around for the nurse, but he's running, looking back at us, giggling before disappearing behind a corner.

The three strangers walk toward us. I pull Mary and move swiftly down the hall. Each door is a black hole waiting to suck us in. I don't dare dive into one.

If every floor is the same, we are heading toward the game room. There is no exit, but what options do I have? I can face the three boys chasing us, but I don't have a weapon. In the game room, I'll have more of a chance.

I shut the doors behind us and attempt to lock it, but they are kicked in before I can get it barred. We back up into the center of the room. Coal Members trickle in like sand, filling every inch, climbing onto furniture, moving tables to the far wall, and sitting on tabletops. There are fifty boys encircling us with evil grins and cackles.

Mary trembles. "Oh, Lord. Oh, goodness me. Oh, Lord."

I do not have a friend among Coal. Every face is dark, dangerous, and threatening. But I will not be afraid. I stand firm, daring. I've dealt with bad odds before. This might be the worst, but that's not the point. I've survived.

The leaders enter, and the crowd parts to let them through. Peat is short and fat. On his bulbous arms are tattooed tally marks of every person he's killed. Nearly forty. He wears a tank top to expose these numbers and his chubby boobs.

Next to him is Noah, Ash's sidekick and newly made leader. Dyed white long hair and black stripes give almost a zebra type of print. He wears white lipstick and a silver chain around his neck. White painted fingernails and tattoos decorate his black body.

Peat grabs me by the hair, shoving me to the floor. He digs his knee into my back, keeping me flat. "I ain't gonna give you a chance, you crazy bitch."

Another boy steps on Mary's back, pushing into her spine. Her fear is vibrant, and she mouths, "What do we do?"

"Get her up." Peat lifts me, gripping my biceps and squeezing them tight behind me, making it nearly painful.

Noah steps to me. He's tall and thin but clearly works out. He keeps his arms behind his back. "Hello, Scream."

"Miss your buddy?"

"You know you did us a favor taking out Ash. He was a creepy ass dude. But then you had to go and blow up our school."

"You want me to say sorry?"

Noah touches my injured cheek, tapping the fracture, and it sends a sharp wave of pain. "Looks like Cola got you pretty good," he whispers softly, sadly. "If nothing else, my girlfriend knew how to throw a punch."

The realization dawns on me. He thinks I've killed his girlfriend. And though it might not matter, I'm desperate for him to know. "She fell. I didn't kill her. She fell."

"Oh." He backs away. "Guys, you hear that? It was an accident. Just a misunderstanding." They laugh at my excuse. I don't know what else to do. Even if I can get out of Peat's hold, there are thirty to forty other people piling in the room. I'm trapped. Our best option is to go with the flow until we find an out. Or pray someone rescues us.

"Did Ash fall too? A stray bullet?"

"I didn't do that." I'm breathless. "I've never killed anybody."

It doesn't seem to matter to him. He's not listening. There is a distant pounding on the door above the commotion and I know Shakes and James are on the other side. They have a pole in between the handles and it rattles.

"You wondering about your little dog? Your heroes?" Noah approaches Mary, kneeling down and removing some of her hair from her face. Mary trembles beneath him, and he basks in it. I can see a knife sticking out of his shorts. "Shakes doesn't have his horde up here. He's powerless. You're powerless. But we're not. We are going to gut each of your pimps. Bleed them dry." Noah gets to his feet, glares at me, and then turns to the others. "Who wants them?"

There's cheers as they struggle against one another trying to decide. Peat keeps his fingers dug deep into my arms, and every twist I make only enforces his hold. He eventually gets tired of me and trips me. I slam back on the floor with his knee buried into my back.

They haggle prices. They wage bets. It's an auction, no different from the one Myers conducted once a month. I shouldn't be surprised. They lived in Coal. They probably watched the proceedings from their own viewing box.

"Stand her up," Noah orders, and Peat aggravatingly gets me to my feet again. He takes his knife out and, with a proud smile, grabs the edge of my shirt and cuts it up the center, the word 'happiness' sliced in two. My breath is heavy in panic and a growing rage that's clouding my rationality. He points the knife at my breasts. "See? It's not a padded bra."

I slam my heel into Peat's foot, and his hold loosens. Just enough to slip one hand out. I snatch the knife out of Noah's hand and swing around, stabbing Peat in the shoulder. I pull it out and wave it as I turn back towards Noah. He dodges, but I slice the top of his cheek.

I circle, holding out my knife with two hands, searching for someone daring enough to try and take it away.

The hyenas are laughing.

Noah holds his bloody cheek, finding no amusement in his pain. He reaches into his other pocket and pulls out a second blade. This one is a bit bigger and a bit scarier. Where the hell did they get these freaking weapons? The best I could find was a butter knife, and it was dull!

"Everyone stand back," he yells. "It's my vengeance."

Peat lifts Mary off the ground. There is a large circle for us. My heart is pounding, my adrenaline running. If I lose, they'll hurt her. I can't afford to go easy.

"Come on, Scream. You want to fight like a man, then you can fight one."

"Then bring him here."

The crowd jeers at my insult. I remove the rest of my shirt and ignore the eager jests. The leggings are a second skin, and as I lower into a stance, I'm happy I'm wearing something so tight for once. I hold the blade out, eyeing the spot I want to cut. How will he move? Is he fast? Is he a quick thinker? Can I trick him? Will he adjust to my ability to use both my left and right hands? I wish the ground were sand. It was always a helpful decoy in a time of desperation.

"So you've never killed anyone."

"Except for your girlfriend." I smirk if only to piss him off. Anger can deteriorate concentration.

He sets his jaw and slips into a stance. "I wasn't going to kill you. I thought I'd much rather have my buddies have fun with you. Now I gotta slit your throat." He darts forward with the tip, aiming for my heart. I ease backward, breathing even, contemplating my next move.

A knife fight is silly. Two people simply trying to poke each other. They seem to forget the basics of fighting, and that's the rest of the body. I've watched multiple knife fights, marking mistakes and highlighting victory moves. It usually always ends up with someone bleeding to death. I don't want that to happen to either of us. But I can't lose.

He swipes the air again, and instead of backing up, I step forward, latching on his wrist and kicking him in the stomach. He stumbles backward, unprepared for the move. "You ever been in a knife fight before?"

He acts like there's some rule I've broken. I smile. "I've held a knife before and fought before. I think I understand."

"Alright. If that's how you want to do this."

He transfers the knife to his left hand, making me nervous. What does he plan to do now? How does this change his fighting performance? He stands upright and motions me forward. "Come on, girl. Show me these famous skills."

I can't attack. That's not my method. I don't know how to start.

Sensing my hesitation, he approaches slowly and my muscles tense. "You feed off fear, don't you? That's when your instincts kick in." He pretends to attack, and I jerk, ready, but he only laughs at me, and quickly, the spectators join in. His smile fades. "Time to get scared, freak." He kicks me in the stomach too fast, and I stumble backward. The people behind me catch, fondle, and push me back. I take the momentum and run, jumping upward and slam my fist in his face. He grabs me and throws me on the ground. His foot rams into my stomach. As I recover, he slices my arm. He could kill me, but he wants to play with his prey. He'll realize his mistake soon. He stomps on my ribs. I choke, unable to breathe, and lay flat on my back. He kneels down and slides the blade along my stomach. I can barely make out the burn of the cut.

"You aren't putting on a real good show, Scream. I'm kind of disappointed. Why don't you cry out or something? Make a moan or a groan. Something really...arousing... for them." He leans over me as

I swallow. "Now I get Tobias. You really are stubborn."

Noah stands and kicks me, but I cushion it and grab ahold of his foot. I dive the knife into his calf. As he falls, I pull it out, and blood squirts the ground. I throw myself on top of him, my knee on his arm to keep his knife pinned to the floor. I press my blade against his throat.

This is the difference between us: I don't waste time.

The shouting stops, and he and I look at each other. His rage is apparent, and I know he'll kill me if I give him the chance, but I can't kill him. I can't. He's still a kid. He's still a person. A person who's just lost someone very important to him. "I'm sorry," I find myself saying. "I'm sorry about Cola. It was an accident."

A kick to the back of my head, and I'm on the floor curled in a ball the next time consciousness returns. A massive headache looms over me, and I can't focus. All their voices seem muffled. I rest against the cold ground, simply blinking, my vision slowly returning.

Noah presses the knife to the side of my neck. He's not far above me. I can feel him breathe. The crowd around him chants, "Do it, Do it, Do it, Do it." But seconds continue to tick, and he doesn't move.

Chapter 19
Mistakes

Shakes

'I hope you realized by now you were simply transferred to a different location. You are still inside Myers' trafficking ring.'

It's everything I feared and worse. My power has been decimated, a mere ten percent of what I used to possess. I am helpless, like a newb, new to a game without knowing the rules. The walls are tight around me, suffocating. I can't win this. I've lost the advantage because I couldn't kill Ember.

I go on and on about how my heart is stone, but it isn't. It's a weak mass of flesh that chains me. I want it because of who I used to be. I keep trying to hold on to my humanity, but it's hindering me. If I'm going to fight monsters, I have to become one.

What's the solution? Push Ember away? Keep her and Mary out of this war? I tried that. Ember is resilient, like a plague that can't be cured.

James and Brick stand to the side, waiting for what I have to say. The girls would only try to talk me out of it, so I left them in the hallway. I can't let their sympathy guide me. I'm a leader. There have to be sacrifices, and they wouldn't understand. Their judgment and constant want to 'do the right thing' keeps me from succeeding.

I stare at the tile, an invisible map unfolding on the floor. "We need to blow this place up."

It's the easiest fix. It's the fastest and most reliable.

But it would kill us.

What's better at this point? Wait to be sold? Wait to be abused? I've spent too much of my time evading Auction to be brought to it willingly. I will not be sold. My hand goes to the back of my neck. The numbers and the barcode are just beneath my hair. And though I can't feel it, I know it's there. It's a constant reminder that to these people, I am only a number, a product on a conveyor belt with a stamp on my forehead that reads 'defective.' I'm something they should have destroyed years ago.

I dart to the window, searching for locks. If we set a fire to the bottom of the hospital, we can escape from the top? As I struggle with the window, I determined we'd have to break it. We'd need something with enough force to shatter it.

"How do we blow up this place up?" Brick asks.

My only answer is gas. "The kitchen. Turn on all the stoves and let the gas pour in."

James replies, "They are automatic."

"What does that mean?" James shifts uncomfortably, and it irritates me. After Mary told me my temper was out of control, all I want to do is lash out. "Just spit it out."

"Stoves are no longer the way you remember them. The flame and gas are contained."

I rub a hand through my hair, blowing out air. I was thirteen when I was put in Myers' school. I was a foster kid living in the most destitute areas. While kids my age walked around with flip phones, I could barely find food. This hospital is one of the best places I've ever stayed in. The flat-screen TVs, the LED lights, hell, even the bed sheets are impressive. I'm out of the loop in this reality. I've dived into a new dystopian world, and I'm the alien.

It's a terrible thought, but I want to go home. And that home is in Boundary. It's becoming clearer as the hours go by that I'm not fit for life outside of Myers' School.

The doorknob jiggles. Mary wouldn't want to be kept out of the loop. She wants to at least know what's going on, even if she has nothing to give. But then the movement stops.

James goes to the door and tests the knob. He looks over his shoulder. "It's locked."

I dart forward, shoving him out of the way, and shake it as if I can get it unstuck. A fist pounds against it, and realization freezes me. We're locked in.

It's my failure. I'm moving too slowly. I'm reacting instead of acting. I can't afford to wait around for something bad to happen. I need to get ahead of it. But I'm too late.

With Mary and Ember on the other side, we lose it.

James pushes me back before he kicks the center of it, but the door isn't flimsy, and it doesn't even register the hit. Brick comes over next and rams a shoulder into it. He comes away whimpering, holding his bicep.

I was reckless. I left the two of them alone. I hadn't even guarded them. That's how out of it I am. This world has made me dumb. I'd never do something so stupid at home. It's such a simple thing: a door lock! And I'm useless. I've no ideas. No backup plan.

I'm fucking pathetic.

James is at the bedside table and types in a number on the hospital phones. I've already tried to work them but they only reach hospital rooms and the nurses' station. I'm surprised when he talks into it, "Room 640. Alert the staff." He slaps it down. "They will be here in a few minutes."

Even though it's more than I was able to come up with, anger is all that comes out. "A few minutes?" I bite. "The girls are out there."

"I know that," he responds too calmly for my patience. "What would you have me do?"

I pace the floor. I'm not helpless. I have never been helpless. But I can't function here. Everything is out of my control. I spent five years molding that school to my whims. I knew every nook and cranny. I knew every person, every layer of their motives, and how to manipulate them. But here, their values have changed. Half of them believe they are going home. They are no longer in survival mode, while I don't know how to live any other way.

I can't use people that have hope.

Standing around like a idiot drives me to insanity. I point to James. "If you had stayed out of this, we wouldn't be in this position. I told you once if I saw you again, I'd kill you."

James stays silent, but I don't want to vent. I want to fight.

I step up to him. "Maybe I should kill you now." I search his face, looking for the beast I know that lives in him. I've seen it. I've watched him beat people to a bloody pulp. I've seen the bodies he leaves behind. And though that should convince me I wouldn't survive a brawl against him, he's one handed now. Easier to take down and it's just enough to make me confident.

"If that's what you want."

I sneer at him, annoyed by his passive bullshit. "You're insane. What are you doing with Ember? You know you don't belong with her, don't you?"

"I can take care of her," he says factually, but even I can hear the slight unsure tone, hiding in his words.

"Can you? I'm pretty sure Zack made such a thing impossible for you."

There it is, a flinch, a tension he tries so hard to suppress but fails. Zack is still in every part of him. He thinks he can just move on and be normal, but there is no normal. Not for people like us. I need him to acknowledge it, so I don't feel like the only one that will never heal.

The door rattles, pausing our conflict. It's too soon for it to be a Special. I dive back to the nightstand, my fingertips on the end of the barrel. I have one bullet and was saving it for Jose, but I wouldn't mind taking out a Coal Member either.

The door pops open and Ink slips his head in. "Hurry, Coal has them cornered in the game room."

Brick slaps a hand on his shoulder and James verbally thanks him before darting out the door. I'll deal with my thoughts on the matter after Mary's safe. Ink betrayed me once, but this action gains him a point.

We move through a crowd of nurses and one of them says, "Help's coming,' but what they don't understand is I don't wait for anyone. We slam into the door like a tidal wave, and it rattles, but remains frozen shut. Even with all of us pounding, it doesn't waver. Thunderous cheers are muffled on the other side. "Mary!" I scream, but my voice is lost among their hollers. I can't stand it, being separated from her. Everything I said to her creeps up in my head. I've never deserved Mary. But I took her because I'm selfish. If she knew that, would she still love me as blindly as she does? When she realizes I'm not a good person, how I've lost so many of my morals, and I'm terribly cruel and hateful person, will she leave me? Is it an inevitability?

Brick rolls out a gurney from one of the rooms and as a team of ten we use all our weight to break through the door. When James' Special friends arrive, it only takes five violent punches to break the pole on the other side and the doors burst open.

I punch the first person I see, and they fall forgotten on the floor. The nurses, all male, intercept, but they struggle with the numbers. The Specials are a consuming force, knocking down kids like bowling pins, leaving only bodies in their wake. This is what I wanted, to take out Coal, to destroy every single person that ever stood against me. It's the vengeance I've been craving.

I search the crowd for Peat and Noah, but it's chaos. The kids are running, diving out the opposite entrance as the Specials devour anyone in their path. James is in the lead, twisting arms and tossing bodies. He is a determined force, violent, talented, and untethered. Even with one hand, he outmaneuvers anyone that approaches, spinning, using his long legs to aid him.

"Adam!" I hear Mary and then she's in my arms. I cling to her, apologizing, burying my fingers into her hair. "You're not losing me, Mary, I promise you. You can't ever lose me. Do you hear me? You'll never get rid of me." Words pour without filter and I don't even feel stupid for it. I need her to know it because she's the only thing in my life worth fighting for. Without her, I'd lose all reason for breathing.

Over her shoulder I watch Ember. She stays seated on the ground with her head in her hands. James is at her side, kneeling beside her. With a single touch, she falls into him. It should be reassuring but it isn't. James is a soldier, lacking more than anyone else here. He's not good for her. And if he's glued to her, he can't be useful to me.

The kind of soldiers I need don't have weaknesses and she is clearly his.

I'll break them apart. One way or another.

CHAPTER 20
Mission

EMBER

A CONCUSSION, THREE STITCHES between my arm and stomach, and the guilt were enough to keep me in bed. I can't remember what happened after I got hit in the head, but I'm missing something. It like a splinter in my skin that I can't pick out. Something about the fight.

Mary sits in a chair at the edge of my bed, doing a word search, but her attention is far from the page. She keeps glancing at the clock, watching the minutes turn into hours. Jose canceled morning recreation and breakfast. He's ordered us to our rooms, but it only leads to panic. Is he planning to lock us in? Is he finished preparing? Or is this simply procedure after the violence of last night?

James and Shakes fought to keep us in their rooms, but the nurses separated us, and even though Mary had been staying with Shakes, she's with me now. Which means neither of us know what Shakes is doing. Will this trigger him to start rebelling? After last night, I realize I don't know to what extent Shakes will go to for survival. He was ready to kill a member of Rain because Lisa failed to protect me.

Will he face the fact that he hadn't protected me either?

And will he admit that protecting me is turning out to be a waste of his time?

A tear builds up in my eye. "Mary?" I shift uncomfortably. "Do you think Shakes regrets keeping me alive?"

Her brows knit and quickly she comes to my side and wraps an arm around me. I hate how it sparks more tears. Shakes went through so much work to protect me and bring me into his family. And I stood in front of him at the school, spitting in his face. If I would have let him take on those police, he'd be free.

"Adam," she begins slowly. "cares about you. You helped him destroy the school, Ember, and

235

no matter what happened afterwards, he'll always be grateful for it." She sugarcoats it, like she's dealing with an eight-year-old child. But I'm not naive anymore. The look on Shakes face when he was standing on the bus with his gun ahead of him, pointing directly at me, told me the truth I'm searching for.

"I have to fix it," I vow. But what can I do?

A knock on the door and in steps Jose. I sit up as he strolls in with his hands tucked into his black pants. He has a buttoned-up shirt and tie. He smiles, but I don't see a sweet caring officer anymore. I see a devil in disguise, very interested in me. "How are you feeling?"

I don't say anything. He's tricked us. He is Myers' reborn. How can someone look in my eyes and pretend so well to care? Why did I so readily believe him?

Because I wanted to. It's a sad reality. I wanted to believe him. I wanted the world to be a better place, but it isn't.

'*Hate me,*' Tobias said. One of the last things he said to me. '*Fight me, fight the teachers, fight against everything you hate. And when you get out, keep fighting because it won't be over. It won't ever be over."*

Tobias knew that even if we got out of the school, there would still be evil in the world. It would just be harder to see.

Jose nods as if my silence is an answer. "I am thinking maybe it is time to get you and a few of your friends into protective custody."

My heart hammers in my chest. I jump out of bed, the swirl of my headache causes me to hold onto the mattress. I hold out my butter knife in front of me ready to hurt if I have too. Mary remains seated, judging the distance between her and the door and if she could run fast enough to escape.

Jose knits his brow. "I didn't think that would upset you so much. I'm trying to help."

"No thanks." He doesn't know I know what he is. He wants to play the game of savior. Men like him think they are the heroes in the story when really they are the villain.

He snorts and shakes his head. Is it the sign of temper brewing beneath his mask? "You are one screwed up individual. If you want to stay, by all means. But stay out of trouble. In a couple of days,

I'm going to be shipping out the ones on my list and hopefully this place will become a little quieter. Have you figured out your name yet? I would love to call your parents."

I say nothing.

"We are on the same side, Scream."

"What side is that?" I ask, if only to provoke him, to make him reveal his big secret.

"What other side is there?" he challenges and then he waits for an answer.

But I give nothing. He will find me a brick wall.

He snickers, backing away, giving in. "Tell Shakes if he tries to attack Coal, I'll have no choice but to have him removed from the hospital."

The threat lingers in the air as he leaves. I remain clenching the knife, the only protection I have that gives me control.

• • • • ● • ● • • •

We are allowed to go to the cafeteria for dinner.

Moving hurts, and I lean on Mary to get dressed more than I need to just because I love her comfort. She makes me feel important and loved. It's what a mother would be like, I imagine. A mother with a violinist's hands and a sweet laugh like bells. I stall in my movement, staring blindly at the floor, reaching for that memory, that moment, chasing it like one chases a rainbow.

But Mary puts her hand on my shoulder, and I pull away from my thoughts, and the door closes so sharply it makes me jump. "Are you okay?" Mary questions, watching with concern.

I nod and keep moving, pretending it is nothing. I don't want to tell anyone because I know what they will say. They'll want me to remember. They'll try like Star tried to get me to grasp those thoughts and gain control of them. But I'm scared.

No matter how much I want to be, I'm no longer the girl I was before I came to Myers. I don't need to know who I was to realize this fact. I am forever changed. I'm afraid to find out who I was because what if that person doesn't fit in with the family I've got now? What if I belong far, far away?

I enter the cafeteria, and it causes a slight wave. Whispers and stares follow me. I keep my head down. I don't want to hear what they have to say. I already know they think I'm crazy.

James rushes up to me and we embrace, clenching tight to each other. He pulls back looking me over, trying to find my wounds, but I assure him I'm fine, even as I fight a headache the size of a cruise ship.

Over his shoulder Mary and Shakes greet each other. He's kissing her, holding her, diving his hands into her hair and she basks in his attention, pretending to swat him away, but eager for more. I love that side of him, the side that knows how to love. It suits him better.

Shakes, holding onto Mary's hand, comes up to me. "Why did you go into Coal Territory?" he attacks, without even hearing my side. He blames me.

Part of me wants to just be silent and take his rage, because I know I deserve it. It's not just about Coal, it's about everything else I do. It's about the fact I defied him and now we are all prisoners to Jose's jail.

But I've never been one to back down, and I can't find the will to do it now.

"I didn't," I snap back. "If you hadn't left us in the hall–"

"Don't try to spin this."

Mary tries to stop him, whispering, but he cuts her off too. "Don't make excuses for her. She knows how to make her own." He glares at me, daring me to make up something on the spot.

People are staring. The spotlight is shining down on me, and I shrink under its intensity. My confidence isn't nearly so high in front of so many.

"Can we sit, please?" Mary pulls on his arm and though he waits for me to talk about it, I remain silent. It hurts my heart that he's so angry with me and all I want him to do is admit he made the wrong decision, but I'm afraid if I provoke, he'll actually say what he's denied—that he should have shot me.

Shakes points. "Sit. Maybe you can handle that without starting a fight."

I clench my teeth and obey, my pride dissolved. I know I'm impulsive. I know I don't follow directions as well as I could. But my intentions aren't evil. I'm trying to help. Don't I get any credit for keeping Mary safe? Why does he only point out the bad things I do?

Ink got food for everyone and he passes it out. he purposely puts a bowl of strawberries down in front of me and gives a small encouraging smile that eases my self-hatred.

"Not for nothing," Brick begins with a grin as he sits. "But I've been hearing some pretty crazy shit." His eyes sparkle with mischief as he looks at me. "Did you really have a knife to Noah's throat?"

Vapor slaps the table. "Man, I can't believe I missed all the fun. These pain killers really knock me out." I'm giggling, while feeling sorry for him. His broken leg remains in a cast as he sits in his wheelchair.

James is not entertained by the direction of the conversation. "We need to talk about Memory."

The group moves their attention to Shakes. He chews his food, ignoring us.

James straightens and tries again. "Memory said–"

"Coal must be dealt with," Shakes carelessly cuts him off.

James clamps his mouth shut, staring straight and unseeing with a stiff back. It appears the tension between them is still unresolved, and I've yet to learn why their friendship is struggling to begin with.

Brick and Vapor glance toward one another before Vapor responds, "Coal is currently grounded." He points to their empty section. Only the ten girls remain, and they are as miserable as ever. "They are not allowed to be here or outside, and there are cops on our floor. This is a good thing, but the girls might still come after you, Ember."

I raise a thumbs up. I'll be extra careful.

"Let's talk about Memory," Shakes decides. "I am not going to rely on her. Are we in agreement on that?"

I almost shake my head 'no,' but everyone else agrees, so I sit still, frozen. Why don't we believe her? She sounded like she knew what she was talking about.

"Alright," Shakes begins. "We can't stay here. Unlike school, where we knew our opponent and their capabilities, we know very little about Jose and his intentions. And a lock down could come at any moment."

I take this moment to warn him, "Jose said if you do anything to Coal, he's going to remove you from the hospital."

"Jose?" he asks. "When did he talk to you? Why haven't you said anything?"

"I am saying something. He just spoke to me—"

"Jeezes, Ember, tell me everything he said."

When James' hand squeezes my thigh, I know what he's saying without hearing it. *Patience,* he orders. But I don't know how much attitude I can handle. I'm trying my best.

"He said—" I bite through clenched teeth. Another squeeze and I breath out, relaxing. "He could put us in protective custody. I said-No. He then said we are on the same team."

"What team?"

"I asked and he said, '*what other team is there?*' Whatever the hell that means."

Shakes rolls the words around his head, nodding as if he's coming to some conclusion that he isn't sharing with us.

Shakes leans back. "We need ideas and good ones. How can we escape this place? First, it's time we start concentrating on ourselves. It's illogical that we can get everyone out. But the seven of us are much easier than the six hundred of us. Am I wrong?"

The statement comes as a shock to me and I'm speechless. Shakes has never been focused on just himself. I thought after what Memory did, he could never decide to leave anyone behind.

Brick thankfully says what I'm thinking. "We can't just leave if that's what you're saying. I followed you because you weren't out for just yourself. Everyone in this school mattered whether they were friend or foe—"

"Are you talking like this because of your girl?" Shakes suddenly accuses.

Brick's eyes widen. I didn't know Brick had a girlfriend, and apparently Vapor didn't either as he leans in and whispers, "You got a girlfriend, bro?"

"Be straight with me, Brick," Shakes demands. "I don't like bullshit."

And though I'm relieved Shakes' temper isn't directed at me, it's unnecessary. He's on a warpath and no one is willing to stop him.

Brick bows his head, his cheeks red in embarrassment. "No, boss. You told me to stop talking to her and so I did."

Shakes isn't convinced. "That's not exactly true, isn't it? You got a letter from her yesterday at dinner."

Brick's jaw clenches. I should probably stop staring, but I'm still. There aren't very many times

Shakes is chastising someone else. As terrible as it sounds, it's interesting to watch.

Brick digs in his pocket and tosses the note on the table. "Then you know I didn't reply. She's the one who told Lisa about the attack on Ember. She thought Lisa would stop it."

Vapor is ignorant of their tension as he asks, "Why didn't you tell me you had a girlfriend?"

"Dude, shut up." Brick bites uncharacteristically, lowering his head in shame.

Shakes picks up the letter, as if he's actually going to read it before he tears it in two. "I'm supposed to believe a Coal Member?" He tosses the pieces back and waits for Brick to react.

Brick silently rages, every muscle tense, and I wonder if he will do something. It takes a moment before the tension fades, and he lifts his head, clear of anger. "Two years ago, you preached that we all deserve a chance at a normal life. That we were kids with the same dreams. I remember that day because I joined Anarchy to fight for you. I'm not abandoning them."

It is silent after that. Shakes stares at the table, and I want to know if he remembers that? Or if that Shakes from two years ago is gone.

Vapor voices his opinion in the silence. "If we get the clans involved, we'll have more ideas, more help, more strength. Tell them what's going on. We don't do it alone. We might find they are more willing to help this time."

Brick clenches his jaw, refusing to look at him. "Rain is just trying to make up for backstabbing us."

"Okay? What's wrong with that?"

Mary picks at her fingers. "We've been trapped for years already. I'm nineteen and don't know how to drive a car. We are just kids. Not everything is our responsibility. When can we go home? When can we have normal lives?" Shakes rests a hand on hers, squeezing her fingers.

It's her speech that triggers mine. "I never cared about the school. About the kids. About anything other than getting out. But then I met Charles. And then you guys. And I realized that we are in this together. I can't leave them."

Shakes scratches his brown locks. He doesn't share his decision, and moves on. "My first thought is we got to get the public aware of us. Our freedoms will be instant."

Vapor questions, "How do we do it? We have no internet access. The phones here only reach others in the hospital."

James interrupts, "I can get a cell phone." He takes a bite of his sandwich, careless of my gaze. I know who exactly he can get a phone from, and it causes red hot jealousy in my chest.

Shakes eyes James. "You think I can trust anything you do?"

James doesn't reply or appear like he's hurt by Shakes, but he's silent and I know it bothers him.

Let Shakes badmouth anyone else, but he isn't going after James. "What is your problem, Shakes?"

"Tell her." Shakes orders. "Tell everyone here, James. Then we'll put it to a vote."

James drops his fork, straightening up. There is only a moment of quiet before he gains the courage to say it. "I stopped the bombs from going off on the day of Grounding."

Those words pause every thought. I remember we talked about the Grounding once. James hadn't been part of the rebellion until I came to the school. He said that day, Zack had given him an order to kill someone, and so he did. He failed to mention the significance of that person.

How long had he known?

I look around at the table, and disappointment causes different reactions. Vapor shakes his head, cursing. Brick sits back, clenching his teeth, and Ink hides his eyes behind his hand. They are devastated by such news. James had become part of their family, and to know he was the cause of their failure hurts.

"I didn't know who I was ordered to kill," James admits, continuing despite their expressions. "I didn't know that doing so would cause the rebellion to fail, though it wouldn't have stopped me. Not back then. I realized only a month ago when I started coming to Anarchy with Scream what my actions did." James stands and turns to Shakes. "But it does not alter that I have done everything you ever asked of me. The day I met you, I transformed everything Zack had ever did to me to be who you needed. I killed Zack for this rebellion. I killed for you. If all that means nothing because of ignorance, tell me to leave, and I will. Because even now, I trust in you and your decisions. And if my absence will help you succeed, I will go without a fight."

I suppress a smile. James is better than most people. He's beautiful in his qualities. I can't get enough of him.

Vapor is the first to speak. "I think he should stay, boss. We've all screwed up at some point. Maybe not as bad as that, but we need him."

It's unanimous, all of us sticking up for James. It pisses Shakes off, and he rolls his eyes. "Get me the phone and we'll see."

James nods once and sits down beside me. I lean into him, and like I knew it, there's a soft relief in his energy. He's happy.

Vapor tentatively begins again. "We might have more ideas if we include more people." Then he adds, "Lisa wants to help–"

"I won't deal with her." Shakes glances over his shoulder, noticing them not too far from us. Lisa and Eric sit side by side with all their friends around them. I find their reemerging friendship annoying, but any ill feelings I have toward them are erased by the fact I hurt Eric. Something I still haven't faced yet. I know I need to talk to him, but I have no idea how to do that.

Eric glances over his shoulder and notices me. He presses his lips tight and turns back around.

Vapor sighs. "Shakes, she can help."

Shakes taps a finger against the table for a minute, contemplating his next move. He needs to realize we need all the help we can get. There's no time for pettiness or grudges.

I say as I hold onto pettiness and grudges.

"Find a pen and a few pieces of paper," he tells Mary. "You gotta write some things for me."

James stands up, announcing he will head back to his room. With no invite, I sit like a chump. But only briefly before I jump to my feet and follow him. "How are you gonna get a phone?" I bulldoze through, keeping my voice soft and pleasant despite the building panic. All I can think about is Grace and their hands touching.

"Grace." He tosses his food in the trash without a flinch.

"You can't just ask for the phone."

"No."

"How are you going to get it?"

He shifts his head to look at me, but James won't find my eyes. "Do you want a detailed description of my plan?"

His defensiveness triggers my own. "What are you going to do?"

"Play off emotion. Get her distracted. Steal her phone. And leave."

"Always so direct, and you are refusing to tell me."

He stops walking and faces me. "I do not feel the need to explain myself. I will fulfill my mission by any means necessary." He spins on his foot, leaving me in a stupor.

James used to be cold when we first started training together. Since then, he has altered, come alive almost, so his harsh response is like a slap in the face. He reveals how quickly he can shut off and be a machine again.

I rush after him, catching the door he doesn't hold open. "James!" He grabs the railing and climbs the steps two at a time as if he didn't hear me. I pursue, holding onto my anger, but confusion is replacing it.

Why has he shut off? If helping Shakes hurts him or puts him in a predicament he doesn't want to be in, then maybe he shouldn't be helping anymore.

After the third flight of steps, exhaustion begins to drag me down. I can't keep up. My head is pounding, and no amount of Ibuprofen will help. I need to rest, and I lean against the wall, taking a moment to recover. James returns to my side just as the intercom comes on, telling us that dinner has ended. The stairway fills with girls, as the boys head out to recreation. He and I stand there and wait out the storm in silence. It's awkward and awful, with so many stares and whispers. A nurse lingers in the doorway after everyone has cleared out, waiting for us to move. I show her my green bracelet, and we continue climbing the stairs until we are out of her suspicious gaze.

On the fourth floor, James stops as he holds the door open, halfway in and halfway out. "You have made the observation yourself that Grace is attracted to me. I will use this to lure her into dropping her guard. I will go as far as I need to in order to take her phone without notice."

I swallow the threatening emotion building in my throat. "So...So you. You umm are probably. .Probably going to kiss her."

"Yes."

"And touch her."

"Yes."

"And other things."

He stalls. "I do not think 'other things' will be necessary."

"But if it is?"

He clenches his jaw. "Then yes."

I hang my head, and my body shakes as I suppress the pain his admittance causes me. It's like he's betraying me when he hasn't even done anything. "And that's just how it is..."

"Do you prefer I kill her?"

I rapidly shake my head.

"This is the part of me you don't know yet, and it's a part I have hidden from you," James softly states, a sadness in these words that scare me. "I'm asking you not to question further. I will not lie to you, but if you persist, it will," he pauses, searching for the word in my face, his eyes flicking frantically. James drops his head, giving up. The distress he exposes is uncharacteristic.

Does he think I'll stop caring about him? Doesn't he know how impossible that is?

I reach for his hand, and his head snaps toward me. "It's okay."

James breaks from my fingers to clench my face, stepping in and resting his forehead on mine. "I am not Light. In many ways, he is better for you.

But selfishly, I beg you to stay with me. Even when I fuck up."

James has never cursed before. Is it pain from his actions that stopped the Grounding? Or is it a sign that the human part of him is breaking through? Despite how hard he tries, he's still an eighteen-year-old boy, far from perfect.

My chest is caving as I stand in front of him. He's asking me to let bad things happen and stand by and do nothing. It goes against everything I am. "You want me to just be okay with you kissing Grace?"

James detaches, pulling away, forming the wall and protection around his soul he has spent years cultivating. "Yes."

I've built walls, too. And I pull up the anger and bitterness to protect myself from the hurt. "Sure." I brush past him and dive into the hallway.

James comes up behind me. "Do not be fake. You can be upset."

"Oh, thank you."

He snatches my arm, stopping my intense pace. "Where are you going?"

"I want to watch."

He sneers.

"If it's just a kiss, nothing to worry about, right? Nothing more than you need to? Isn't that what you said? I want to see your 'skills' in action. I'll let you know if it's anything to brag about." I yank my arm away and continue to his room.

"You are making this more difficult than it needs to be."

I cackle insanely. "More difficult? I'm sorry, tell me, what's more difficult than watching my boyfriend try to...do stuff with another girl? You don't have the right to tell me what's difficult here, okay?"

I leave him in a stupor, going down the hall, passing the nurses' desk without being seen, and enter his room. It's not long after he comes in, shutting the door. "Where are you going to hide?"

"In the bathroom."

"No. Behind the curtain. You'll have a better view."

I follow his instructions, slipping behind the thick curtain and sitting on the windowsill. I tuck my legs in, and he pats the fabric in certain areas, ensuring I can't be seen. He steps back and nods his head. "Don't make a noise."

"Yeah. Wouldn't want to ruin the mood."

He chooses to ignore my comment and toes off his shoes. He carefully unlatches the sling and slides his hand out of the holster. I ask if he needs any help, but he continues on regardless. I roll my eyes at his independence. Why can he never accept help? It wasn't like I was stealing any pride. He removes his shirt next, and my thoughts get slightly off-topic.

Was that how he was going to get her, by showing off his chest?

Sure, it had its finer qualities, but she was a grown woman, a nurse at that. She'd seen a fair share of male pectorals. He pulls down his pants then, and I shield my view. He still had his boxers on, which imprints in my mind, but I just hadn't been prepared for such a move.

He gets into bed and clicks the button. "Stay."

"Yeah. I got it."

Our eyes are on each other, and he is so obviously troubled by my presence. I can make out the tension in his shoulders. He doesn't want me here, but he allows it if only in an attempt to make this less awful, but I might have only cursed myself.

Why do I even want to be here? Part of me is to make sure it doesn't go more than it needs to.

Another part wants me to protect her and ensure a man doesn't take advantage of a woman. And still, a distant third part of me is curious.

What will James do?

Chapter 21

Fear

EMBER

I'M SITTING HERE WAITING for James to make out with another girl, and I can't honestly say I know what I'm doing. It sounds wrong and stupid, but I'm here anyway.

What can I gain from this?

I've been scared of physical contact since I can remember. Tobias made every touch terrible. Whenever he looked at me, I would silently beg the universe to strike me dead, so I wouldn't have to endure.

But it's different with James. I'm scared, but in a complete opposite way. I'm dying for his touch, but I shouldn't be, right?

With a knock on the door, James loses any emotion in his face as he plays his role. Grace pops her head in with a pleasant smile. "You're back! I heard there was a problem upstairs last night." She pulls her cart behind her. Her blond hair is in bright wavy curls around her shoulder. "No Ember?"

"She got hit in the head. She's fine; she just needs to rest for a bit. You look different today."

Grace smiles, shrugging. "Just did my hair. I always wear it up."

"It looks good."

A rush of heat hits her cheeks as she unrolls a blood pressure cuff. "Let's take your blood pressure. You look better. Is there a lot of pain?"

"A bit."

She sticks a temperature gauge in his mouth and watches the screen. "I'll get some meds for you before I go. Blood pressure looks fine. Temperature's good, too." She puts all her equipment back on the rack. Then she leans over him, close enough where the tips of her hair touches his blanket. It's purposeful and so ridiculous, I clench my fist, imagining what it would be like to punch her in the face.

Her fingers pull at his gauze, checking his wound. "When was your last antibiotic dose? You refused an IV, but we have to keep you on antibiotics so you don't get an infection. The site looks good. A little swollen." She grabs a pillow from the edge of the bed and props his hand up. She removes the stethoscope around her neck and attaches it to her ears. "Let's listen to your heart."

He watches her every move, and she knows it; her cheeks are red as she tries to dart her gaze in different places. "Odd tattoo."

The black tattoo on his pectoral is a simple '28.' A tattoo that matched the number on the door of his room in Zack's house.

When she pulls away, his hand is on her wrist. "Can I see?"

"What? The stethoscope?"

"My father was a doctor. I was going to be one before I was kidnapped."

Her brows knit, and she removes it, handing it over. "I can't imagine what you've been through. I've been hearing horror stories. Some are hard to believe."

He struggles to put it on with one hand, and she readily comes to his aid, sitting on the bed leaning in to help. There is a moment of silence as they stare at each other. "Thank you," he murmurs. "Can I listen to your heart?"

Speechless, she nods. James presses the end against the top of her breast, and she sucks in a breath. "Here." She pulls the edge of her shirt lower. "It better against the skin."

"That's true." He smirks, slipping it back against her skin. His fingers meticulously touching her. "Your heart beat is a little fast. I don't make you nervous, do I?"

She giggles. "Why would you make me nervous?"

He doesn't respond, allowing the insinuation to linger in the air.

Grace pulls back, taking back the stethoscope but staying on the bed. "So are you and Ember serious?"

James leans forward, his lips nearly brushing against hers. "Is that what you want to talk about?"

She shakes her head. It would be a perfect time to kiss her, and the dread rolls in my stomach Every muscle in my body is tense, and I dig my nails into my skin to keep me from jumping up and interrupting them. This is what I wanted to see, right? It's my fault for being an idiot. Now, I don't want to be here. I want to be far away and ignorant.

Why had I ever asked him? I could have remained dumb and blind and never the wiser.

His eyes flicker toward the curtains, toward me, and he leans backward. She is taken off guard by his sudden pull and stutters, "I'm sorry, I didn't mean—"

"No." He latches onto her hand, keeping her seated. "It's the pain. It's distracting."

"Let me get you something."

She rushes out of the room.

James hisses, "Stop staring."

I scoff. "Where do you want me to look?"

"I can't concentrate."

"Oh, is this difficult for you?" I throw the word back in his face in a hiss. "What are you going to do now? Whatever's necessary, right?"

James is unamused. "Jealousy is a weakness. Try to work on it."

I shrink when Grace comes back in with a pill in between her fingers. "This will make you feel better."

James latches on to her fingers, sits up and pulls her sharply against him. "I have something else in mind."

She doesn't fight, and she doesn't push away. She sinks into him, sitting partly on the bed with her hands on his shoulders as she giggles. "Oh? And what's that?"

He leans in, and I clench my eyes shut, terrified he's about to kiss her. Then I hear whispering. I peeked an eye open. He's talking into her ear, but I can't hear it over this distance. Her face and neck redden, and her hands boldly clench his shoulders, moving up and down his skin with a desire I don't want to see. She giggles and makes odd sounds as she listens to every word out of his mouth.

She bites her lip, and groans, "I'm working. I can't."

"I can wait."

"And that will help the pain, huh?" She giggles. "Well, I am your nurse. I do have to care for you."

"It will be hard work." His hand is on her side, nearly at her ass. "When your shift is over, come back."

"You make a lot of promises for having only one hand." She runs her fingers down his arm and I want to barf.

"I have other resources."

My brows knit, *whatever that hell that means.*

Grace sucks in a heated breath like she knows and I hate her for it. She pulls out of his arms in a daze, giggling and tucking her hair behind her ear. She departs with a lick of her lips. James gets up and locks the door.

I slap open the curtain. "Great job," I sarcastically nip.

James keeps his angry gaze on me as he returns to his bed. He pulls out the phone from under his covers. My mouth falls open as I blink. "How?" I gap openly, more afraid he used some sort of magic that I hadn't noticed. He tosses it on the bed before he sits next to me on the windowsill, quiet, no doubt waiting for the avalanche of questions.

I feel gross, and though nothing happened, it's like it had. He didn't put any effort into it at all. What words had he said? What if it was like hypnosis or something? Could he use it on me? What kind of defense did I have against someone like him? He's intimidating on a different level now.

"You did it." I break the terrible silence, but the victory is depressing.

He sighs and nods.

I'm stuck on how he looked at her. It felt like the way he looked at me, with intensity and seriousness. But I couldn't tell from here. What else had been reflecting in his eyes to get her so compliant? Desire? Lust?

"Do you have questions?"

"I can't...figure it out." I find myself saying. "Tobias was only ever brutal and demanding. But you..."

He shifts his head toward me with knit brows.

"For so long, any physical attention was frightening. But she wasn't afraid. She doesn't even know you. Why wasn't she afraid?" I look at him, desperate to understand.

"What do you feel when I kiss you?"

My face heats up, unprepared for such a question. I stutter and try to word it but fail.

James smiles adoringly, and he licks his lips to suppress it. "That feeling is what you are supposed to feel, Dream," he murmurs, using my name as a sweet caress. "What Tobias did was associate physical attention with negative emotion. That is not a normal response. Do you understand?"

"He screwed me up."

"Yes."

"How do I fix it?"

"Time."

I nod, disappointed with that answer. I want to forget Tobias with all my heart, but he lingers like a bad aftertaste.

The doorknob jiggles, and we both snap our attention to the door. "James? It's me, open up." Grace calls from behind the door.

He doesn't move from my side. "Sorry, Grace, I'm exhausted."

"Oh. Yeah. Okay. I can't find my phone. Did you hear it? I called it."

"No. Nothing."

"Alright. Um let me know if you find it."

It's silent between us again, and I pick at my jeans. Does he realize he's in his boxers? I certainly noticed, and it's getting near impossible to avoid glancing at his legs. I've circled around the entire room eight times, and the only place left are his naked legs. I slap a hand over my face. "Put some pants on!"

James chuckles but gets up and grabs a pair of cotton pajama pants. They are easier to slip on with one hand. He even puts on a shirt before he sits back down beside me. He yanks my foot down, ending my curled position, and his hip touches my own. It's assuring, and my walls aren't nearly so high. I relax against him.

But I'm still worried.

"Why were you so good at that?"

James swallows, keeping his head straight. "I was taught many things in Zack's care."

I stare down at the ground. It's more indirect that, if I asked correctly, he'd tell me. But I don't. I stay silent, trying to say to myself it doesn't matter.

"Are you scared of me?"

I watched James brutally kill someone, and yet it's here and now that I find him the most dangerous. How can he lie so well? I don't want to hurt his feelings, so I say nothing.

"You will always be safe with me," he assures me.

"I know it's stupid. I'll fix it." But how can I trust him when I don't know what he's capable of?

"I'm in love with you."

I snap my head up. His brown eyes glitter in the light, and a soft smile dances on his lips. His fingers come up and touch my jaw, brushes my lips. I can't think as I try to form words. How can I respond? What should I say?

I can't say anything. So I run.

Tobias fills my head like a dust storm. Every nook and cranny of my vision becomes cloudy with only him, a frozen statue in the wind. *'Love me,'* he whispered, so close to my face I could smell the nicotine and mint. He wanted something I could never give.

I stop at the door. James hasn't moved, resigning against the window sill giving me the space I desperately crave. He's always revealing how different he is from the man in my nightmares. Even when James clearly wants more than I'm ready to give, he doesn't take it by force. He waits.

I turn back to James. "Why?"

His brows knit in a sadness I rarely see from him. "There's no reason, Scream." He says my name instead of the nickname he gave me. Because right now, it's not a dream we are in, but a full-on reality that I'm fighting. "Not the kind of reason you're looking for. I don't want anything from you."

"Then why?" I ask again, insanely. Why else say that to me?

James continues to watch me, to let me soak in his admission. Being loved is an insane thing. I've been wanting it on so many different levels. Through friendship, through siblings, through parents, and yes, even through romance. I've been wanting to feel special and deserved.

So why am I fighting it?

James walks toward me. I flinch, a thought to flee, but I stay still. I'll never know the answer if I run. He stops inches from me as if wanting to touch me but afraid too.

"How do you know?" I ask, desperate to understand what this means. If it's real. If it's something that can be ripped away from me like Charles was.

"I couldn't kiss her," James reveals as if that makes sense.

"Because I was watching?"

"Because the thought sickened me. Why? It was a simple procedure, done countless times before–"

"What does that mean?"

His brows knit, and he shakes his head. "Don't ask me that."

"James–"

He holds the side of my head, pulling me closer, his broken hand wrapped around my waist. I lean into him, when I should pull away. "I'll tell you one day, but not today," he murmurs, leaning down to touch my lips.

It's impossible to stop my heart from pounding or the desire in my belly from building. His touch, scent, and presence aren't calming but radioactive. I find myself out of breath just standing there doing nothing, silently begging him to kiss me, to show me what real love feels like.

James rests his forehead on mine. "I never thought I would get to tell you how you have taken my whole world and blown it apart. How everything you are, is everything I love about you. And how everything you've become is everything I believed you could be. I've been waiting for you, Dream. Not just for months. But for years."

I stare at him, amazed by such a devastating confession. He's so brave to say it, but that's James. Never embarrassed about anything. The weeks we've known each other play back in my head. Every moment he glanced at me, hoping I wouldn't notice, every moment his fingers graced mine, every time he watched me from across the room, suddenly had more meaning to it. I always felt something in how James looked at me; now I know what it was.

From the moment I could remember, I've felt too dirty, stupid, ugly, and insignificant to be cared for. Charles was the one to make me see there was something good in me because he wouldn't have loved me if there hadn't been.

But James makes me believe I'm worthy of all the love in the world.

"Are you still afraid of me?"

The only thing I find myself afraid of now is losing him.

Chapter 22

Dream

James

I STARE AT THE ceiling. Dream is curled into my side, and it is unreal, replaying the last hour in my head. Words that I thought I'd never get to say came out of me without force or manipulation. I wasn't coerced or threatened. I exposed a weakness I tried so hard to smother. And now I'm free.

For months, I followed Dream, sitting on the edge of buildings, observing everything she did. She spooked at every sound. She flinched at every loud voice. Initially, she was a broken shell, the kind I've seen numerous times in my career. But despite how much she feared, she somehow managed to be courageous. Some would call it stupidity, but when all around are demons, there's nothing wrong with keeping a knife in your hand

and sharp wit ready on your tongue. It made others afraid of her and isolated her, which, in turn, kept her safe.

Month after month, I watched her evolve. She became a scavenger, agile on her feet, and quick to learn. With every battle, her skills increased like a War of Warcraft character. She would get angry when she lost and prideful when she won. It was a little taste of the person she didn't know she was, and it enthralled me.

Because, like her, I had no idea who I was. Though I didn't suffer from amnesia, I grew up in Zack's service, which gave little room for personality. Perhaps if I had amnesia, I could make excuses for the things I've done.

Observing her helped me dig out pieces of who I could be, of who Zack tried so hard to destroy. It was addicting like the first hit of cocaine before the aftermath sneaks in. I don't want to stop; if anything, I want more.

Am I coming on too strong? She has only known me for a few weeks. We've only just kissed a couple days ago, the first reveal of the unspoken attraction between us. To tell her so quickly and with no shame that I was in love with her was foolish and a risk.

But I've waited long enough. I cannot slow down.

I slip out of her hold, sitting on the edge of the bed. My broken hand lays in my lap. The pain pulses and distracts me. I lean over to the nightstand and open the drawer. Numerous white pills roll freely, and I stare at them.

I close my eyes as Zack's voice threads into me. *'Take your vitamins, my babies. I need you to be nice and healthy.'*

I slam the drawer shut and wince when Dream pops up, wide-eyed. "Sorry," I whisper and lay down beside her. "Go back to sleep."

"You okay?"

Her concern warms me, and I kiss her temple. "Sleep."

Soon, she relaxes against me, but I stare at the ceiling, seeing Zack's face. I took ten pills a day for ten years. Vitamins, he called them, and though some of the pills were for our health, there were also steroids and testosterone boosters, and sometimes, if the mood hit him, he'd surprise us with drugs like Molly, PCP, or Ativan. He liked to experiment. Especially with new recruits or the younger children because it affected them worse. Made for good entertainment.

My fingers run through Dream's brown hair, and she shifts only slightly. Zack disappears from my thoughts as I rest my palm upon her arm, her skin soft and warm. I pull her closer, and she wiggles instinctively nearer, sighing contently. She is like armor. I need her like I need air.

I did not think I would be granted peace. I have done nothing to deserve it. I could reflect on every sin I have voluntarily committed, but I find myself unable. If I had not taken every step, I would not be here. How can I then feel remorse? How can I regret it? It does not make it less horrible. It does not make my actions good in any way. I understand evil and that it exists within me. But I will not stand in front of a crowd and lie and say I would not do it precisely the same way.

Will Dream accept this about me? I have merely hinted about my past misdeeds. She knows so little despite living in hell. She had barely begun to scratch the surface. There were darker levels that she could not fathom. Levels, she would not make it out of.

I had given up on freedom. I had no choice if I wanted to survive. I had seen Death take those who fought. I wasn't ready to die at ten because I still believed that I could one day find a way home. I had to fight because my sister, Anata, relied on me.

When she died, I knew her spirit wouldn't be set free until I brought her killers to justice. So I allowed myself to be swayed by Zack with the intention that karma would follow every horrible action and one day, Anata's killers would know terror. But as the years stretched, accepting my life, I began to sink into foulness. Years drowned my religious beliefs, and too much rancor buried me. I lost myself. I lost my reasoning. And now I will never be the boy I was.

I could never go home.

Home. I can barely remember it. We were there six months before my sister and I were taken. I close my eyes and try to picture the house. I've forgotten names. I've forgotten faces. I couldn't find my home even if I got free.

Not that I would try.

My parents came to America as Japanese immigrants, hoping for better opportunities for my siblings and myself. My father was a doctor, while my mother stayed home with three younger children and my older sister. We were home schooled and lived in an Asian community in a very small section of South Jersey. Every day was the same as the day before. Chores, school, chores, dinner, bed. My mother liked consistency and discipline. It kept us well-behaved, and five children were difficult for her to handle. She was 90 pounds and 5 feet and did not yell or get angry. She had the best patience, and we tended to take advantage if she didn't give us a proper schedule.

Anata liked to be rebellious. Because I was the eldest male, I was responsible for looking after her. She tended to run away when my mother wasn't paying attention, and I went with her, constantly yelling at her to return home before our mother noticed.

Inevitably, it was one of these times a man was walking down the same street as we were. We tried to slip by him, but he grabbed my sister. He didn't even care about me. I could have run away and gotten help, but she was calling for me, reaching out her tiny hands, and I could not leave her. He clamped a hand on her mouth and threw her in the back of his van. My little punches did nothing but aggravate him. He pushed me in as well.

I will never be that little boy again. It is impossible to take away eight years of treatment. I can hear Zack in everything I do. Even now, his voice whispers in my ear. 'Do not fall asleep. You are not being paid to snooze.' Or 'STD and you're in need.' His stupid singing voice. 'All they want is your special talents. If I hear anyone ask for a phone or a favor, I'll remove a testicle. Everyone has two chances.' He'd giggle and dance around.

What I want is to walk away from the school, capable of moving on. I don't want to hear Zack. I don't want to look back and think about the what-ifs and the should-haves. I want to keep stepping further and further away and not hold on. But it's hard because I don't know how to be anyone else. What is life without missions? Without clients? Without Zack?

It is scary to think about. I killed him, and I almost stopped myself from doing it. I needed him to tell me what I should do next. Where I should go. How do I live normally after eight years of life as a servant? Is there such a thing as normal for me?

My hand hurts and I stare at it, attempting to move a swollen finger. Zack would have moved me to the 'unseen' section of his garden. He doesn't like to keep damaged goods, but he wouldn't have gotten rid of me. *'Waste naught, want naught.'*

I sit up. Dream only moans in dismay, but she stays asleep, snuggling into the pillow. I gently dig under the mattress. I managed to steal a phone from one of the nurses. An insecure woman is an easy target to distract. Any man with nice words makes them swoon.

In the bathroom, I stare at it. I don't think about calling home or calling for help. These are childish things that I am no longer privy too.

I type a number I memorized years ago. And immediately, it is answered, "Hello?" The familiar male voice answers, much to my horror. I click it off.

I'm frozen in place. I am far from free.

With urgency, I go out of the room, and a Special stands beside the door. "Mic." I greet and motion him down the hall. I hold the phone out to him. "Call a client."

He does as ordered and only two rings in, and she answers just as easily. He doesn't understand. "Why aren't the cops going after our clients?"

I reach into my pocket and pull out the small USB. This was what I climbed through crumbling buildings and quicksand to get. It contains all of Zack's files. Every single person that ever walked into one of our doors. "Because this isn't real, Mic." I, like everyone else, wanted it to be. I ignored the obvious signs. I even tried to ignore Memory. But this is the solid proof I need to shatter the shroud over my eyes. "This is just another school. Let the Specials know I plan to fight if they want to join me. Select a leader among yourselves. Shakes will meet with whoever you decide."

I return to the room. Dream is awake and wide-eyed, and upon seeing me, she visibly relaxes. I hug her and kiss her, and she clings with intensity. "I thought. I thought." She shakes her head and lowers her gaze, "Don't leave like that."

Her need to be in my presence is part of what will heal me. She will make me a better man simply because I don't want to disappoint her. I want to undo all her own damage, and by doing so, it will undo mine.

The bell for morning Recreation comes on. She groans and tries to ignore it. Dream slips on her shoes, uses the bathroom, and brushes her teeth. I put on more appropriate clothes, and though it is a struggle, she does not witness it. Only a few days of being unable to use my hand, and I can already see the problems. Trying to save it may be a better alternative. But I am not used to physical limitations, and it's aggravating.

I squeeze in the bathroom to brush my teeth, and Dream slinks backward in the corner, bumping into the showers, primarily intimidated by the lack of space and my form in front of the only exit. I continue, watching her from the mirror. I have done uncharacteristic things to gain her trust. I have admitted to emotions I have denied for too long. I have succumbed to these said emotions even with no intention of doing so. There is really nothing else I can do. And it is here, I decide it is not me. She needs time. Her wounds won't heal overnight, and neither will mine. We all assumed that life would resume once we were out of school, but it's not reality. It may take years before we reach a point where we find a bit of normality.

I open the door, leading her just on the other side. She doesn't understand what I'm doing and that's fine. I'd rather her be ignorant. Grace eyes me from the nurses' station. I pretend not to notice. I lean down and kiss Dream with a little more eagerness than she's ready for. When my hand slips below her waist, Dream peels away from me completely embarrassed and annoyed, but she smiles anyway and waves goodbye.

After watching Dream go in the elevator, I turn my head and meet Grace. Her expression is anything but happy and I smirk, driving home her conclusion. I want her to think I'm a womanizer. Her anger will keep her away from me. Grace will figure out I stole her phone, and I'll completely deny it. She won't be able to go to her superior because she'll have to tell them that she's been flirting with a patient. Which would get her fired, and this job means more to her than revenge.

I close the door.

Zack's in the corner of the room, pleased with my performance.

CHAPTER 23
Squabble

JAMES

I WAIT FOR DREAM at the table in the cafeteria. Shakes sits at the head, and Brick, Vapor, and Ink occupy the opposite side. All we're missing is her.

All I'm missing.

Then I see her walking in with a surprising smile on her face. She shines like the sun, leading a small circle of girls. She's talking and laughing, and I see who she used to be for a moment. I could imagine Dream was a team captain for a sport. More than likely soccer or track because of her quick reflexes and uncanny instinct to run. She leads like there's no other place for her.

Shakes glances back but swivels his eyes away with an annoyed sigh. He chews with attitude, ignoring my glance. I know what he's thinking because I've spent the last five months diving into every word he speaks like they are carved into my skin. He's seething, a brewing boiling pot about to blow. He wanted Dream to recover before he fought with her, and now it seems it's come to a head.

I hope Dream is ready for it. I should have asked her to sit and take whatever he says. But suppressing Dream is like putting a chain on a dragon. It's pointless. She's going to do what she's going to do.

Shakes greets Mary with a kiss on her cheek, helping her sit. Then he addresses Dream with a fake smile, "Hey, how are you feeling?"

Dream takes my hand when offered, and she sits beside me, leaning against my side like it's natural. She doesn't notice how Shakes fidgets, trying to gain control of his temper. "Good. You?"

"Got a fan base," he says off-hand, gesturing. Mary can hear it, and she turns away, aggravated with him already.

Dream giggles, shrugging. "They want to know about the fight. I can't really remember much after getting hit in the head. But none of them can believe I had Noah on his back."

This is a new piece of her: pride. She doesn't have much of it, she typically is consumed with guilt for everything that she does despite the need for survival. But the girls managed to get it out of her. She wants friends, though she'll never admit that.

"Ember." Light approaches the table timidly, but it doesn't stop him.

She turns to greet him, her eagerness obvious. "Hi."

"Are you alright?"

"I'm fine."

A concussion, a broken rib, bruises on her face, and three stitches on her stomach, and she says, 'I'm fine' with such authenticity.

"Can we talk?" Light asks, glancing around, avoiding my face. Without thought, Dream moves to follow him. It's another blow to Shakes' temper. He doesn't ask us for much except for complete control over our decisions. I monitor his face, wondering what he'll do. Mary whispers in his ear, and he smiles, returning to his breakfast despite how his eyes continue to flick her way.

In an effort to take his mind off her, I slide the phone across the table under a napkin. He takes it up and slips it into his pocket but says nothing.

The praise I yearn for doesn't come. Without it, self-loathing creeps in like a tide, pushing all the trash up on the beach. I clench my fingers against my thigh.

I don't know how I'm supposed to get back into his good graces when everything I do is discarded. I know the only reason he tolerates my presence is because of Dream. She'd put up too much of a fight, one he's not willing to participate in.

To recover, I force myself to ask, "What are we going to do about Coal?"

"We? *We* aren't doing anything." His suppressed anger seeps like slow-moving lava. Shakes glances at Dream again, gnashing his teeth. Mary keeps a hand on him, a temporary sedative that can wear off at any moment.

I retreat once more. Shakes' disappointment in me is worse than suffocation. I'd rather that punishment than his disregard. I need him more than he realizes. He's the only replacement I have for the master I killed.

Mary fights for me and says to him, "If I were you, I'd be thankful. James came after me when he didn't have to. He's still family–"

"Mary–"

"He's protecting Ember, just like you asked. He's protecting me and you. It wasn't his fault Ember and I were left alone last night, was it?"

Shakes slams his fist down on the table and then proceeds to get up, pounding his way across the lunchroom to get Dream. Shakes puts forth his sweet-talking skill as he interrupts, slapping Light on the back with a friendly smile. But gently, forcefully, he pulls at Dream's arm, helping her stand before slipping that hand to her back, guiding her toward our table. His smile falls when he faces us.

Dream curls her lip, cursing under her breath. She twists away from his hand. "I can't believe you are acting like this." She sits roughly beside me. "I didn't know there were rules to people I could talk to."

Shakes sits and growls back, "You are a part of this family; you eat with this family."

Mary slaps a hand over her eyes. "We aren't in the mafia."

"How can I keep you all safe if you are spread out like stray cats? Just do what I say, and maybe, just fucking maybe, you won't be kicked in the face and in a knife fight."

Dream narrows her eyes. "I feel like you are directing that towards me?"

He looks right at her and bitterly asks, "Why? Were you in a knife fight recently?"

"I didn't go looking for a fight!"

"No, you just stepped dumbly into Coal territory. How many dumb things are you planning to do? I would really like to know."

Bewilderment spreads over her features. She looks at me, but I am already on Shakes' bad side. I can't afford to be displaced any further. And besides, this is a fight between him and her. I can't protect her from him. IIe is the leader and an alpha male. I am in his hands, just like she is.

Yet, as I am thinking this, Dream is particularly headstrong. She is independent, and no beating from Tobias ever made her submit. This will not end well. I decide then to intervene. "You need to eat."

She lashes out. "If you ever trusted in me, maybe I wouldn't do stupid shit. But all you want to do is shove me under the table. I can help, Shakes. I'm not weak."

"I don't want your help."

The reveal is more than she can handle. Dream leaves the table.

Mary once more interrupts, "You are mad about Memory. Don't take it out on her."

"Maybe this time it will be a gunfight." Shakes leans back in his chair, glaring after her. Dream heads out of the cafeteria, and the moment she's out of sight, her endangerment comps his anger. "Shit." He snaps to his feet and goes after her.

I stand unsure whether to go or stay. Specials watch me from across the lunch room, wondering what I am doing. Sometimes, I wish they didn't care so much. I understand they are thankful for what I have done, but simple gratitude is enough. They are no longer soldiers. But if Shakes were to tell me to sit and do nothing, I would lose myself in self-pity. I need objectives just as much as they do.

I signal them to stay before I follow. I open the doors to the stairwell softly, peeking in. They are on the foundation of the next floor, and as I predicted, it's not going well.

"That's no excuse. None." Dream speaks in a low, bitter voice. "I'm not one of your lackeys. I wasn't

Tobias', and I'm not yours. What are you going to do if I don't listen? Hit me? Chain me up?"

Shakes runs a hand through his mohawk, trying to keep his voice low, but the more she attacks, the harder he fights back. "Would you stop comparing me to Tobias? I am not him. Does my wanting you safe really bother you that much? Why can't you just follow directions?"

"Just admit that you hate me!"

"What?" he scoffs, dropping his head. "Ember, you are driving me nuts! I got Mary on my case already. I don't need you making shit up."

"I put us here," she finally says, her voice nearly breaking. I was wondering when she would bring it up. We haven't discussed it; some things get overlooked in the constant struggle to survive. But I knew it was affecting her. "You were gonna fight, and I stopped you. I went against you when you knew this hospital wasn't safe. Why didn't you kill me?"

"I don't know," his response is too quick to stop what he really wanted to say, and he backs up. "I don't know."

Dream's face contorts in confusion. She drops against the wall. I want to know what she's thinking. Why did his confession hurt the way it did? Logically, killing her would have been the best plan when she interrupted his takeover of the school. By all accounts, we'd be free. Less of us, for sure, but free.

Shakes steps forward, and a hand reaches out, but he drops it and shakes his head. "There is so much about this world that you don't know. And I keep asking you to trust me."

Dream softly replies, "I do trust you."

I'm thankful their conversation is going better. I step back, willing now to leave them alone.

"Then please, just follow directions." Shakes hardens, and I don't move. "It's not that hard, Ember. Stop doing everything yourself, stop ignoring the clan boundaries, and realize there is a world outside of yours. We are fighting together."

"I was alone for months–"

"You were never alone," he bites harshly. "And you aren't alone now. You may not want to be a part of this family, but you are. I need you to be a little bit more conscious of what your actions do."

"I do want to be a part of this family," she screeches. "The knife fight wasn't my fault."

"You're right. It's mine. But I'm going to rectify it."

She's silent, staring. "Who are you going to kill this time?"

Shakes shrugs. "Stay within our family, and I won't have to kill anyone."

"Tobias used to say something like that."

Shakes sneers. "You are un-fucking-believable. Why do I bother?" He snatches her wrist and pulls to bring her down the stairs.

Her instincts kick in, and she knocks his hand off, kicking him in the shin. I leave the doorway and move to the bottom of the stairway. "That's enough."

"She's overreacting," Shakes defends himself, rubbing his leg.

"You're overreacting," she mimics childishly.

"Good one." Shakes jots down the stairs, shaking his head. "Hope you can see how screwed up in the head she is. Not really girlfriend material."

Dream stomps her foot. "Don't talk about me like I'm not here!" Shakes is through the door by the time she finishes, and she growls, "What?"

"You need to eat."

"I'm not sitting at the table with that control freak."

I hold the door open and wait. With a few deep breaths, she pounds her way down and zips by. I suppress a smile. Her temper is her best feature.

We all sit and eat in silence. The two bull-headed siblings do not speak and have rotten faces. Mary and I struggle to make the best of the awkward situation. We are, however, thankful when breakfast ends.

I have a hand on Dream's back when Mic approaches me. His standing there indicates something serious, and I hand Dream over to Mary. Shakes is hesitant to leave, eyeing me, a silent order to tell me what this is about later. I nod in understanding before he leaves.

Mic and I have both served Zack for a long time. He is number twenty-seven, living in the room across the hall for the last five years. We interacted the most, though our conversations were typically silent as we waited for clients together or received Zack's punishment together.

Mic leads me to the Special's Table. All fifteen remain sitting, quiet and controlled. "What is this?"

Mic answers, "I've told the others about your USB."

Though I'm surprised he felt the need to tell others, I wasn't withholding the information from them. They are part of Zack and, therefore, privy to what I plan to do.

I stand stiff and boldly say, "I will take it to the police." There is a shift, and they glance at each other. I am unsure what it means. "Does this upset you?"

Mic once more speaks for them. "Some of us believe it is not the best course of action."

Another kid gets to his feet and approaches me. Glass is a new recruit, barely thirteen years old. He's thin, with hardly any muscle on his pubescent arms. He is nearly a foot shorter than me, and I do the courtesy of not looking down on him. "A client knows my address."

"Why?" I shift my gaze toward the table. There is a collective look of guilt as I realize they have all made the same mistake. This is a fault in their upbringing. It seems Zack was getting sloppy during the recruitment process. He was cutting corners in places like their hope.

Perhaps I didn't need to join Anarchy. I could have waited for them to rally.

This is, however, a setback.

The Specials were worried about their families because they stupidly asked for help. We have laws in our world. Asking for help would have gotten them gelded if Zack had found out. These new recruits had never seen that kind of torture. It is not something one forgets.

"If our clients are free and unknown, you are in more danger," I point out. "But if the cops are after them, they are less likely to come for you. When you are home, uproot your family and run. This is our best plan."

Glass is unhappy with this and he curls his hands at his side. Would he challenge me? I trained him for his first year and gave him his name. He was fragile when he came to us. So timid and scared. But now, the name does not suit him. He is cocky despite his small stature. "Some of them weren't bad. My client...He...You don't have to turn him in."

A few are in agreement. I cannot blame them for this thought. Two clients of my own have treated me well over the years. At thirteen, I met Jasmine.

She was a fifty-year-old government official with tons of money and no husband or kids. She had six cats but was incredibly lonely. She was the first to ever buy me a birthday present. It was an Xbox, and with every visit, she brought me a new game and many clothes I never wore. Zack took everything.

But there is a problem with this thought. Our clients are not good people. They are pedophiles. They prey on the weak and devour us. No matter how friendly or pleasant their company was, they still took advantage of children. And they need to be punished for it.

"I will turn in all of them," I proudly say.

Mic steps to my side to have a better look at the faces that dislike this decision. I can see the calculation tallying in their eyes as they contemplate their next move. Can they disarm me? Can they win? Do I have the USB with me or in my room?

Three more shift to my side as the Specials split apart. I did not want this, but I don't know how to undo it. Five of them back up, separating, gaining distance to add more defense to their line. Glass does not take his eyes off mine. When they are far enough away, they turn and leave our area.

The seven left undecided or careless look to me for a decision. "I will negotiate with the police. I will protect your families. But your clients are not your friends. They paid Zack money to use you. No amount of kind treatment can erase that."

CHAPTER 24
Secrets

EMBER

INSTEAD OF SULKING ALONE in my room, I sit in the game room, hoping I could somehow be coerced into a better mood. But all the girls are chatting, so oblivious to the rage in my chest that I can't stand them. It's not their fault; it's Shakes' and his ridiculous control, but I'm bitter regardless.

I stare out the window, eyeing the horizon, wondering what it would be like to have the freedom to run. To go anywhere. I used to think running in the compound was freedom, and now I know I was more like a hamster on a spinning wheel, never really going anywhere, no matter how fast or hard I ran.

Where would I go? I haven't put much thought into it, having no clue about the difference in cities.

I once saw Greece and imagined what it would be like there, but now I know it's too far away.

Charles said I could go home with him. The thought only brings sadness. Do his parents know yet that he's dead? Will they ever learn? Or will they be stuck in limbo, searching every face that walks by whenever they are at a store?

Mary sits next to me and nudges me with her foot. I press a smile to my face, and the sadness is quickly dissolved by aggravation.

"How do you deal with him?" I spout at her.

She giggles, keeping her attention on the word search in her lap. "With grace and God."

Lisa, and her two sidekicks, Daisy and Blizzard join us, pulling up chairs or sitting on the floor. I pretend not to notice as Mary talks to them. I hate how I've started to like them. I'm not a girly girl. And they talk way more than I'm comfortable with, but they make me feel normal. I see myself in them sometimes, like I could be careful and loveable, if I didn't struggle with fear. They make me want to be prettier too. I haven't had the time or the sanity to care about my looks, but that isn't to say I wouldn't like to learn. I want to feel beautiful.

Lisa nudges me and slips a piece of paper into my hand. She keeps talking like nothing happened. As normal as I can, I look down at it. 'What's Shakes' plan?'

I'm relieved that despite how calm and docile everyone acts, they are just as paranoid as I am. I slip the pen out of Mary's fingers and quickly write back. *'We have to get out. Need Ideas. Twenty-four hours.'*

When she reads it, she nods and pockets the paper. She laughs at just the right moment as if she's been paying attention the whole time, while I'm the odd one, staring wide-eyed and wondering what I missed.

Daisy turns her attention to me. "So everyone wants to know," she begins with a weird grin. "What's it like dating a Special?" Interest perks in the girls around us. They look over their shoulders, quiet as they pretend they aren't listening to a private conversation.

"Ummm." I shift, pulling my legs tighter.

"Don't be nervous," Blizzard assures. "It's just us."

Like that means anything. Two days ago, they let a psychopath in my room to kill me because I betrayed their friend. Now they sit in front of me, ready to have gossip hour.

"Come on, details. I've heard some crazy things about Specials." Daisy glances toward the other girls. Mary bows her head to keep from being involved. "He seems so empty. Can't imagine him being a great conversationalist."

I defend, "He's more emotional than I am."

"Aww, that's so cute!" Blizzard whines. "She's blushing." The girls all 'aww' together, and my face worsens.

Why am I here? I should not be here. I attempt to get up, but Lisa presses down on my shoulder, "We're not done." She smiles brightly. She's lucky I don't have a knife.

A different girl comes toward our group. Heather, Blockade's girlfriend and the leader of the Boundary girls. Lisa and the girls share their annoyance with a glance at each other. "Think the real question here is why would you want to be with a Special? They're basically murdering prostitutes."

I stand to confront her. "Shut your mouth. He is not."

Mary claps her hands. "Okay, that's enough. Let's all go about our business. Shoo. Shoo." She grabs my arm, pulling me out of the room. My eyes don't drift from Heather's as she watches me with a smug little smirk. Mary drags me like a toddler heading to timeout.

Once the door to my room shuts, I turn on her. "You expect me just let someone bad mouth him and say nothing?"

"You want me to braid your hair?"

My anger pauses. "Huh?"

"Sit down. I'll braid it." She dashes into the bathroom to get my hairbrush and search for supplies while I stand in the middle of the room, ready for a fight and not receiving one.

Is this how she deals with Shakes? Am I being 'dealt' with?

I despise the thought, but she ushers me to the bed, and I don't fight it. With her fingers through my hair, my eyes close, and within seconds I'm calm as a kitten, enjoying the sensations. I wonder if I ever had a mother who did this. Her thin sleek fingers brushing against my temple. Her painted red lips kissing my forehead and she laughs as she rubs the smeared lipstick off my skin.

I stare ahead, seeing it and feeling it.

Resenting it.

"Shakes wanted me to talk to you about James," she admits softly. "But I really don't know what to say. He treats you wonderfully. He's completely enraptured by you."

A smile teases my lips. "He said he loved me."

She squeals. "Aww, I love that. Did you say it back?"

"Was I supposed to?"

Her eyes widen and she makes a weird face. "Yes! Unless you don't feel that way."

"I don't know," I admit. How am I supposed to know? I've known him for only a month. Isn't there a time limit for such things?

"Well, I think it's wonderful. You two fit each other."

"So why does Shakes not want me to be with him?"

She doesn't answer right away, but the silence only aggravates me. Shakes doesn't get to decide who I date. He can voice his opinion on the matter all he wants, but he better not be going on making orders or he'll learn just how petty I can be.

If Mary's going to respond, I don't let her. I don't want to know why Shakes doesn't like James. It shouldn't matter. "I was terrified of Tobias. When he touched me, I hated myself for it. But I couldn't always stop it. I began to think I'd know nothing but disgust." I stop myself from diving any further. Thinking about Tobias never brought me any peace. "But James erases everything. I feel safe and cherished. He gives me a choice and that means everything to me."

"I'm happy you found someone, Ember. You deserve to feel safe."

"But everyone seems to think I'm an idiot."

Mary sighs out. Her fingers never stop twisting my hair.

"Last night—" Sharing this makes me sick. "I watched him flirt with Grace. He got her distracted enough to get her phone. He was totally different. No longer this quiet, shy boy, but confident and eager. He manipulated her so well. And then it hit me, every time he spoke to her, he was setting it up. Making a path to when it came time to use her, she'd be easy." I twist, looking at her. "Is he doing that to me?"

Mary only greets me with a sadness on her brow. "I don't know."

"But what could he want from me? I've nothing to give." And then the answer comes out and I'm frozen. I can't say it out loud, it's too personal. But what if he wants sex? It seems to be what everyone else thinks about.

"Mary, what's a prostitute?"

Her brows knit, and she looks away, putting the hairbrush on the table. "I think–"

"Don't tell me to talk to James. He doesn't want to talk about it, and he asked me not to. Shakes won't tell me what Spread was about either. Please, just tell me."

Mary turns me back around and keeps her fingers twisting my braids. "A prostitute is someone who is paid to have sex."

Confusion slips over me.

Mary struggles as she whispers, "Zack took children to groom. For clients to take to bed."

I shake my head, not fully understanding. "But they're kids."

"Yes."

"No," I whisper, my heart pounding as I sink. The reveal is too much, overwhelming, and sickening, and I bury my face into the pillow. All the rumors that led to speculation now bombard me. I was stupid for believing someone couldn't do something so sick and twisted. I knew how terrible our world was, but Zack and his role in our society would prove that not only was Myers' world horrifying, but the *entire* world.

I hear James' words, moments where he slipped, and the realization is more than I can grasp. What has James gone through? How can he ever recover from something so revolting?

Mary leans on me. "Oh, baby girl. I'm sorry."

I can't speak, imagining a life like his and everything he was forced to do. I don't know how he stayed alive. I can't break out of the darkness, and I keep barreling downward. Tobias never raped me, but the fear of it consumed me so badly that I could barely function. Was James assaulted in such a manner? How can he walk around nearly normal, indifferent?

"This is one of the reasons why Shakes wants you to break things off with him. James is trying, Ember, he is, but we don't know how much Zack affected him. And I hope you understand Zack *has* affected him."

I rub the wetness from my face. My protectiveness is like a galloping white horse barreling through, unstoppable. "James is fine," I bite harsher than attended. "Shakes needs to keep his mouth shut."

"Ember—"

"I'll take care of James. I can help him."

"How? Honey, you need help, too. We all do. Who's gonna take care of you?"

She pisses me off. James is stronger than anyone here. He only listens to Shakes out of respect, but he could easily be a leader. James has made it through hell and come out better. There is nothing wrong with him. I don't know how he's managed to do it, but he really is okay.

A swift knock on the door, and it opens. "Hi, Ember." Doctor Yugi walks in with my nurse behind, shutting the door. "Can we talk in private?"

I don't let Mary leave, keeping her seated beside me. Doctor Yugi looks back at the nurse, and the woman takes out a medical film and sticks it up on a board, turning a light on. It's a picture of a brain. "So, as I told you, your cat scan was fine for the concussion. But—" She turns and circles a particular spot. It means nothing to me because it all looks odd. "This here is an old injury on your brain. Sarah spoke about this, and I wasn't too sure, but now I can't deny it. This section is specifically designed for your memory, which would explain why you don't remember anything."

So there was an accident. I don't know why it matters, but to know something terrible happened to me before this place doesn't sit well in my stomach. I fear remembering because what if the reason I can't remember is because the life I had before was worse?

"There's always a chance you'll regain your memory as your brain heals."

Mary leans in. "Perhaps stop getting hit in the head."

I giggle, slightly ashamed.

Doctor Yugi takes a deep breath. Her eyes sparkle as she attempts to hide her grin. "When we did a physical when you were first brought in, I noticed a couple scars that were older than the many you have now. Scars that were medically attended, meaning you had stitches at some point. We've been scanning the DNA database for you, but I couldn't narrow it down further because there are so many things we don't know about you. Instead,

I focused on people who were in a car accident this past year. It was really a shot in the dark. But-" she pauses. "We found you. We found your name."

CHAPTER 25
Allies

EMBER

"WE FOUND YOUR NAME."

The bed beneath me falls away, the world itself drops from existence, and I'm in a white room, and it's empty. In front of me, Myers stands, lighting my folder on fire, but that folder becomes me and my existence and everything I am, and I am a flame, running and screaming, and no one can hear me.

I have chased after my name more than I have pursued freedom or happiness. I have yearned for a name to replace the horribleness surrounding me. A name, I imagined, would protect me from Tobias. A name, I believed, would break the hell I stumbled into. A name, I hoped, would return my parents and restore my innocence.

Now, I see this unknown name as a thief. It will tell me who I am supposed to be, and it will destroy everything I have become. It will take me away from this family that I've created. It will deprive me of their care and their love. I will lose everything I have gained in the last few weeks since Shakes brought me into his world. I cannot give it up, not for a name, not for anything.

"Ember?" The doctor inquires, and the room zooms back into place.

"No."

"No, what?"

I snap to my feet, "Get out." I push her, shoving her into the nurse, "Get out."

"What?" She stumbles and twists, trying to explain, but I don't stop till she is out the door. Mary attempts to talk to me, but I push against her, and with all my weight, I lean against the door and lock it. My breath is heavy, and I can't figure out what to do. I want to run away from everything. I want to spring across school and get lost in the rat buildings.

I stand before the windows, looking off into the dark distance. It's completely black, and aside from the stars in the sky, there is no telling the earth from the heavens. I want to disappear into its vacancy. If I start running, they will never find me, and my name will never catch up to me.

I snatch my bag of clothes and open the drawer to the nightstand. Heaps of food I've stockpiled, and I hurriedly toss it in. My body's shaking. I'm afraid to go, but I'm afraid to stay. If I stay, they'll force someone's name upon me, and I won't be me anymore.

So I run.

One glance down the hall, Mary is talking to the doctor at the nurses' station. I slip against the wall, flinging to the other side, pressing the elevator button, and when it opens, I dive in, pressing my wristband against the security box and slapping the bottom floor. The dings and beeps alert Mary, but the doors close before she can reach me.

The exit to the recreation area is unlocked, and I'm out the door, and free. I can't believe it was so easy. I run as fast as I can, diving into the darkness. The pathway leads nearly two blocks backward. There are crickets singing, and the night is caving in. In school, there were no places like this. It is open and bare. Here, every tree is a hiding place. Every bush is a place to jump out and snag unsuspecting prey. My eyes can't be wide enough. It's scarier than home, and I find myself missing its simple demographic design.

My feet stall. The thin moon shines low in the sky, but it's just enough to expose the fence that separates me from escape. It is tall, nearly ten feet, and at its head are curvy spiky thorns. My fingers reach out, curling around its thin metal. I shake it softly at first and then with brutal strength, but it barely moves, sunk deep into the ground.

"Just like home," a voice whispers.

I am already in position to attack. I scan the ground, searching for a weapon, but the dark does not help. My fists are tight in front of me.

Noah steps out of the shadow of the trees, holding up a hand. In his other, a cigarette burns, and the smoke swirls in odd shapes as it floats into the air. He stands slouched, unafraid.

Noah holds the roach toward me, "Take a hit. Might help you. You are way too tense."

I twist my nose in disgust. He shrugs and takes a long inhale, holding his breath as he steps closer, limping slightly. He blows the thick smoke through the metal wire of the fence, and it swirls in the moonlight. "You shouldn't be out here," Noah says.

I haven't adjusted my position, and my fists are still ready to break any bone in his body. But I notice the bruising on his face that I didn't give him. "You get in a fight?"

He chuckles cheerlessly, shaking his head, toeing the grass. "I lost a fight to a girl my entire clan despises. Guys don't let things like that go."

"Your own clan is beating you up?"

Noah shrugs. "It's what they do." He notices my stance and scoffs. "I ain't gonna hurt you, girl. Think I could win if I wanted."

The fight between us is still hazy, and I struggle to remember. I could have sworn I won, though. I put a little more space between us before I relax. As a Coal member, he poses more of a threat to me than a normal kid. They aren't like everyone else. They are diluted in their thinking or brainwashed. Shakes gives everyone a chance, but not a Coal member. So why am I giving him a chance?

Noah glances down at my bag. "You trying to run away? Don't think you'll get very far. There's a roadblock north and south, and if you stay off the roads, well, the coyotes will get ya."

"How do you know that?"

"Mike's been messing around with that nurse who led you to us, you know, the one that got fired. He was a talker. We probably know more than your good pal, Shakes."

"I doubt that."

Noah doesn't say anything else, taking a last big inhale and holding it in for a long time. He flicks it outside the fence before he blows it out. The distance is further than either of us can get. I grab my bag and step away.

"Scream."

"My name isn't Scream."

He looks over his shoulder. "It's not Jennifer, is it?" He doesn't ask it like a question. He says it like a jab, and I hate that it stings.

"I go by Ember."

He nods, turning and leaning back against the fence. "Never thanked you for taking out Ash. He was a prick."

I'm surprised by the admittance, but relieved. I noticed Noah's dislike for Ash. At least, my instinct was right on that one. It reassures me, I'm missing something about our fight. And if I could think clearly, I'd find it.

"You got the wrong impression about Coal."

"Me? Or everyone?"

He shrugs. "We get what you're doing. We don't want kids to be sold at auction. Why do you think we stressed Clan recruitment? Every month, we supplied endorsements to Rain and Boundary so they could provide for new recruits. We kept Myers happy. That was our job so that our lives within the School didn't change." He looks around him, gesturing. "Do you see what we were afraid of? This! There are worse places than the school. We have no control here. We have no weapons. No money. No resources. We are ants marching to their beat. You destroyed the very thing keeping us safe."

At least someone has the gall to say it. I'm to blame for all of this.

"The kids that have 'gotten out'. Two of them were suicide. Ask your Special about that, and the other two were Coal Snatchers. And that mute, Kevin... Well, he had a secret, didn't he?"

My eyes widen.

Noah puts a finger to his lips as if saying it would provoke some higher power. "I don't know, maybe you're right. Maybe he is home. But I guess we will never know because we don't really exist here.

This is worse than the school. And I hope your boy is doing something. Because if we ever needed help, it's now."

I stare at his face, remembering how close he had been during our fight. I can see it, him leaning over me with a knife at my throat and everyone chanting.

"You could have killed me." There it is—what I've been wanting to tell Shakes.

Noah shrugged. "I was playing the crowd."

"No." I smile, knowing I'm right. "You were waiting."

"Don't smile like I'm a fucking saint," he growls, and I take a step back, bending my knees. "Yeah, I knew they were coming. I kill you, and then what? Your Special comes and mutilates half my clan? I'm getting out of here. This is not the end for me." Noah hands me a folded piece of paper. "Give this to your pal. I know he's talking to the other clans."

"Why should I? Coal has done nothing but bully us."

"You owe me, *Ember*. I saved your life. Clan decorum: an eye for an eye."

CHAPTER 26
Orders

JAMES

I STAND IN FRONT of Shakes with my hands behind my back. He sits with crossed arms on the gurney, listening to my report. It's as it should be. I am his soldier, willing to put my life in his hands. This is the life I am made for, and I cannot survive without it.

"Show me the USB."

I pull it out of my cast and lay it in the palm of my hand, holding it out for him.

His shaking fingers take a hold of it, analyzing it. "All that information is on this?" Computers have evolved since he has been in the world. He finds it hard to believe but I assure him. He shrugs, and instead of handing it back, he puts it in a zipped pocket in his shorts. The tension in my shoulders

319

tightens and a part of me wants it back, but I keep my mouth shut. I believe he understands how valuable it is, and I accept his decision to keep it.

"Glass, you said the kid's name is. Do we got to worry?"

"I think it needs our attention."

"Kill him," he says simply, but he watches me.

I stand stiff, and unresponsive. He knows what he's asking. If I kill someone, I will be removed from this hospital. I will be taken away from Dream, and there is no telling if I will ever find her again. It's exactly what he wants. He is against our relationship and he has taken no effort to hide it.

"Kill him and I'll trust you again."

It's an ultimatum, leaving me with little choice. It's impossible for me to choose between him and Dream. I cannot live without either. But the chance to get in Shakes' favor might not come again. I cannot risk losing it.

And Dream?

She will be in Shakes' care. I'll find her again. No matter where I am, I'll always find her.

"Yes, sir."

I spin on my foot, and the realization of what I've just agreed to hits me harder than I am prepared for. I make it through the door before my back hits the wall. There has rarely been a time when I've questioned the motives of my leaders. Zack was easy to understand and his aspirations drove his movements. As long as I performed as he needed, he never asked from me more than I was able to give. It wasn't until the last year in his service, after the Grounding, that his motives altered and confused me. It caused me to question, because he wasn't consistent. It is like being fed chicken every day. I don't question it. I eat it and I move on. But then a salad is in front of me. I cannot act like it is the same, even while I pretend it is the same. It's not. Something different has occurred and I have to figure out why I'm being fed something so strange.

Shakes moves in the same manner. His actions are typically for one purpose: escape. But this order he's given me is not for his plans. This order is spiteful. He's punishing me for stopping the Grounding. Or perhaps it's his protection of Dream. He's scared I'll hurt her. Either way, I'm sitting here questioning, when I should be obeying.

If I could talk to him, would he listen? I could claim I would protect her even from myself. I could explain how I know my faults. I am very self-aware of my limitations. I know what I can and cannot give. But he is biased. He believes he knows the kind of man I am. I cannot convince him otherwise with words. It would have to be by my actions. I'll gain his faith in me with how well I treat Dream.

But I can't, if I'm away from her.

Mary comes bursting into the hallway and I snap up straight. "Ember took off," she huffs out of breath. I follow her into Shakes' room and she repeats, "Ember took off out the back."

Aggravation is instantly on his brow, but he stays laid in bed. "What else is new?" His lack of panic elevates mine. It means he won't do anything to go to her aid. "I'm done worrying about her. I've got other shit to think about." I stand in front of the window, searching the recreational area. The moon isn't bright enough, but I swear I see her form by the gate.

"I'll go for her."

"No," Shakes says. "Go do what we talked about."

I stay unrelenting. He waits for me to disobey, even sits up, daring me to go against him. The movement shatters my defiance, and I instantly reply, "Yes, sir."

As I leave, I hear Mary, "They learned who she was, and you're not going to believe it."

• • • • • • • • • •

I return to my room, take a shower, and wait in jeans and a t-shirt and wet hair. Dream will come here, I have no doubt. And I'll say goodbye without her realizing it. She'd fight it if I explained to her what I needed to do so instead I'll wait till she falls asleep and then lock her in.

I had doubts before, but after learning who she is, I know my place is not at her side. She is meant for so much more than I can offer her. It is a shattering revelation that would ruin me, if I didn't know how to shut off my thoughts. I will not falter now. I have come too far.

It was never my intention to be an active role in Dream's life. I was always meant to watch from the outside looking in. In my dreams, I was not the one sitting on the couch with my hand in hers. I was in the shadow of the trees outside her house, constantly wishing she knew who I was.

It's ten minutes before there is a soft rap at the door, and I rush to it and whip it open. Dream is there with a sheepish smile. I yank her in, locking the door behind me. I don't speak, continuing my nighttime ritual. I am upset about her latest run, but fighting is not particularly something I want to do. She stays by the door, timid and small, holding her arms around herself like she is waiting for chastisement. I figure Shakes said all I wanted, and she's feeling guilty enough. One day she'll realize how much she means to people. She'll stop putting herself in danger. She'll love herself as I love her.

I slap off the light to the bathroom and pass her, going to the bed. I remove my shirt and pants, folding them neatly back into the drawer, and slip on cotton pajama pants instead. I sit on the bed, and I wait for her. She doesn't move.

"Where did you go?" I begin since she doesn't.

Her brows knit in question before aggravation rolls around her face. "You have spies on me?"

"Of course."

She scoffs. "You are just as bad as Shakes. I just went for a walk. I'm sorry, it won't happen again."

The apology is obviously fake. My muscles clench at her level of disrespect. I am not used to it, but it only means she is getting more comfortable in my presence to be who she is. It's a good thing, but as a person who spent countless hours speaking with proper form and diction, it cuts a nerve.

I decide to drop it. I don't know why she doesn't want to talk about the doctor finding her name. I don't understand why she ran. Her name is important to her. She's been searching for it since she realized she lost it. I'm missing something, but if she wanted to share more, she would have. "Let's go to bed." I lay down, leaving room on my left for her to lie with me. I snap off the light, leaving the TV to shine through the darkness. I'm withdrawing before it is necessary. If I pull away too quickly, she'll notice something's wrong. I have to act like nothing's change. Like I'm not leaving her in the middle of the night to kill someone, like I may never see her again, like I don't deserve a single glance.

Dream doesn't move from the doorway, and after a minute, I end up flicking on the light again and sitting up. "Was there something else?" Something scared her. She is keeping her distance for a reason. "Did someone hurt you?" Her head shakes, and the sudden panic recedes. "What happened?"

Dream struggles to speak, her eyes dancing on the floor. "I know about Zack."

Perhaps I should be shocked or taken aback, but I am neither. I knew she would find out. If not from someone else, then from me eventually. But it does not matter.

"Okay."

I wait for whatever she has to say. Will she break up with me? Will she be disgusted that I even touched her? Whatever it is, I know I can handle it. I'll be fine. It will be easier this way to leave.

"I'm sorry."

My brows knit. "For what?"

"I complain about myself all the time. I'm so inconsiderate. I've been selfish and terrible to you. I can't imagine what you've gone through, and here I am, acting like I'm the one who suffered. But you're the one in pain."

"Pain is subjective."

She growls. "Don't be annoying right now."

I smirk. I'd rather her anger than her pity. Though neither does anything for me, at least her temper is humorous. I want to move on. "Can we go to bed, please?" I turn and pull the cover back, hoping to entice her, but when I look over my shoulder, she has not come any closer. I sink on the bed with a sigh. "Anything else?"

"Why are you being so careless about it?"

"Because it doesn't matter. Zack is dead. I am here."

"But it does matter. What you've been through-"

"Will take me years to repair. I am aware. Would you rather I wallow?"

"I would like some human response."

"Perhaps I am less than."

"James-"

"Scream." Her first name comes out thoughtlessly. "This conversation is pointless. I thank you for your sympathy, but what I would rather do is never talk about it again."

Being dismissed is something Dream responds poorly to. She huffs and steps forward. "We can't *not* talk about it, especially after what I saw."

I wait for clarification, but she struggles with saying it.

"The way you talked to Grace-"

"Is irrelevant." Irritation sparks like a small piece of ash. I should have never allowed her to stay. "It was a mission."

"I was a mission."

"What is your point?" I ask sharply. "That I will fall in love with her?"

"That you use people."

My eyes widen at this sudden accusation. "Do I?"

"You were so meticulous. The way you flirted with her from day one."

"Flirting and having common manners–"

"There's a difference, and you know it. Stop acting like it wasn't on purpose. I know you, James." Then she stutters and shifts uncomfortably. "I'm getting to know you," she corrects.

In a mild attempt to see it from her point of view, I admit, "Yes. I knew Grace was attracted to me." I shift, finding myself uncomfortable. Flaws are not something that I like to face. "I was 'friendly,' I suppose to keep her on my side in case we needed to escape. But it was not mutual, if that is the problem. Otherwise, I fail to see why this bothers you."

"Are you using me?"

"For what?"

"Sex?"

An uncontrollable sound, much like a snicker, escapes me before I could catch it. I realize how rude it sounded, and her expression exposes that I've managed to hurt her feelings. If I could truly explain it to her without sounding like a douche bag or mentally unhinged, I would, but I do not want her to understand that part of me. I want to keep those secrets behind locked doors and bury them in the sea.

"I apologize. But if I am using you for anything, Dream, it is to selfishly escape the life I had. I want to enjoy this time with you, because I don't know how long it will be before it is taken away."

Tonight, it's going to be taken away tonight.

The distance between us hasn't gotten smaller. I don't know what she is looking for at this moment or how I can fix it. But I am incapable of giving anymore.

"What makes you think it will be?"

Zack never let me keep anything I loved.

"Just a theory."

"You and your theories."

When a soft smile stretches on her lips, I get to my feet and move closer. She doesn't step back or flinch. She trusts me, and that alone can heal what years of solitude never did. I touch the tip of her braid, admiring it. She could shave her head bald, and I'd still find her to be the most beautiful woman on the planet. I lean down and kiss her softly, barely touching her skin, and to my delight, she leans forward, wanting more. I kiss her harder and place my hand on the back of her neck to tilt her just enough for my tongue to grace her lips. I kiss her like I may never do so again.

Dream pulls back, slightly out of breath, and she looks up at me. "Not for sex, huh?"

My stomach aches at the thought. If I knew she wouldn't overreact, we would never leave the room. But no matter my desperation, I cannot take advantage of her. Taking from her and then leaving would be the worst thing in the world I could do.

"Is it so bad?" she wonders, her hands on my shoulders. "All I know is what I hear. Tobias used to touch–"

"No, Dream, don't compare anything to Tobias."

She shrugs. "I have nothing to go on otherwise." Her blue eyes lift up, a little mischief in their reflection. "Maybe you can help?"

This is a different side of her, one I'm happy to see, but it's strange. It's not like her. And I search her for the answer. She's redirecting. She doesn't want to talk about the fact the doctor found her name. It bothers her enough to make her want to escape. And what better way to escape than through physical relations?

Who's using who?

I am not upset by it. In fact, it derails some of my control. I think of kissing her again, touching her in places that I've been dying to explore. This will be my last chance to show her how much I love her. But I hope it shows in my restraint.

"Go lay down. I'll be right back." I watch her go to bed before I move out the door.

In the game room, a few guys hang out playing on the Xbox. They look at me in surprise. I rarely come out of my room and never come here. But I still have friends who chatter about the details of this hospital. Underneath the couch is a box full of DVDs, and when I pull it out, the boys chuckle and joke, but I ignore their banter. A few are missing already, and I scan the first layer, scanning the names before I pull a few out to read their descriptions. Most I have to put back before I find a decent one.

I return to the room, and Dream is curled up in bed, staring at me. I slip the DVD into the slot in the TV and take a seat on the windowsill.

"You're not going to lay with me?"

I point to the screen and lean back. I'm watching her. Her facial features. Her body language. She wants to learn about sex. Perhaps this will help cure her fears. Or make them worse. It's a gamble, but I don't know how else to explain it.

The movie is slow. It's about a couple stuck during a snowstorm, and eventually, they lose power, so only body heat will keep them alive. It is a mediocre film at best, and the scenes are obviously for a female-driven audience as it plays more on emotion and romance than physical need. But it is good for Dream to witness. She stares at it with wide eyes and speechlessness, never taking her attention off it for a moment. Only when the couple becomes more hands-on, she becomes uncomfortable, shifting, dropping her gaze, her cheeks red from embarrassment, but it doesn't stop her from glancing back at it. Moans fill the room, and I hit the mute button on the TV, easing her discomfort.

"Do you—" She snaps her head toward me as if she forgot I was there. I chuckle softly. "Do you have any questions?"

She continues to watch it and swallows, "Is that um.." She clears her throat. "Is that normal?"

"Typically." I would go on, but I do not want to overload her with details.

She shakes her head. "Tobias—"

"No," I finish her thought. "Nothing that Tobias did was right. But this. This is a mutual desire between two people. Sex. Lovemaking. It is quite different from what you experienced."

"It...It makes sense then." She darts her eyes at me but quickly looks away, "Why people talk about it."

"I guess."

"You've..." My brows knit, concerned where she is going with this. "You've done this... a lot, then?"

It's a dull spoon digging into my chest and ripping out my beating heart. I stand unfazed while I'm falling into a deep, endless hole. I never thought I would feel shame. But I swallow, and the emotion is a thick wad that won't go down. I clench my teeth and force out, "No. I've never done that."

"But–"

I walk away, slamming the door to the bathroom, hiding. My back hits the wall, and I struggle to stay on my feet. My reflection is in front of me, showing every uncaged emotion on my face, and I despise it. I want to destroy it.

A soft knock on the door and Dream whispers, "I'm sorry. Can you talk to me, please?"

What kind of person does she think I am? I want to know, when she looks at me, what does she see? Does she see a Special? An escort? A fucking prostitute?

I know who I am. I will not wallow in my past, in my future, or in my present. I will take each step forward without regret because I have made it through the fire.

But it matters what she thinks. Does she see a person who has overcome hell? Or will she pin the labels upon me like everyone else?

I open the door, keeping my back against the wall, and stare at the ceiling. Dream leans against the doorway and observes me. Can she tell I'm teetering on the edge of sanity? That if she were to question or comment about my lifestyle, I'll crumble?

"I said something wrong," she whispers. "But I don't know what."

I shake my head. "It's fine."

"It's not fine." She takes a step forward but changes her mind, sticking to the door frame. "Will you tell me, please?"

I look at her, and she stands there with her arms crossed, looking at me with a face full of sympathy, like I'm some hurt dog she doesn't know how to treat. I don't want her to understand. I don't want her questions. I have no intention of telling her anything about my life with Zack. I thought I could, if only in bits and pieces, but now I know I can't even do that.

"Why did you run?" I change the subject, having nothing else to say.

Dream nods, accepting my decision to change the subject. "They found my name," she murmurs. "But I like who I am now. What if...What if it changes everything? What if who I am now isn't who I'm supposed to be? What if I can never be that girl again?"

I understand her reasoning too well. We are all different now, covered in slime that can't be washed away. But Dream is still new. She can recover with therapy and rejoin society like this never happened.

Once more, I'm faced with an example of why she and I shouldn't be together. What kind of life could I give her outside of this screwed up world?

I approach her, my hands on her arms. "A name doesn't change you."

Her brows knit, tears building in her eyes. "Yes, it does. As Scream, I was a scared girl—"

"No, you were the girl who blew up a school. You refused to follow Tobias, lived on your own, and defied every rule he put before you. But the names weren't what made you that way. Even without a name, you'd still be you."

She shakes her head. "No. Without my name, I wouldn't be here. Don't you see? Even if I was never supposed to be Jennifer, that name's a part of me, too. It's because of these names that you are here. That I have a family. And I'm thankful. I am. Now, what if this name takes you away?"

I wrap her back in my arms, burying my fingers in her soft hair. "Nothing will take me away. Nothing."

I hold her. With every kiss, she melts into me. Her fears are forgotten and she concentrates only on us. Her want is a fire and it could consume me if I let it, but I pull back, bringing her to the bed.

I wait for her to fall asleep, staring at the ceiling. When there is a knock at the door, I don't get up to answer it. Nor the numerous times after that. I stay.

I know what I'm choosing. For some reason it comes with no guilt. With no hesitation.

I'm choosing a dream.

And praying reality doesn't notice.

CHAPTER 27
Left Field

SHAKES

FROM THE FIRST LETTER until the last, I wasn't sure if I could trust it. The clan leaders wanted to meet. It would be the first congregation since Carbon, Memory, Tobias, Star, Hail, and I formulated the clans and set about Myers' destruction. The anxiety of it all is overwhelming, and I can't sleep. Mary felt none of my anxiousness simply because I didn't tell her. She sleeps quietly in her bed, and I find myself watching her in an attempt to ease the stress.

Not many pleasant memories surface when I think of the school, but I yearn for it regardless. In that world, I made friends that would alter my brain chemistry. They became a part of me, like the sun or the air.

And I lost them all, one right after the other.

It makes no difference to me that Memory is somewhere here in this building. She died the day she left. Seeing her again was like seeing a zombie. I'm obligated to kill her if only to give her real self peace.

It wasn't that Memory betrayed me that ruined me. It was afterward I had to watch each of my family members die. Hail fighting for Ember's safety. Star threw herself off the roof because she had given up hope. Tobias sacrifices himself to revitalize the spirit of the rebellion and bring us our victory. Carbon, dying in my arms.

And Memory suffered nothing. She was free and living happily.

I stare at every note spread out on my bed. Ember had brought me Noah's message, and then we got into another argument. Ember still hasn't gotten it into her thick skull that her survival is important to me, but she keeps putting herself in danger without any care for anyone else. She continues to act like she is alone. Needless to say, she ran off. Can't say she isn't good at running.

After much deliberation, I have decided to meet them. Brick and Vapor will be with me, but James and Ember have yet to respond to my impatient requests. I will have to do it without them. As much as it irritates me, they are now in a relationship. I've seen it too often and understand it. I still have that need to be alone with Mary. But now isn't the time for love.

I remove the gun from the nightstand and tuck it behind my back, fixing my shirt. I write a scribbled note and lay it near Mary's hand. She knows how to read my chicken scratch. When I kiss her temple, she shifts, and her eyes flutter open. I kneel down, "It's alright, go back to sleep."

She moans tiredly, her eyes shutting while my fingers play with her velvet brown hair. Even angry, I admire her. She manages to get under my skin, and I hate how I let her. She is so sweet and kind to everyone else, but I get the brunt of her brutality, and I know why. She calls it tough love. That I need an ass-kicking because too many people are 'ass-kissing'. It's probably why I'm infatuated with her. She knows how to push the right buttons.

I'm coming to the idea that maybe I'm holding a grudge. I don't know Memory's story. Maybe there was a valid reason she did what she did. It was always so hard for me to understand how, at the very last minute, she betrayed us. It never made any sense. She was not a malicious person. The first time she killed someone, she threw up and cried for days.

But that's where I get tangled up in my resentment. Whatever the reason, could it justify the death of a hundred and sixty people? Or justify shooting me? Leaving me? Would it make everything instantly better? The answer to that is no. It wouldn't. So why should I listen to it?

Mary opens her eyes. "How come..." she begins slowly. "You never told me you kissed Memory?"

It's a question out of left field, and at first, I struggle with the memory. I almost deny it until it hits me. With confusion on my brow, I rest my arms on the bed, getting close to her face. "That was a really long time ago, babe. Years. What made you think about it?" Her silence makes me continue. She actually wants me to answer such a ridiculous question. "It didn't mean anything. W e..um...We were patrolling, I think, and a Snatcher chased us. We almost got caught, and we dived into our hideout at the last moment. I was fifteen, and she was a girl." I shrug. "That was enough for me at the time."

"I saw it."

I had always wondered if she had. When the light switched on, and Mary was standing in the doorway, my stomach filled with dread. But then she smiled and asked us where we were.

"We had just started dating."

"Why didn't we talk about this then?"

"Because you never brought it up."

"I honestly didn't think about it again. Why are you thinking about it now?"

"Because I think you love her."

Tears build in her eyes, I realize this is a real thing to her. I'm speechless. I've already asked her to marry me. What else does she need to understand how much I feel for her?

She sits up, holding her legs in for comfort. "She was your first kiss."

I roll my eyes, standing up. "I guess, but that doesn't really mean anything to guys."

"You idealized Memory. I used to have nightmares about it and stress about it. I waited for you to leave me for her. Even when she was with Tobias. She was funny and beautiful—"

"So are you—"

"And you two were always together planning your war, and I was in the background having nothing to participate—"

"You're blowing this out of proportion."

With a voice full of conviction, Mary says, "From the moment I saw her again, I've been counting down the hours. You are going to leave me for her."

I can't remember when I've been disappointed like this. I almost want to lie and hurt her because that's how it works in our world. An eye for an eye. But I love her and can't intentionally inflict pain, even when it's right on the tip of my tongue.

"Has everything I've done, everything I've said, meant nothing up until now? I mean, God, Mary, how can you say this to me?"

She hangs her head. "She and I are complete opposites. How could you kiss her but like me? It didn't make any sense."

"I don't just like you, Mary. I'm in love with you, so let's be clear on that. And this was years ago when I was a fifteen-year-old boy. She was a girl, and it just happened, and it never happened again afterward. And are you forgetting she shot me?"

"No."

"I just don't understand you right now. You haven't been this insecure in years. What do you need me to say? You know how I—" A knock on the door interrupts, and I clench my teeth, frustrated. There is always someone or something interrupting us. "We'll talk when I get back."

"Where are you going?"

"It's not to cheat on you, so don't worry about it."

She huffs. "Oh, I'm gonna sock you one of these days, honey."

I smirk, looking back as I open the door. "That will be really hot." She flings a pillow, and I cackle, shutting it behind me.

Brick and Vapor are antsy about my late arrival. Vapor's out of the wheelchair and leaning on crutches. I check to ensure they have weapons before we head downstairs. Brick picks Vapor up and I hold on to the crutches. The tension is displaced with humor as Vapor wiggles, fighting against the baby hold. We all nearly fell down the stairs in our laughter.

We walk the long hallway toward the game room on the fifth floor. It doesn't have a camera that we know of. Nervousness twists in my gut. I could be walking into a trap. I don't know if I'll be alive by the time this is over. Am I ready to die? I stopped being afraid of death a long time ago, but for some reason, I'm hesitant. I should have told Mary I loved her. I can't die knowing she has doubts. But how much proof does she need? I want to marry her. I can't fight her self-esteem. That's something she has to work on by herself. I don't care about her weight, but I know that's where this sudden uneasiness stems from. All these girls around her are anorexic and fit, but it doesn't instantly make them attractive. I never had feelings for Memory deeper than a brother for a sister. She had the ability to make me feel like an idiot. That's not exactly something I find desirable in a girlfriend.

The closer I get to this den of enemies, the more my hands shake. I resent its foul disease more than I have ever. I don't want anyone to mistake it for fear or weakness. Especially in front of the people I am about to face.

I take a deep breath and enter the game room.

CHAPTER 28
Meeting

SHAKES

COAL, RAIN, AND BOUNDARY in one room together. The three selected clans that became the largest inside the school. We never intended for the clans to get as big as they did. But then again, we didn't have control over how many kids would get abducted every month.

The leaders of Coal, Noah, and Peat, stand in the opposite entrance, and our eyes meet. Instinct kicks in, and my hand slips around and grips the base of my gun, but Brick is quick to touch my wrist, whispering into my ear. I clench my teeth and let it go.

Rain consists of Light and Snow. Light is taking the lead as per my request. I will not speak to Lisa anymore after she failed to uphold our bargain. She is lucky I haven't killed her.

In Boundary, Blockade, Dave, and Plank sit at a round table, appearing the least concerned about our tedious meeting. They are tired and have a hard time hiding their yawns.

Blink is in the center. She was a Sky member at one point, also a Snatcher and leader of my assassination team. I submitted her as a neutral party and mediator, and if only to please me, they accepted this. She will, however, act as a shield for me if this turns south.

Brick shuts the doors behind us, and Peat shuts the doors on his side. Now we are locked in, like a cage match. Being the only one with a gun, I like my odds.

"Let's take a seat," Blink instructs, pointing to the chairs provided. She keeps her eyes on Coal. They are the only real threat among this lot. I twist the chair around, bringing the back against my chest as I sit. I observe Noah. I haven't met the new co-leader of Coal. But I know he's the one who sent Cola after Ember and then challenged Ember to a knife fight when Cola failed to kill her. But he's also the one who wrote to me. He has bruises on his face, a swollen lip, and his knuckles are wrapped in bloody gauze. I can only assume losing had not brought pride to his clan. But the fact that he remains a co-leader demonstrates his fighting skill. How, then, had he lost to Ember? She is a good fighter and quick on her feet, but knife fighting isn't her style.

"Who wants to start?"

Noah is quick to answer. "What are you going to do to get us out of this mess you've put us in?"

"Excuse me?"

"Don't act like you did us any favors. We ain't gonna give you a fucking round of applause here."

I swing the chair out from under me. "I don't want a thing from you or your clan.

Lisa pleads. "Can we talk without the animosity for once?"

Noah sits back in his chair, holding up a hand. Was that an apology? I retake my seat, my leg bouncing, and I chew the inside of my lip, trying not to take my gun out and shoot him between his bruised eyes.

Blockade looks much like his name. He's black, short, and stout and probably weighs about 200 pounds. Once he sets his feet, he can't be knocked down. It's funny to watch new rats attempt to fight him. "What I think dickhead here is trying to say is we're screwed. These doctors and nurses know shit, and that guy Jose doesn't seem to be in a rush to get us home. We're trapped here, and we have ninety percent less freedom than we did at school. We got no weapons. No information coming in or going out. No one knows we're here any more than they did before. At least with Myers, we could protect ourselves, protect our clans. But here, we are separated from each other, and I don't like my girlfriend in the same damn ward as the Coal bitches. So we need answers. What are we doing here?"

Everyone rests their eyes on me. I'm used to it. Everyone always expects an answer. It's why I'm always searching for one. I have to have it, or my credibility is shot, and I won't be much use to anyone.

I'm trying to decide if I should share my information. What will happen if I do? What chaos will ensue? I've rarely relied on the clans for obvious reasons. They are loyal to themselves. I've relied on my family, and we've done just fine. But it's getting harder to do with just us. I don't have the resources

I used to, and contacting everyone who helped in Anarchy is impossible. But if we manage to work together, there will be many benefits.

So, against my better judgment, I share. "Jose is finishing the last touches to the hospital, and then we are all going to be locked in our rooms. Sold off individually."

There is a collective curse around the room while they speak amongst themselves. I give them time. I'm not going to reveal Memory. She's not anyone else's kill but mine. And who knows, they might choose to protect her, considering she fulfilled her promise despite betraying them.

"Jose's making a list." I break into their conversation. "Of kids to take first." I look expectantly at Coal. "That is harmful to his new society."

The two of them become alarmed and on their feet. "Wait, us?" Noah steps forward, and the three of us get on our feet, preparing for an attack. "You help make that list? Bet you got every Coal member on there, fucking prick."

"It is not my list. But hell yeah, I would."

He whips out his knife, and I respond by holding out my gun. They gasp in surprise when they see my weapon. I am perhaps the only one in this entire building that smuggled a gun inside. I only have one bullet left, but any bullet used on a Coal member is worth it.

Noah doesn't move, keeping his knuckles gripped, but he's not as confident as he was. I step forward, boldly, daringly, unafraid of his blade. Blink is beside us, keeping her eyes on Noah for any sudden movement. She tries to interrupt, but I don't hear her. "My girlfriend and every single member of my family is on that list for doing everything they possibly could to take Myers and your selfish ass clan down." I step back, addressing the room. "I'm getting my family out of here. If you want to tag along, I don't care. But you'll obey my orders and the orders of my family. That includes Ember. If any of you attempt to harm her, or" I look expectantly at Light since he's the representative from Rain, "fail in protecting one of my own, there will be no second chances." I turn to Coal. "We'll start new. A clean slate. Can you manage it?"

Noah looks to Peat. "We ain't got a choice."

Peat spits tobacco into a plastic cup. "The others aren't going to follow this. The Snatchers are already forming their own group. We'll be killed by our own before the end of the day."

Noah chews on his thumb and glances toward me. "Help me remove this ban on my clan, and I'll be able to make this happen."

"Tsk. No way. You threatened my girlfriend, and you gave Ember a concussion."

"My girl's dead. You're lucky I didn't string your girl up from the roof."

"Your girl is dead because she was dumb."

Noah slams his fist in my cheek, and Brick yanks me back only to swing his own fist, but Noah has his arms up covering his face, and Peat nails his fist right in Brick's rib. I push around Brick and kick Peat in the stomach, and he falls against the wall.

Light comes out of nowhere, punching Noah across the jaw, and he flings off his feet and lands sideways into the double doors. He shoves Brick backward, and the giant bumps into me. I stumble in a vain effort to keep him from falling. "Enough." Light barks. "We are in this together. We can't fight like this anymore, or it will take another five years to get out. I'm not turning eighteen in this prison. You all may like this petty crap, but I'm sick of it. There will be no more revenge killings. Or clan beatings or rape or murder. Enough is enough."

"How do you expect to make that work?" Peat holds his stomach and kneels beside Noah. Noah keeps to the floor; his nose is bleeding and he puts pressure against it, but there is too much pain, and his eyes water.

"If we are one, we are strong. No more clans. We become united. Us vs. them. The way it should have always been."

"And who leads this united front? You?"

I step out to the center of the room. "That's the way it was once. Carbon, Star, Nail, Memory, Hail, and myself. We ruled equally, and it worked well."

"What changed?"

"We were young and stupid. But if we had managed to stay together, we would have gotten out years ago."

We all look at each other, deciding what to do, who would be best to lead this united clan, a mass of six hundred. Brick calls out, "I vote for Shakes. If my vote counts."

With a round of approval, it's a swift unanimous vote. "Alright." I take a breath. "Who else?"

"You'll need one from Coal." Noah gets to his feet. "If you want any hope of them following you."

"Then you'll have to do."

Behind me, Plank speaks up on behalf of Blockade, and he joins our growing squad. Light gets nominated, and the vote passes quickly.

"Is that it? The four of us?"

Blink scoffs. "All men? I don't think so. I vote for myself."

I struggle to hide a smile. Her feminist attitude is what got her on my assassination squad, but her skills are what made her the leader. I second the vote, and no one objects.

"Alright, the five of us. Let's spread the word, we attack at breakfast—Together. We can't wait any longer. It will be messy and complete chaos, but it will be unexpected. We take their guns, and we take over this hospital."

"Yeah. Perfect." Noah waves a hand. "Except Coal's still grounded."

I smirk. "Two cops stand in your way. You're telling me you can't get rid of them?"

Slightly embarrassed by my insinuation, he curls his lip and spins around. "Let's go before they hug."

Peat looks over his shoulder with a smirk. "Tell Scream we said Hi."

Noah shoves him out of the room, and he glances back, again apologetic-like, before walking out the door.

I can't figure that guy out. He shouldn't have lost against Ember. He's the type that can take a hit and keep going. It's apparent his pain level is commendable. I've had my nose broken a couple times before, and I've never been able to be quiet about it.

Vapor pops over to Light, slapping his hands, excited for his promotion more than Light is. His cheeks are red, and shame diminishes the confidence in his shoulders. Lisa won't like being pushed out, but it gives me a small taste of vengeance. It's not wholly satisfying, but I'll take what I can get. Boundary passes me by, and Brick and Blockade knock elbows in greeting, talking.

It's a rare moment I'm out of place. Usually, I am the center of attention simply because I am a symbol to the masses, a mascot to their hopes, but as for friends, I don't have that many. All of the people I connected with over the years have either been auctioned off or are dead. Since the Grounding a year ago, I've made no further attempt at those fleeting connections. Ember is perhaps the last person I've befriended, and that was simply because of who we thought she was. Before her, it was James on the day Ember arrived when I stopped him from taking her.

Thinking about Ember brings guilt. More of Mary's doing, I'm sure. I can't have both women important in my life mad at me. Mary might take a little longer to fix. But I can make things right with Ember. She's arguing with me because she thinks she's blame for our current situation and all I have to do is tell her I don't.

But the problem is there is a small part of me that does blame her. It's so very little that it shouldn't even count, but I know she'll see it if I try to lie and it will hurt her and do damage.

What she'll fail to take into account is what she's done for me, far outweighs the blame. Ember has fulfilled every dream. And even now, stuck here, I know somehow, she's going to help get us out. She's what Memory was supposed to be. She's my hope, and I've put all my faith in her.

It's why I get so pissed when she puts herself in danger.

I should tell her this, make her understand that I could never hate her.

The intercom instructs the female populace down to the recreation quad, and I jog to get to James' door. If he did what I ordered him to do, I'll take him back into the family. But I don't know if I'll ever be good with him dating Ember. Especially now that I know who she is. James doesn't belong with someone like her. He'll only weigh her down.

The guard at the door changed out, and I look a little uncertain at him before I knock, calling for James and Ember. He seems a bit young to be a Special, but Zack had weird qualifications.

James opens it to my disappointment. I'd hope he'd be gone already. "Is it done?"

The barrel of a gun presses against my temple.

Chapter 29
Threat

EMBER

SHAKES STANDS RIGID WITH a gun pressed against his head. The person holding it is clearly a Special. His clothes are ironed. His hair is flat, parted, thick with gel. He's stiff, like a gun handle, hard and full of power.

James steps backward, a hand behind him reaching out for me, and I take it desperately. Despite how well I can fight, I'm no match against a Special. I've seen James fight too often to have any confidence of victory.

The boy pushes Shakes forward till he can close the door behind him.

"Glass," James introduces him. "What are you doing?"

"Once the hall is clear-" the Special instructs, "-you three will follow me down to the first floor."

I meet Shakes' gaze. He is subtle in his movement, telling me to wait, to remain calm. But my instincts are telling me to run.

"Is this the route you choose for a client, Glass?" James asks.

"Boss agrees that the three of you are the most dangerous to her future."

Her? Shakes and James notice the reference. Does it make any sense to them?

James boldly asks, "And if we do not go quietly?"

"Then I will have no choice." He cocks the gun, pressing it harshly into Shakes' temple, making me flinch. Shakes clenches his teeth, keeping his shaking hands at his side.

James grips my arm. "We'll follow you. Don't do anything you can't take back."

"Ember," Shakes whispers. "We're gonna listen, and we're gonna be fine, okay?"

I nod dumbly, panicked, fighting tears. He knows how stupid I can be, how reckless. He knows me so well, and all I do is annoy him. All these stupid fights we've been having mean nothing. I don't want to lose him, but I'm pushing him away because I know all I do is cause him trouble. I don't want him to care about me, but I also don't want to be without him. Why am I so stubborn? Why can't I just listen to him without being a bitch about everything?

"Zack always talked about you," Glass says with bitterness on his tongue. "You were his favorite."

"Because I made him money."

"He loved you."

James scoffs. "That wasn't love. You're young, Glass. You have all the time in the world to fix what he broke inside you."

"I was gonna be better than you. I was gonna get everything you had and more."

"I had nothing."

"Why did I look up to you? How could you betray him?"

James can't stand it. "He betrayed us. By promising us a life and then destroying everything we were. He deserved what he got. Killing him was the best thing I ever did."

Glass swings the gun on James, and we both step back. I grip James' shirt, begging him to be silent and not make things worse.

Glass grounds through his teeth. "I worked so fucking hard to erase my parents. My sisters. My life before he took me. I can't go back. So what am I supposed to do? With all that I've done, what am I supposed to do?"

James lowers his hands to his side. "I can't answer that."

Shakes slams his elbow into Glass' chin and reaches for the gun. But Glass recovers faster than any of us could have thought and smashes his fist into Shakes' stomach. Shakes drops to his knees, holding his ribs, panting. Glass puts a hand on Shakes' shoulder and presses gun to the back of his head. "Anything like that again, and I'll kill you."

James quickly assures, "We aren't going to do that again. Right, Shakes?"

Shakes readily agrees.

"Take your finger off the trigger," James warns.

"Fuck you." Glass moves for the door, keeping the barrel on us as he pokes his head out. I flinch, seeing an opening, but both James and Shakes flinch to stop me. I have to follow them. They know better than I do what a Special is capable of. His emotional distress only makes him twenty times more dangerous. My heart's pumping as I struggle to stay calm. I don't know how to get out of this without one of us getting hurt. "Let's go." Glass pushes the door open, and with his eyes trained on every moment, he directs us out of the room and down the hall. We hope for someone to spot us, but it's annoyingly empty. I could call for help, but I'd die before finishing.

"Where's Mic?"

"Dead," Glass replies.

The information does nothing to James. He doesn't flinch or react, his hand keeping tight around my fingers as if to keep me from escaping. We pass the nurse's stand, and Grace sits there at the computer. She pretends not to see us. I don't know if it's because she's a part of this or because she learned James stole her phone, but it doesn't matter. If she had only glanced up once, she would have seen the fear in my eyes and perhaps helped, but she didn't, and we passed by, our last line for help gone before we were through the doorway for the stairs.

The first floor is a little trickier. There are strangers walking around that I've never seen before. They were odd clothes: black leather, chains, and most are covered with tattoos. Glass doesn't need to hide his gun and any hope for a savior drifts away. One main thing sticks out. They have the same tattoo, a spider web on the back of their hand, like a weird cult.

"Do you see it?" Shakes whispers.

"Yeah," James replies. He looks down at me and attempts a soft, assuring smile, but all it does is stress me out.

We enter a small room with a table and two chairs. It's cold, and I lean into James, hoping for his warmth. He holds onto me as we stand, facing the door where Glass remains. He shuts it on us, and we are alone.

A minute passes, and nothing happens.

I rush to Shakes' arms, and he wraps me up, clenching tight. "I'm sorry, I'm sorry. I'll listen to you. I swear."

He chuckles, clenching my hair. "I'm sorry, too." He kisses my temple and holds me tight to him. "I don't hate you, Ember. You are everything I wanted Memory to be. I just wish you had talked to me beforehand." Feeling him laugh makes me giggle. It's awful, though. We're laughing in the middle of a frightful situation. Our trauma is showing.

Shakes grips my arm. "Don't do anything unless James or I tell you, okay? He's a Special. Neither me nor you can handle him." I nod, rubbing the silly wetness from my cheek. I can't hold him tight enough. I fear something terrible will happen, and I don't want him out of my arms.

I sigh against his shoulder. "What are we going to do?"

James leans against the table. "We will find an opening and take it. Pay attention to us. When there is an out, be on our heels."

Their confidence calms me. They don't appear scared at all. I shouldn't be either. So many things have gone wrong these few short days that I should be immune to fear.

The door opens, and Glass returns with his gun pointed at us. "Against the wall," he orders.

Shakes guides me over, and James latches onto my arm. I can't help but feel the most protected out of all my other situations. Having my best friend on one side and my boyfriend on the other, I could believe nothing terrible could happen to me.

And yet, the sound of chains is loud, and they drop on the table, jolting my nerves. I stare at them wide-eyed as Tobias's voice echoes in my ear.

"Scream. That's all you have to do. Just scream."

Chapter 30
Faith

Ember

I STARE AT THE chains on the table, but in my mind, I can see them hanging from the rafter. I smell the dank basement in Tobias' house. I feel the cold stone floor against my legs while my head rests on a lumpy mattress. My body is limp, and the burning on my back keeps me from trying to move. I'd rather sleep or die. It doesn't matter which.

"She's not gonna help anyone," Tobias bragged, *standing above me.*

"How do you know?" Myers asked, studying me from beside him.

"She doesn't remember."

"Are you sure?"

"*I'll make sure she never does.*" Tobias touched my forehead, making me shiver. "*Shhh,*" he mocked.

"*It would be easier just to get rid of her.*"

"*True.*" A different voice sounded from the stairs. It's a woman. "*But where's the fun in that?*" Her heels clicked against the ground, getting closer till she was at my head. I twisted just enough to reveal her shadow. "*Take care of her, Tobias. She's special.*"

Myers chuckled. "*You're playing a risky game. The rebellion came too close last time.*"

"*Can't have a good show without some thrill. It's why I'm letting her in. Besides, you've told me the rebellion is dead. Or did you lie?*"

"*No-no,*" he stuttered. "*No, I took care of it.*"

"*Good. Then, all she will do is cause a little excitement. If she stirs up too much trouble, sell her. Just remember, you are the one trying to start a new system. I must find all the cracks before I think about instituting the idea with the other schools. Think of this as a test drive.*"

"*Four years of tests. I think I've proven my experiment is working.*"

"I said, we'll see." Her heels ring sharp against my ear, like a high-pitched bell. It calls to me, and I whimper, trying to find her, a pathetic hope that she'll help me. But I only see her sharp pink heels. *"Don't hurt her too much, Tobias. She's going to sell for a large sum by the time she's ready."*

The tap, tap, tap of heels clicking against the ground freezes me where I stand. My breath is ragged, waiting. Every second, I'm slipping further into quicksand. I don't try to escape it. I'm not dumb enough to attempt.

A woman enters the doorway. She's beautiful with long red hair and sharp green eyes. She smiles wide, her white teeth almost as pale as her skin. She wears a dark black dress that goes down to her knees, wrapped tight around her form. But it's her heels that keep my attention. They are bright bubblegum pink.

"Scream."

Any hope that this woman could help us dissolves, and I stiffen myself, preparing for her threats.

But then she starts clapping. "What an amazing end! You really brought my whole show to a standstill."

"Who are you?" James asks.

Her gaze flickers to him, her smile never fading. "We've met."

"No," James replies. "I'd remember."

"Hm." She stares a little longer. "My name is Faith."

I snap my head to Shakes. Memory mentioned a woman by the name of Faith.

"I am the leader of the G.O.D.S. and owner of the schools," she proudly exposes, full of cockiness. And she nods at James. "You understand now."

Part of me wants to punch her in the face, but I'm terrified and can't move. If she could own the school, then she's capable of evil I can't possibly fathom.

"I can't thank you enough, Scream, for stopping Shakes. It would have been a bloodbath, and I would have lost so much money but instead, only a few casualties, and you all got on the bus with no hesitation. It's why I like working with kids. They're so easy to manipulate."

My inner walls cave in. Everything she said is rolling around inside of me. I can barely feel the ground beneath me.

Faith steps around the table, her heels taping against the white vinyl floor. The boy, Glass, lingers against the wall. He keeps his hands tight behind his back, but his eyes are on James. He may believe I'm not a threat, but unpredictability can be seen as a weapon, too.

If I could stop being afraid to actually move.

Faith sways in front of Shakes. They are nearly the same height, but her heels give her just an inch more. She eyes him like he's dessert. "My prized stallion. You made this experiment so entertaining."

"Fuck you."

She giggles and nudges her head to the side. "Don't lose your temper now. Those chains are for you."

I look over at the table. It's only one set. Does she think I'm gonna stand here and do nothing? She must not have been watching her own show.

Faith reaches up to play with a strand of his Mohawk. "One of my best friends has been waiting to get hold of you. He thinks he knows exactly how to break you. I hope you don't disappoint."

Shakes snatches her wrist and grips it hard till his knuckles turn white. It makes Glass move, but she stops him. There's an odd excitement to her. She runs her gaze over his face, eager to feel the pain he causes. "Show me," she dares in a whisper. "Show me the evil I'd love to taste."

Shakes sneers in disgust and shoves her hand away. "Aren't you fifty?"

Faith's smile stretches.

I know Shakes thinks about punching her, doing something violent and terrible, but he keeps his hands fisted at his side. Nothing he can do can get us out of this, not with Glass at the door. But there are three of us and only two of them. Shouldn't this fight be in our favor? Why are we doing nothing?

Faith shifts her attention to James, moving just slightly to stand in front of him. He's taller, and he watches her from down his nose.

"I have the perfect spot for you, Special. Even one-handed, I'm sure you can find ways to fulfill your duties." She winks at him, and it breaks me.

I latch onto the chain, more than daring to swing and see how much damage I can do. Even with

Glass' gun on me, I don't fear it as much as her. I swing, but she snags it, letting it curl around her arm, bruising her skin. She pulls, bringing me toward her, twisting me until her hand wraps around my neck and her breath is at my ear.

"I know what a fighter you are." She clenches, her nails digging into my throat, making breathing difficult. "It's why I decided to take you home with me, Scream. We're gonna be best friends."

With grit teeth, I reply, "No, thanks. I prefer friends that aren't three times my age."

A gunshot goes off. It's like a bomb right next to my ear, and I fall to the ground. I'm holding my head, looking around. Shakes holds his shoulder, blood slipping between his fingers. A gun is on the floor between his feet, but Faith snags it before I can. She backs away, dropping the chain back on the table. She checks the mag. "One bullet. That's all you got?" The crisp sound of the cock of a gun is her reply before she rests it on the table.

Shakes knells on the floor with blood dripping through his fingertips. I take off my flannel, ball it up, and press it into his wound. He doesn't look at me; his attention and rage are one hundred percent on the woman behind us.

"You have been so interesting to watch," she says, sitting in a chair and crossing her legs. "But I can't afford to humor it anymore. Too many do-gooders sniffing around. They can't see how I contribute to society."

"And how's that?" Shakes countered. "By destroying lives?"

She snickers. "You think your life matters? That's why you fight me. You're delusional." Faith nudges her head toward James. "He knows, don't you, Special? What you really mean to the world?"

James doesn't speak. There's a panic beneath his visage that he's trying to suppress. I thought there would be more anger to him, like how Shakes can barely contain his, but instead, James is pulling away, shutting down.

Faith is scaring him.

And if she can scare him, she should scare me.

"Why are you doing this?" I ask. "We are just kids."

"Just kids," she mocks. "Just kids." She pretends to cry and then smiles. "Do you think a fish says, 'Don't eat me, I'm just a fish?' It is the fact that you are 'just kids' that I make the money I do. Don't blame me that people suck. I'm just a smart business woman." A beep on her phone interrupts, and she looks at the screen. "Your cars have arrived."

Shakes dives for the gun, but Faith slaps her hand on it, laughing, enjoying the thrill like a mad woman. With a flick of her fingers, Glass accosts him, taking the chains and yanking Shakes' hands down in front of him. He groans in pain, the gun wound on his shoulder soaking his shirt. "Make them tight." She watches every flinch he makes. "Make it hurt."

I step in front of him. I don't like how our fight is some sort of fetish to her. Faith's green eyes are on me, humored, and she holds the gun lazily in her hand, like it's a wine glass. "Are you two lovers? Cheating on Mary, are you?"

Shakes bucks and I latch onto his arm. "Don't fucking say her name."

A giggle, a carelessness and then a change of topic. "Do you remember me, Scream?"

I don't want to admit that I do. She used Tobias to control me.

"No? Not even a little?" Faith leans her elbows on the table, tossing the gun back on the metal. Her feet shift out from under the table. The hot pink of her shoes catches me again, and I stare at them, diving into a memory I didn't have before.

'I love your shoes!' I shouted.

There's a driveway.

I'm reaching for the handle of a car door.

'I'll buy you a pair!" a voice shouted back, but it was so distant like it was submerged in the water.

My eyes flick across her face. Why do I hear her in my head differently from before? It sounds familiar, like—

Faith leans down, a secret on her lips that she's been keeping. "We were neighbors."

I fall back against the wall, gripping my head.

'How was the game?' I hear her voice echo in the darkness. 'Sorry, I couldn't make it.'

My knees weaken, and I fall to the floor. I repeatedly see Faith by her car with her brilliant pink shoes. Nothing else exists. It's black around her, like a blurry picture. She wears a knee-length skirt and a white blouse with her hair down, curled over her shoulder. She looks ready to go to the office.

"You look so much like your mother."

"Shut up." My head vibrates in pain, it sounds like an avalanche, and I don't want to let it in.

I clench every muscle, stopping it from coming. There's agony in the memories. I know it, and I won't make it through.

"Don't know how sorry I was to learn your memory had been broken. Barely even a scrap of what you once were. But you're in there, sweet girl. I see it. I'll help you bring her out again."

Tears drip down my cheeks, and I peer at her through my hands. Could she? Could she find me?

But like Tobias, it doesn't matter what she knows. I'd never sell my soul for her help.

Faith fingers the gun. I stare at it, eager to grab it.

"Shoot me," she dares, sitting back and giving me room to seize it before she can. "Shoot me, and you're free."

Shakes moves for the gun, but James presses a hand against his chest, keeping him against the wall. There's a look between them. James knows we can't make it out of here. So now it's a different kind of game. We must watch every move and wait for an opportunity instead of grasping at straws. It's the kind of game I hate playing.

"Come on, Scream. I've got a bet going on that you have the balls to shoot me. I know you better than you know yourself. Shoot me. Find that old you." She sits back, leaving the gun on the table between us. The confidence in her is as strong as the insanity.

Would she actually let me grab it? If I did, what then? I couldn't pretend to threaten. No one would believe I would actually shoot her. Even I know that. I've never killed someone, and I don't want to.

But this is different. This woman would deserve it.

"Ember," Shakes hisses. "Do it."

The desperation isn't lost on me. This is a way to freedom. All I have to do is take her life, and it will all be over.

"Do it, and we're free."

"Don't." James stays stiff against the wall, staring straight. "You can't."

"Hell yes, she can." Shakes grips my arms with his hands, the chains wriggling. "Do it, Ember. This is your kidnapper. Do you understand that? She stole you from your home and brought you to the school. She's to blame for everything that ever happened to you. Kill her, Ember."

My head is shaking. My body is shaking.

She's giggling. "You can't, can you? Even knowing it will free you. I'll give you something better. If you shoot me, I'll let the whole school go."

I stare at the gun, imagining myself picking it up and firing. The loud boom. The blood. What makes her any better than Charles? He died with a bullet to the head. She should, too. She's the cause, right? The cause of every terrible thing that happened. But I can't project my hate onto her so easily. And even if I could, would it be enough to take her life?

Shakes grabs my hands. "Look at me."

"I can't."

His grip hardens against me. "You want to be somebody, then be somebody. This is it. If you don't do it, we will be sold, Ember. We will be used for whatever fucked up fantasy some old pervert has for us. We'll die." The softness comes back to his green eyes, and I see Charles in them for a moment. "Please. Fulfill your promise."

My promise, I repeat, knowing it was a promise I made to Charles that I would get home. I thought I had fulfilled it when we came to this hospital, but I'm not even close, am I?

"No." James clenches his teeth, refusing to look at me. "She's trying to force you to be somebody you're not. Don't let her win."

Shakes snaps, "It's not about winning! It's freedom. Nothing matters, not her soul, mine or yours."

"Times up." Faith snatches the gun between her manicured fingers. "Just cost me a shipment."

Glass reminds her, "Jose will be back soon. We have to go."

Faith nods, a sad fake pout on her lips. "I don't want to go, my loves, but your cars are waiting. I'll see you soon, Scream. And then the fun can begin." She stands, straightening out her skirt. Faith backs out the door. "I'll let you say goodbye. I'm not completely cold-hearted."

Glass shuts the door behind him, and the silence echoes. My breath is the only sound, escalating along with the panic. I run to it blindly and tug at it, but it's a deadbolt and no amount of pulling breaks the knob. I pound a fist, my knees giving out, and the cold tile shocks my skin as I collapse against the ground.

I've screwed us all.

CHAPTER 31
Run

EMBER

I SIT AGAINST THE wall, staring at James and Shakes. These two have saved my life numerous times, and I have failed to do the same. I want to go back in time, take up that gun, and shoot Faith in the face. Never mind I'd never feel good again. Shakes is right. It's not about my soul or my conscience. It's a sacrifice for freedom. How many people has she ruined? How many children has she stolen? How many bags of trust has she taken and never given back? I've condemned us because of my weakness and stupid desire to be good in this hell of a world.

"What do we do?"

I have to make up for it. I can't let them give up. James looks like he's sinking into a tank of tar-soaked memories, unable to resurface. Shakes sits defeated in a chair, his bloody hands dangling between his legs, and the chains glitter like a wind-chime.

"What do we do!" I yell. "What's the plan?"

No reply.

I kneel in front of Shakes. "Listen to me. It's not over yet. I don't know what's out there, but it doesn't matter. We run. Like a bulldozer."

His brows knit.

"Just run."

A fan turns on, and we look around for the noise. White smoke billows out of the vent. James snaps to life, a burst of fight left in him. "Don't breathe it in. Get on the floor. Take off your shirt and put it against your nose and mouth."

Shakes and I obey, laying down. James looks over at us. "When that door opens. We run."

"Run where?" Shakes struggles to hold his shirt against his face. The chains are tight, and his arm is in pain. "There is nowhere to run."

"It doesn't matter. We cannot be sold. We have to run and find another way."

We lay on the floor, staring at the ceiling, watching the smoke fill the room. Waiting with James on my left and Shakes on my right. I don't know if it will work. I don't know if, in a second, I'll pass out, and the next time I wake up, I'll be in a stranger's house, separated from my family, lost in the world, forgotten, without a single hope of ever finding them again.

"Ember," Shakes muffled voice sounds. "We know your name." His green eyes slip to me. "Mary said you were afraid."

My brows knit, hating how such a silly thing got me to run while I'm faced with odds like these. It sounds stupid now.

"But you shouldn't be," James says, and I fling my head towards him. "Be proud of who you are."

I have never been. I don't know how he can say it like it's a possibility.

"Because we are." I turn back to Shakes. "You are everything I hoped you'd be, Maya Bennet."

Tears drip down my temples as I stare at the ceiling. The name soothes me like a warm blanket when I've been frozen to the core. It wraps around me, familiar and pleasant, and I know without a doubt it's mine. *My name is Maya Bennet.*

I grab Shakes' hand, and he squeezes my fingers. We lay in silence, watching the fog thicken.

I look at James, and he is already watching me. I'm terrified to breathe, and the last I want to see is him. Because I know I wouldn't have made it this far without him. Without either of them. And no matter what my future holds now, I have something in my past to be thankful for.

"I'll come for you," I whisper to him, full of conviction. I don't care how long it takes or how far apart we grow. I'll never give up. I'll rescue him from whatever fate that lies ahead.

Tears build in his eyes, and his black brows knit in pain. "Don't."

My muscles weaken. The drugs are shifting through my veins despite how hard I try not to breathe it in. I take long pauses, nearly suffocating myself until I can't hold my breath longer. I won't make it. I'm going to pass out, and the fear of this fact only makes my heart beat faster and my need for air more urgent. My eyes shut on a will of their own, heavy and thick.

Distantly, the door opens, and I hear the pounding of footsteps approach.

A jolt of movement, and I snap my eyes open. The air around us clears from a vacuum in the ceiling. I hear terrible things that force me to roll on my stomach. James has Glass against the wall. He smacks the gun out of his hand, and they move at a speed I can't process. It's a bunch of kicks and punches until James latches onto his waist and lifts Glass over his shoulder, slamming him down on the table. But Glass wraps his arms around James' neck. He holds him harshly and no amount of flailing arms and punching reduces Glass' hold.

I turn on my side. Shakes is in worse shape. He struggles to lift his limbs. He'll be no help. But the gun is in my reach. I stretch out for it and latch onto the handle.

Glass twists off the table and locks an arm around James' throat, pinning his only good arm against the side of his head. Their backs face me. Glass can't see me. I kneel on weak legs and lift the gun. James is faltering. His knees are giving out as he suffocates. He's dying, and I can stop it. Unlike last time when Zack was peeling off his fingernails with pliers, and I stood by and did nothing, I can stop it this time. I'm no longer that girl I was. I have people to fight for now.

'Be proud of who you are.'

I fire. Glass drops to the floor. His body limp and motionless. I wait for him to get up. I look at

James who coughs and struggles to breathe again. He holds onto the table, his legs weak and his eyes meet mine, unwilling to answer the question that won't leave my lips.

A dozen more people come into the room, screaming orders, and have us on the ground with our arms pressed against our backs. Someone ties them up. I don't struggle staring at Glass' face. His eyes are closed. A small line of blood dribbles out of his mouth. But he doesn't wipe it away. He just lays there as if he can't do anything else.

A foul-smelling rag is pressed against my mouth and nose. The hit of it burns and makes my eyes water. My mind goes blank, but only one thought remains: *Why won't Glass get up?*

• • • • • • • • • •

The ambulance sirens are distant, miles away, and yet they vibrate my body, disturbing my sleep. My eyelids are heavy like tape holds them together. I try to lift my hand to feel it, but even that is a struggle.

"Shh," a stranger whispers in my ear, making every muscle in my body tighten. "Boss wants to take you to her home." Fingers tickled in my hair. I'm panting, panicking, trying to fight the heaviness of my body. "You're lucky." The man declares, "I hear she treats her girls very well."

For so long, I dreamed of a moment when I would leave the school and pretend it never happened. Everything about it and everything in it would be nothing more than a distant nightmare. I'd recover and learn how to be someone new.

Now, the further I get, the more I realize it's the only life I have. I know nothing of the outside. I don't know how to be normal, to be anything but Scream, the girl that can fight with two hands and run faster than a mob.

I cling to the idea that being good is all I need to be redeemed, but I'm not good, and I doubt I can ever be good. It's a pathetic attempt to keep the school from getting into my veins. But it's too late. It's been inside me since the day I arrived.

The regret is staggering. It builds tears.

"Don't cry." A finger runs along my skin, wiping it away. "You'll be just fine."

I try again to move. A finger twitches, but it took so much effort. This man above me doesn't scare me. I've been beaten, abused, and left for dead. He is but a fly above my rotted corpse.

It soothes me. If I am genuinely a corpse, then I cannot feel. And if I cannot feel, I am a machine. The thought numbs me. I can turn it off, like a faucet; stop the flow of emotion and just be 'off'. James taught me how to flip the switch. It's better this way. All the overwhelming loss ends, and there is nothing now. No pain. No fear. No regret.

What fills in that emptiness is anger.

I will get revenge.

I will get out.

I will find Shakes and James and save them from whatever fate awaits them. Even if it takes me years. I will never give up because this is all I have out of life. It is that school. And that school exists inside me. And because of it, I know what I must do to survive. And I will survive. Faith will regret letting me live. Because even though I failed to kill her today, I won't make that mistake again.

The ambulance slams on its brakes and turns so sharp the gurney falls over. The jolt spurs senses to life. Pain is acute but welcome. I can finally move my legs. Gunshots boom, an unmistakable sound I'm not fully familiar with. My wrists are chained to the gurney, the metal saving me from being shot. I curl as small as I can as bullets strike the walls around me. Glass shatters, and screams sound muffled through the door.

There is quiet, and my panting is the only sound I can hear.

"Get the ax. Stand back, Scream!" My name opens my eyes. With every hit of the ax, more senses spring to life. When the door opens, the sun shines, and I turn from the bright light.

Hands pull at me. "She's alright!" They uncuff my hands, getting me to my feet, but I'm weak and fall against them. The stranger holds onto me, helping me out of the truck.

"Hurry, we got to move."

I look over my shoulder, and beside the ambulance I was riding is, is the body of the man that was talking to me. He is wide eyed and riddled with bullets.

I'm not afraid; maybe it's the drugs, perhaps I've reached my limit, but I keep moving. I know what I have to do in this life. I've finally figured it out. I'm going to destroy everyone that hurts kids. I will come after this organization and burn it to the ground.

Even if I'm inside it.

A door to a van opens up and my happiness boils over seeing James. I throw myself at him, and he grips my hair, clinging to me. All the emotions I had shoved down moments ago spring forth like vomit, and I cry into his neck. I'm weak with him like he breaks down every wall I try to reinforce. He whispers in my ear, wiping my tears away, kissing my cheeks and lips, "We're okay," he assures me. "It's the FBI."

I'm not so easily moved by the declaration. I need proof before I dumbly put my trust in it. Too many times, I've been lied to.

"Fucking Memory." Shakes climbs in the car. He holds his shoulder and babies a new cut on his forehead that drips blood into his eye. "She has to be as dramatic as possible." he bitterly growls. "She must have cameras somewhere. That girl is always thinking ahead." Despite the apparent aggravation, he's relieved. She came through for him, and though he hates her, he's thankful.

Shakes nudges his head, pointing to the people around our car. They wear yellow jackets and jeans. "FBI. About time. Now we can go blow up that damned hospital and get everyone out." He tilts his head back with a heavy sigh. "God, I almost lost it." Shakes' green gaze is on my face while I stare at the ground. He nudges me with his arm. "You alright?"

It's sign of forgiveness, that I didn't screw us as terribly as I thought I did. But yet, I'm still confused. I don't know how I am. I was on the verge of a massive downward spiral, and now I'm unsure if I should be afraid or happy. I'm drained currently, and though we've been rescued, I'll need more proof before I can actually believe it. I rest my head on his shoulder.

The car takes off, but when Shakes sits up, I stiffen.

We are going the wrong way.

Shakes flips his head about, shifting in his seat, looking back, and glimpsing the hospital in the distance. "What are you doing?" he asks the driver. "Turn around."

The man doesn't flinch. "I'm taking you to our headquarters."

"No, the fuck you ain't." Shakes reaches for the steering wheel. "Turn this car around."

The man shoves him back. "I got my orders, kid."

Shakes slaps the seat in front of him. "Turn around. Turn around now! My fucking girlfriend is in there. My family is there!" Shakes dives through the front seat and grabs the steering wheel. The car jerks to the right, but the man stomps on the break, stopping us.

He shoves Shakes back. "We can't do anything for them!" he yells. "We risked our lives coming after you three. We aren't ready to take on the entire building. Or Jose."

"I don't give a shit–"

"Shakes," James interrupts.

"What!" He snaps his attention to him. "Tell me that we're leaving them behind. Fucking tell me. Tell me we're abandoning everyone. Go ahead. Say it. Say it!"

I bow my head, sinking into James' side. Misery is a familiar feeling, soaking up any form of happiness. We aren't escaping. We're running away. And though it's something that I'm typically okay with, I now see the problem with it. People get left behind. The car continues to drive away. Every member of our family could suffer the consequences of our actions.

Shakes unexpectedly punches the seat in front of him. He hammers into it, screaming, gripping the fabric, trying to rip it off. I cover my mouth as tears flow down my face. He kicks and shakes it, pounding violently into it, but it does not break, a robust wall to his distress. He drops his forehead against it, squeezing the seat with his eyes clenched tight. A sob breaks out in a horrible scream, "Shit!"

CHAPTER 32
Epilogue

EMBER

THE DRIVE CONTINUES FOR hours. We've abandoned our friends in a sporadic moment of rashness. Now, we are stuck in a colossal bubble of guilt that cannot be popped.

The driver keeps looking in the rear view mirror. Whoever he is, we are at his mercy. If he betrays us now, I don't know what I'll do.

When we enter the city, my eyes are wide, and my excitement grows. The buildings, the cars, the people, the noise. I have trouble believing it simply because it's so much at once. How can all these things be going on at the same time? It's impossible to describe a single scene, let alone a street or a moment because a million things happen within that time frame. I can't observe it quickly enough as the car continues forward.

People are walking on the sidewalks. Women, men, children. Fathers. Mothers. Siblings.

I want to talk to them, meet them, tell them everything, but I'm afraid. What if they work for Myers? What if they are just as evil as the teachers in the school? How do I know who to trust?

The car maneuvers underground, underneath a building, and twists a bunch of times before it parks in an empty parking lot. The driver gets out of the car, and the sound of the door closing echoes. I remain seated in the car, looking around, searching for something familiar. Shakes blocks the exit, and I'm in no hurry to get out. What waits for us in this place? Will it finally bring us to some salvation? Or is this another level of Hell?

The door opens. Memory proudly grins, "I told you—"

Shakes' hand is around her throat as he climbs out, twisting her around and shoving her against the side of the car. James and I rush out after him, but we don't know if we should stop him. James cuts in front of the driver, keeping him back as he yells as Shakes to let her go.

"How did you know?" Shakes grits through his teeth.

She moans against his hand, digging her nails into his skin. "Cameras," her squeezed larynx hums.

"You're gonna take us back."

Her face is turning red. "I can't," she forces out. Memory hits his hand in desperation, struggling to breathe.

James keeps hold of the driver, but calls out, "We need her. Kill her when we have finished destroying the hospital."

Shakes doesn't let go. The rage is brilliant on his face. His teeth clench the muscles in his jaw. He trembles with the effort. But then, thankfully, he shoves himself away. "You are going to help us."

Memory coughs and sucks in breath. The driver goes to her side, holding onto her, glaring at Shakes. "What the hell is your problem?" He steps toward Shakes, but James moves in front, putting a hand against his chest. "Is that the thanks we get for saving your life?"

Shakes grips his hair, squatting, a little ball of pain and rage that can't explode.

"We're not leaving them, Shakes," Memory assures him. "We're gonna help them."

The driver and Memory walk toward the building. I don't know what to do, so I'm still waiting for my brother to swallow all his emotions and return to the calm, rational man I know.

"Well?" Memory barks across the empty space.

I touch Shakes' shoulder. "Don't," he warns. As he stands, Shakes rests his gaze on me, and for the first time, they are dark and unfriendly. "You did this."

James steps up. "We didn't have a choice."

"We had a choice. She chose to let that fucking psycho go. Now everything that happens to Mary, Vapor, Brick, Ink—Everything can be laid at your feet."

My brows knit as tears press against the back of my eyes.

He finally admits, "I should have killed you months ago." And then walks away.

I clench my lips and harden my gaze. I find it easy to switch off any pain or sadness. He's upset, and he has every right to be. We left our family behind, but we are getting them back. I will not stop until we are free. I will win this war. And if I have to do it without him, then I will.

James slips his hand into mine. "Don't listen to him, Dream. He's lost in grief."

I smile, unfazed, unconquered, unbreakable. "Call me Maya."

• • • • • • • • • •

Next book in the Scream Series:
My Name is Loss

After being rescued by Becca; Maya, James, and Shakes find themselves in the hands of the FBI. There is little else they can do but play their game and join as pawns if they want to bring down the hospital and save their friends. But as they get their first taste of freedom, Maya deals with feelings of jealousy when a new girl joins their pack who understands James' past more than she ever can. And while James struggles to find order in his chaotic mind, he makes a painful mistake that will destroy their future and ensure the reality that all dreams must come to an end.